Big-Headed Son
and
Small-Headed Dad

Written by Zheng Chunhua

New Classic Press

2024

NEW CLASSIC PRESS

Published by New Classic Press (UK) ★

5th Floor, 99 Mansell Street, London, E1 8AX, UK,

Great Britain ★ Established in the year 2008 ★

Seeking business opportunities worldwide

Big-Headed Son and Small-Headed Dad

Written by Zheng Chunhua

Translated by Anthony Rash

Proofread by Xie Jiahang

Original Edition © Changjiang Children's Press (Group) Co., Ltd 2016

This English Edition Published in the United Kingdom of Great Britain and

Northern Ireland

by New Classic Press Limited in 2024

ISBN 978-1-917143-08-0

First printed in the United Kingdom of Great Britain and Northern Ireland

10 9 8 7 6 5 4 3 2 1

DESIGNED BY

The publisher's policy is to use paper manufactured from sustainable forests.

CONTENTS

001 Two Little Houses

010 Waiting for Dad

020 New Neighbourhood

030 Fragrant Road

040 New Year's Eve Dinner

050 Writing and Reading Letters

058 Alien Car

068 The Retrieved Swing

078 Animal Inn

089 Surprising Apron Mum

098 Green Frog by the Pond

107 Not Afraid of the Real Tiger

115 Searching for the Alien

124 Magic Hat

133 Big-Headed Son's Disappearance

142 Football Oasis: Arena of Big & Little Heads

151 Candy Dentist

161   The Trouble of Being a Celebrity

170   Apron Mum's Weight Loss

179   Subway Circus

188   Rugby Ball

196   Welcome the New Year

205   The Puppies

213   Toy Hospital

220   Mama Bear's Hotel

229   Flea Market

236   The Dad Who Can Make Toys

243   Tiger Bear

252   Share the Joy

261   Story of the Glasses

269   The Hunter Changes His Profession

277   Ghost in the Attic

285   Captain Daddy

293   Days in the Countryside

301   Red Chinese New Year

310   Emergency Rescue

318   Joint Battle

326   Home on the Map

334   Invitation from a Small City

338   Remote Control Toilet

342   Scooter City

346 Eating Apple Penalty

350 Haha Laughing Children's Hospital

354 Statue of the Mayor in the Square

358 Path at Night

362 Super Sleepy King

366 First Day of Kindergarten

370 Strange Gardener

373 The Boat on the Floor

376 Ouyang Dad

380 You Adults Are Weird

384 Very Stupid Idea

388 Let's All Escape Inside

392 Two Ears on a Big Bed

395 The "Big Bear" on the Quilt

398 Seeing No Animals at the Zoo

402 It Was So Much Fun to Paint!

406 A Total of 25 Big Bags

410 Pants Kite

414 Cold, Cold Night

418 Catch a Big Fish

Two Little Houses

Small-Headed Dad and the shop attendant brought back two enormous cardboard boxes, one containing a washing machine and the other a refrigerator.

Big-Headed Son, observing the images on the top of the cardboard boxes, remarked, "Ah, the large one is a fridge, and the smaller one is a washing machine."

As the washing machine and refrigerator emerged from their cardboard confines, the two now-empty boxes seemed even more substantial.

"A box this size could accommodate me too!" exclaimed Big-Headed Son, promptly clambering into the cardboard box, and indeed, it proved a perfect fit.

Small-Headed Dad chuckled, saying, "Shall I transform them into two little houses for you?"

"Yes! I want that!" eagerly responded Big-Headed

Son, quickly vacating the box.

Small-Headed Dad found a pair of sizable scissors, producing a "click" sound as each cardboard box received a door and a window. Big-Headed Son joyfully fetched a red pen and inscribed "101" on the 'big house' containing the refrigerator, while on the 'small house' with the washing machine, he wrote: "102."

Small-Headed Dad bagged "101," and Big-Headed Son bagged "102." They shut the door behind them, stuck their noggins out the window, eyeing each other, then tilting their heads, causing Apron Mum to burst into laughter.

Come evening, Apron Mum rustled up the grub and hollered, "Dinner's on! Come on out!"

Small-Headed Dad cracked open the window and quipped, "If you're a top-notch missus, fetch me my supper."

Big-Headed Son also popped open the window, declaring, "If you're a good mum, you won't mind me dining in the little shack."

Apron Mum shrugged, had to dish out two hefty plates with rice and dishes, and ferry them over.

Small-Headed Dad took a plate from the window, saying, "Cheers, good lady!"

Big-Headed Son snagged a plate and chimed in, "Thanks, good mum!"

Apron Mum found herself alone at the table, unable to eat, as if she had no appetite. But in a jiffy, she spotted the door of 101 swinging open, and an empty plate emerging; 102's door also creaked ajar, with another empty plate following suit.

Apron Mum sighed, muttering, "They've got quite the hunger!"

Night fell, and still no sign of them. Apron Mum drew the curtains, flicked on the lights, and then rapped on the doors of 101 and 102, "It's getting dark, come on out!"

Small-Headed Dad poked his noggin out and quipped, "If you were Mrs. Nice, you'd send me some light." He wrapped it up with a flying kiss.

Big-Headed Son thrust his big head out and remarked, "If you're a good mum, you'll come up with something good." Following that, he showered her with two flying kisses using both hands.

Apron Mum frowned, pondered for a moment, and then grinned. She opened the fridge and retrieved two vibrant red lantern chili peppers, placing lit candles within. Ah, the peppers illuminated, resembling two miniature crimson lanterns!

Proudly, Apron Mum positioned the little red lanterns into 101 and 102, transforming the two small houses into two substantial lanterns.

After making a large bed and a small bed, she called them, but they refused to emerge. Apron Mum reluctantly retired to sleep alone. Shortly after, she heard, "We're cold! We are cold." Hastily, she provided two thick towel blankets to warm them.

As time passed, the lights of the two little houses dimmed, accompanied by a purring sound: "Whirr-whirr-whirr-"

Apron Mum pressed her ear against the door of 101, then the door of 102, and burst into laughter. Shaking her head, she turned off the living room light and entered the bedroom.

In the darkness, the two little houses continued to "purr."

Abruptly, the little houses transformed into cabins, situated in an open field beneath a sky adorned with stars.

Surprisingly, one by one, the stars "giggled" and descended from the sky, forming a large circle as they spun and laughed simultaneously. The laughter awakened Big-Headed Son and Small-Headed Dad in their cabin; they peered out, astonished and unable to close their mouths. The stars twirled, changing hues from red to green, ultimately becoming vibrant and encircling the two cabins. Big-Headed Son and Small-Headed Dad stepped out of the cabin, joining the joyous circle surrounded by stars.

The little stars climbed onto their heads, sliding down their arms like a playful slide. These mischievous little stars slipped and slid repeatedly; their happiness evident.

Suddenly, in the distance, two fierce eyes appeared, fixating on the little stars. Beneath the eyes, two rows of sharp teeth materialized.

But the little stars were having a whale of a time with Big-Headed Son and Small-Headed Dad, and none of them cottoned on to it. Ah, those wicked eyes turned out to be on the tiger's mug, and the tiger opened its mouth wide, sucking hard – "whoosh," like a magnet pulling the little stars into its gut one by one.

Big-Headed Son and Small-Headed Dad hurriedly took cover in the cabin, peering at the tiger through the window. Lo and behold, the tiger's belly was swollen and luminous, resembling a lantern, filled to the brim with little stars. The tiger strutted around with great pride, patting its belly with its front paws.

Big-Headed Son and Small-Headed Dad exchanged

hushed words through the window, "The little stars can't escape; what should we do then?"

"Humans are cleverer than tigers; we'll figure out a cunning plan!" declared Small-Headed Dad. "If we keep the little stars trapped, they'll croak from suffocation!"

"I've got an idea; you fetch the pepper, and we'll make the tiger sneeze, spraying the stars out."

They stealthily crept out of the hut, each wielding a bottle of pepper. Slowly but surely, they inched behind the foliage, then stood upright and showered the tiger with pepper as though it were rainfall. The pepper coated the tiger's head and body, and before the tiger grasped what was happening, it began to sneeze repeatedly. With each sneeze, a cluster of stars, resembling fireflies, soared out of its mouth and shot straight up into the sky.

The tiger's belly descended, and the light extinguished. Enraged, it emitted a fierce "ah woo" scream, then, spotting the cabin, it charged towards it.

The modest wooden house reverted to its original state, with 102, where Big-Headed Son resided, collapsing onto 101, where Small-Headed Dad lived. Big-Headed Son yelled, "Tiger's coming!" and hastily scrambled to escape. Confused by his surroundings, he surveyed the unfamiliar home. Glancing at the small house, he realized it wasn't made of wood. The revellation struck him – it was just a dream. Quickly, Big-Headed Son carefully assembled the little house and crawled back inside.

Come morning, Small-Headed Dad and Big-Headed Son emerged for breakfast. They decided to lock up the little house to see if it resembled a genuine abode, hence the two locks hanging on the door. While enjoying their meal, they glanced at the hefty locks and felt genuinely satisfied. Recollecting his dream, Big-Headed Son shared, "Small-Headed Dad, last night I dreamt of playing with the stars!"

Small-Headed Dad questioned, "Why did you yell 'Here comes the tiger' if you were playing with the stars?"

Big-Headed Son chuckled and explained, "The tiger devoured the stars and is now approaching to devour us."

"What?" Small-Headed Dad tilted his head, asking, "Did you include me in your dreams as well? No wonder I had a restless night!"

Big-Headed Son suggested, "If we sleep outside for real, I'm sure we'll have a peaceful night sleep."

Small-Headed Dad agreed, "Really? Then let's give it a try tonight."

"You bet!" cheered Big-Headed Son gleefully.

Come evening, Big-Headed Son and Small-Headed

Dad lugged the little house downstairs together and shifted it to an empty plot.

Big-Headed Son was over the moon, doing a couple of victory laps around the little house. He suddenly halted, raised his arms, and declared, "Brilliant! I'm genuinely sleeping outdoors tonight!" "Then don't freak out!" Said Small-Headed Dad.

Big-Headed Son, bringing out the pepper, retorted, "I'm not scared of the tiger. Not scared at all!"

As darkness fell, they retired into 101 and 102, respectively.

But before long, a mighty gust of wind swept in. The wind rustled the tall trees, and leaves descended like rain upon the little house. The two tiny abodes quivered in unison.

From 101, Small-Headed Dad's voice piped up, "It's blowing a gale; we better head home and hit the hay."

"Nope, I'm sticking to my plan to sleep outside," echoed the voice from 102.

The wind intensified, and then the rain began. The raindrops were the size of beans, pelting the trees, the foliage, and the little house. Gradually, the little house started to get damp.

"It's pouring buckets; we better head back home!"

"No, I'm sticking to sleeping out here!"

As time passed, the small house gradually became damper and less stable, succumbing to the wind and rain. Eventually, it softened and collapsed, leaving Big-Headed Son and Small-Headed Dad seemingly frozen in place amid the wreckage. They clutched a soggy piece of cardboard over their heads, the remnants of the "window" of the house.

Big-Headed Son, now infuriated, shook his fists and yelled at the sky, "Nasty rain! Pesky wind!"

Small-Headed Dad pulled him up, and together, they sprinted towards their actual home, with the wind and rain relentlessly pursuing them from behind.

Waiting for Dad

At noon on this day, Big-Headed Son was coming back from his uncle's house out of town where he spent summer vacation. Small-Headed Dad hadn't eaten his lunch yet, and Apron Mum kept urging: "Hurry, hurry, the train is coming! "Small-Headed Dad swallowed the last bite of his meal while tying his shoelaces.

He ran up the street as fast as he could, just as a bus stopped, and Small-Headed Dad jumped on like a rabbit. There was a loud bang as the door closed so fast that it caught his small head. The conductor hurriedly reopened the door and said: "I'm sorry! I'm sorry! "

Small-Headed Dad rubbed his small head and said: "It's okay, ... I'm happy! "

Passengers all laughed, thinking that Small-Headed Dad looks funny, and his words are even more fun.

Small-Headed Dad hastened to say: "I'm happy because I'm about to see my Big-Headed Son! "

The car arrived at the passenger station, and Small-Headed Dad jumped down like a rabbit again, and then rushed in like a whirlwind ...

At this time, a red train is slowly coming into the platform, and Big-Headed Son is sitting on this train. He was sticking his big head out of the car window and looking carefully for his Small-Headed Dad.

The old grandfather sitting beside him asked: "Little boy, is your family coming to pick you up? "

Big-Headed Son nodded his head: "It's daddy coming to pick me up. I can see my daddy at once, because his head is the smallest small head in the world. "

The travelers laughed, and the old grandfather laughed so hard that he touched the big head of Big-Headed Son.

The train stopped, but Big-Headed Son sat in his seat and did not move, as his dad told him on the phone to stay put. He said, "Bye, Uncle! Auntie, goodbye! Bye bye grandpa", while watching them take down the big bags from the luggage rack. The luggage rack, which was full just a moment ago, was now so empty that it could be used as a bed.

After all the people in the compartment had left, Big-Headed Son stood on the aisle and looked at the long and empty luggage rack, thinking it was really funny.

Suddenly, out of the window came the voice of calling "Big-Headed Son". He froze, and when he listened carefully, he realized that it was true, and that it must be Small-Headed Dad coming to pick him up! Big-Headed Son rushed to the window and said loudly: "Small-Headed Dad, I'm here! "

Hey, how come there is no Small-Headed Dad, but the voice of "Big-Headed Son" is still there? He wondered, so he stepped down from the carriage and followed the voice, and the voice became clearer and clearer: "Big-Headed Son, please stay in the carriage, Small-Headed Dad will be here soon ..."

Oh, it was the radio shouting "Big-Headed Son".

Big-Headed Son went back to the train, but he got on the wrong train and didn't know it. There were many trains on the platform, and there were several red trains.

Big-Headed Son sat down in his seat again, and he wanted to wait for Small-Headed Dad to come and say that he was really well behaved. But after waiting for a while and not seeing Small-Headed Dad, Big-Headed Son raised his head to look at the empty and long luggage rack, and when he looked at it, he stood up without realizing it, climbed to the back of the seat, and then climbed from the back of the seat to the luggage rack. Big-Headed Son has been on the train several times, but never on the luggage rack, this is too much fun!

I am hiding here, Small-Headed Dad will not be able to find me! Big-Headed Son so thought, on the back lying on the luggage rack, also spread arms and legs, stretched himself.

Suddenly, the train "clang" shook a little, but slowly started. Big-Headed Son strangely turned around on the luggage rack looking out on the outside, only to see the platform kiosks, lights, chairs, newspaper columns and so on, all moving in the backward. The whole platform are moving back, and faster and faster!

"Wow ..." Now Big-Headed Son became anxious, "Stop the train! Stop the train! "He cried and screamed, but the train didn't care about him at all, it was still "whimpering" as if it was deliberately mocking him.

Train conductor heard the sound of crying from the next compartment rushed over. She looked for the source of the cry, and finally found Big-Headed Son in the luggage racks, crying, face full of tears. She hurriedly called out to another conductor, and together they hugged him down from the luggage rack.

Big-Headed Son stood on the chair, and when he saw that the train was still running, he jumped down and rushed towards the door: "I'm going down! I'm going down! "

At this time the conductor also came, he picked up Big-Headed Son and said: "Little boy, you can't get off the train while it's running. I will arrange for you to get on another train when we get to the next station. "

Big-Headed Son was still crying: "When we go back later, Small-Headed Dad has gone away, I don't recognize the way home, oh ..."

The conductor wiped away Big-Headed Son's tears for him and said: "Don't worry, there are many uncles and aunts on the platform who will help you later! "

Big-Headed Son nodded, and stopped crying.

The conductor put down Big-Headed Son, took his hand and said: "Go, now there are no passengers on the car, I'll take you to visit the locomotive. "

Awesome! Big-Headed Son smiled and hurriedly followed.

The conductor said as he walked: "I can also let you pull the whistle. "he said, rounding his mouth and imitating the train's cry: "Oh—", which sounded quite like the real thing.

Big-Headed Son looked at him, growing at once to like him!

They walked into the locomotive; the conductor held Big-Headed Son sat next to the driver. The train driver was a big bearded man, he smiled at Big-Headed Son, and explained to Big-Headed Son about the buttons: Red is to speed up, green is to slow down, yellow is to reverse the ... Big-Headed Son listened with great interest, while watching the train through the fields, drilling through the caves, around the beautiful village. Look, there was a cowherd boy on the slope squinting at the fast-moving train and waving at them! Big-Headed Son also rushed to wave back at him ... Suddenly, he remembered, hurriedly pulled the whistle: "Woo – Woo – Woo –" ah, cattle herder understands. Only to see him jump up at once, rushed down the dirt slope, towards the far away train raised two waving hands!

Small-Headed Dad rushed onto the platform, spotting the red train that carried Big-Headed Son. He shouted urgently from window to window, "Big-Headed Son! Big-Headed Son!" However, his calls failed to bring Big-Headed Son out.

Without hesitation, Small-Headed Dad leaped

onto the train, searching through each compartment and occasionally checking under the seats, suspecting that Big-Headed Son might be hiding. "Come out, Big-Headed Son! I've spotted you! I've seen you!" he declared deliberately, even turning around abruptly, attempting to catch Big-Headed Son hiding behind him. But there was no sign of him. Small-Headed Dad continued his quest, racing to the last carriage, but still, there was no trace of Big-Headed Son.

Anxiously, Small-Headed Dad sought out the station duty room. The duty chief listened and informed him, "I just received a phone call. Someone reported a boy fitting the description you provided. He boarded the wrong train and is currently on the way to Hangzhou ..."

Small-Headed Dad was rendered speechless, his mind unable to register the commander's subsequent words. Suddenly, he made a decision: "No, I must catch up with that train!" With determination, he dashed out and sprinted vigorously.

The red train continued its journey along the tracks, emitting a piercing scream and expelling a cloud of smoke, resembling an iron dragon traversing vast fields.

Simultaneously, on the highway running parallel to the tracks, a blue cab was in hot pursuit. Moments later, the small head of Small-Headed Dad appeared from the cab's window. He waved, shouted towards the train, and even whistled with his thumb in his mouth. However, Big-Headed Son on the train remained oblivious to the frantic pursuit.

Oh dear! Small-Headed Dad let out a sigh and sank into his chair when, out of the blue, he felt a pinch on his buttocks. The pinch stung, prompting him to reach out and touch, his brows furrowing in surprise. What do you reckon Small-Headed Dad laid his hands on? Well, it was none other than Big-Headed Son's cherished Iron Armor Dragon Warrior, which had somehow slipped out of Small-Headed Dad's pocket where he had stashed it while heading out.

Small-Headed Dad joyfully brought the Iron Armored Dragon Warrior to his lips and planted a kiss on it, saying, "Big-Headed Son will surely be able to spot me!"

Meanwhile, Big-Headed Son was seated on the train, munching on candy and engrossed in a picture book. As he flipped through the pages, he stumbled upon an illustration of an Iron Dragon Warrior identical to his own. Big-Headed Son exclaimed in amazement, "I've got this Ironclad Dragon Warrior too!" He tossed the book aside, stood on the chair, and mimicked a robot with vigorous up and down arm movements, producing a "kwok" sound.

In the midst of Big-Headed Son's antics, he glanced to the side and noticed a blue cab cruising alongside the train – behold, in the cab's window, an iron armor dragon warrior was indeed waving at him!

Big-Headed Son lunged towards the window, shouting, "Ironclad Dragon! Ironclad Dragon!" As he yelled, the iron armor dragon transformed, revealing itself to be the small head of Small-Headed Dad, swaying towards Big-Headed Son.

"Small-Headed Dad! Small-Headed Dad!" Big-Headed Son was even more thrilled than if he had seen the iron armor dragon warrior. He was practically itching to leap off the train and dive into the embrace of Small-Headed Dad.

The train let out a prolonged whistle and entered a tunnel. The darkness inside was so deep that Big-Headed Son couldn't see a thing. When the train emerged from the tunnel, the blue cab had vanished. Big-Headed Son scowled and was on the verge of tears when, like a magic trick, the cab reappeared from behind a tree.

Big-Headed Son spotted Small-Headed Dad once again, and Small-Headed Dad saw Big-Headed Son. They waved at each other until the train pulled into a station.

The moment the train halted at the station, Big-Headed Son hurriedly descended. However, as soon as he reached the foot of the ladder, he found himself enveloped in the arms of Small-Headed Dad, who had dashed over. "Finally caught you now!" exclaimed Small-Headed Dad with relief.

Big-Headed Son reciprocated the embrace, giving Small-Headed Dad five hearty kisses. They bid farewell to the conductors and proceeded to board another train for their journey back.

New Neighbourhood

Today, the new neighbours were moving in.

During breakfast, Apron Mum suggested to Small-Headed Dad, "Later, we'll tidy up the entrance aisle and extend a warm welcome to our new neighbours."

Small-Headed Dad nodded attentively, "Write another sentence and stick it on the door: 'Welcome new neighbours.'"

Big-Headed Son, after gulping down a big glass of milk and wiping his mouth, inquired eagerly, "New neighbours moving in? That's fantastic! I wonder if there are any children?"

Small-Headed Dad replied, "I guess they would have a dog or a cat even if they have no kids."

"I'm not a fan of dogs and cats, but a boy my age would be great," declared Big-Headed Son, leaving the table and assuming a boxing stance. "We could play and have fun every day!"

After breakfast, Big-Headed Son quietly made his way to the vacant house next door. Gently pushing the door open, he peered inside and discovered it to be empty. When would the new neighbours arrive?

Entering the house and closing the door behind him, Big-Headed Son found himself alone in the empty space. He extended his arms and pretended to fly like an airplane, finding the experience enjoyable.

After some play, he stopped and surveyed the empty house. Realizing that the new neighbours might not appreciate the emptiness, Big-Headed Son took out a few coloured pencils from his pocket. He proceeded to draw a spaceship on one wall, two monsters on another, three bears on yet another, and four balloons on the last.

Satisfied with his artwork, he closed the door and left.

A little while later, Small-Headed Dad brought red paper with "Welcome New neighbour" written on it, neatly pasting it on the door. Apron Mum joyfully added a big handful of flowers to the doorknob, completing the warm welcome.

Come evening, Big-Headed Son sneaked out of the house again to check if the new neighbours had settled in.

This time, the door was firmly locked, and Big-Headed Son couldn't budge it, so he gave it three knocks: "Duk! Duk! Duk!" The door swung open instantly. Big-Headed Son looked up and saw a shiny belt; lifting his gaze again, he spotted a white sweatshirt adorned with a flying horse picture. Straining his neck further, he came face to face with a black visage sporting a substantial beard. Big-Headed Son hesitated and took a step back.

The bearded gent reassured him, "Ah, don't be scared. I'm not a big bear; I'm Big Beard." With a hearty slap, the bearded man ushered Big-Headed Son into the house.

All of a sudden, from behind the thick legs of the bearded uncle, another little face peeked out. This tiny face had two tiny eyes fixed on Big-Headed Son. In a soft voice, she recited, "Big head, big head, don't worry 'bout the rain, people have umbrellas, I have a big head." After finishing, she giggled and hid behind her father's legs.

Big-Headed Son chuckled, touched his substantial noggin, and joined in the laughter. He glanced around the living room and unexpectedly spotted the mural he had painted on the wall, a detail he had completely forgotten!

The bearded man guided Big-Headed Son into the living room, pointing at the paintings on the wall and inquiring, "Did you paint these?"

Upon another look into the living room, Big-Headed Son realized that all their furniture was huddled in the middle of the room. They probably didn't fancy the paintings and intended to erase them before arranging the furniture, Big-Headed Son surmised.

Feeling a bit anxious, he shook his head, then nodded again.

The bearded man promptly lifted him up, expressing his gratitude, "Thank you, thank you so much for beautifying the house with your paintings!"

Small Eyes interjected, "My father mentioned that these paintings are superior to his. My father happens to be a renowned painter."

Big-Headed Son smiled reassuringly and remarked, "I reckon you guys don't fancy plain white walls because there's nothing to see, and it can get quite dull, can't it?"

"Tomorrow, I plan to paint all over that as well. Would you like to join in?" the bearded man asked, pointing towards the ceiling.

Big-Headed Son eagerly nodded, "Absolutely!" The man suddenly seemed like a kid to him.

During dinner at home, Big-Headed Son enthusiastically shared with his parents how much fun the bearded man next door was, adding, "And he's really, really tall …"

"What? Taller than me?" questioned Small-Headed Dad, not entirely convinced.

Big-Headed Son asserted, "Certainly! If he's as tall as a ten-story building, you're only two stories tall."

Small-Headed Dad, hearing this, grumbled, "Boasting!"

"Don't believe me? Go see for yourself!" urged Big-Headed Son impatiently.

The following day, as Big-Headed Son went to assist the new neighbour, Small-Headed Dad sneaked over and peered through a small window. To his surprise, he only saw half of a grown man in the living room – two stubby legs standing on a stool. Small-Headed Dad then crouched down and looked upward, witnessing the bearded man creating artwork on the ceiling with a brush as large as a broom.

The father was taken aback, staggering several steps backward and thudding the back of his head against the aisle wall. His glasses nearly tumbled off, so he steadied them and hurried home to call Apron Mum.

Small-Headed Dad and Apron Mum peered through the small window together, only to find the ceiling transformed into a forest, complete with wildflowers, mushrooms, and birds fluttering about.

Suddenly, the bearded man hollered, "The sun's red!"

"Coming right up!" Small Eyes handed up a bottle of red paint.

A moment later, the bearded man shouted again, "Green for the grass!"

"Here we go!" Big-Headed Son handed up a bottle of green paint.

Small-Headed Dad exchanged glances with Apron Mum, wanting to say something but holding back. Eventually, they walked back to their house together.

By now, darkness had fallen, and dinner was laid out on the table, yet Big-Headed Son had not returned.

Small-Headed Dad glanced at the closed door and remarked, "Big-Headed Son seems quite taken with that bearded man."

"Look at him having so much fun; he's forgotten about us," Apron Mum said, a hint of irritation in her tone.

Small-Headed Dad added, "What an eccentric new neighbour, doodling on the ceiling!" Glancing at the clock, he noted, "It's already seven o'clock; I'll go and call our son back."

Just then, the doorbell rang. They both rose and rushed to open the door. However, their beaming expressions turned into dull faces as they saw Big-Headed Son standing outside, his face and body adorned with a riot of colours, as if he had taken a tumble in a paint bucket. On his open palms, he proudly displayed a red spider and a green frog, both freshly painted.

The following morning, Big-Headed Son woke up early and began searching for something among his toys.

Apron Mum approached and inquired, "What are you looking for?"

"I'm looking for the easel," replied Big-Headed Son.

"Why do you need an easel?" questioned Small-Headed Dad, who had hastily emerged from the bedroom. "Are you planning to go out with that bearded guy to learn how to paint?"

"Huh?" Big-Headed Son nodded curiously.

"I knew it! I just knew it!" Small-Headed Dad declared confidently, and Big-Headed Son thought he was rather remarkable.

On the path leading out of the new village, the bearded man carried an easel, Small Eyes carried an easel, and Big-Headed Son had his own easel in tow. A bit further away from Big-Headed Son, another woman carried an easel. This lady wore sunglasses and sported a flowery silk scarf tied around her head.

They strolled towards the countryside, where the winding path was bordered by ponds, wildflowers, and meadows with lively chickens, ducks, and cows ...

Small Eyes and Big-Headed Son observed, walked, and paused.

In front of a row of fir trees, Big Beard halted. He surveyed the surroundings, chose a satisfactory spot, and set up his easel.

Small Eyes and Big-Headed Son followed suit. The big bearded man proposed, "Let's paint this row of fir trees together, and let's do it with vigour."

The woman with the silk scarf on her head set up her easel not far away but seemed to be constantly looking around, as if she were more interested in her surroundings than in her painting.

After completing their paintings, Small Eyes and Big-Headed Son began chasing butterflies in the grass. While engaged in this activity, they noticed the woman with the silk scarf.

Big-Headed Son suggested, "Let's go over and see what that woman is drawing." Small Eyes agreed, and they walked over together.

Just then, a gust of wind blew, whisking away the woman's silk scarf. Swiftly, she dashed after it, with Big-Headed Son and Small Eyes joining the pursuit. They watched the silk scarf dance in the air like a magnificent butterfly, landing gracefully on top of a fir tree.

Big-Headed Son looked up and remarked, "Oops, can't reach it."

Turning his head, he noticed the woman had short hair, so short it resembled Small-Headed Dad's! "So you're Small-Headed Dad!" Big-Headed Son exclaimed in surprise, joyfully leaping towards his father and inadvertently bumping his big head into Small-Headed Dad's small head.

Small-Headed Dad, delighted to be embraced, hugged Big-Headed Son tightly, saying, "Ah, you still like me!" He gently put Big-Headed Son down, their heads playfully touching.

Small Eyes chimed in, shouting, "Cheers! Cheers!"

The cheers startled the bearded man engrossed in painting. He dropped his paintbrush and rushed over, brandishing his two large fists and shouting alongside Small Eyes, "Go for it! Come on!" The bearded man's booming voice even spooked the little birds, causing them to flutter from tree to tree, still a bit uneasy.

As they made their way home at sunset, Small-Headed Dad no longer needed to carry the easel at a distance. Instead, they all walked together, sharing conversations and laughter along the way.

Fragrant Road

Apron Mum, laden with groceries, strolled homeward, meeting acquaintances along the way. They all took a deep breath and complimented Apron Mum, saying, "Ah, you smell delightful!"

Proudly, Apron Mum pointed to the white orchids adorning her chest and declared, "Look, it's white orchids, fresh from the grocery store!"

Upon entering the house, Big-Headed Son and Small-Headed Dad simultaneously exclaimed, "Wow, it smells amazing!"

Setting down the grocery basket, Apron Mum chuckled, "You both enjoy the fragrance? That's wonderful!"

Entering the kitchen, she began sorting the groceries. Shortly after, she heard Big-Headed Son's enthusiastic voice from inside the house, "Apron Mum! Let's play hide-and-seek, shall we?"

"Sure, sure ..." agreed Apron Mum, recalling her fondness for hide-and-seek from childhood.

After washing her hands, Apron Mum returned to find Small-Headed Dad blindfolded with a flowery silk scarf.

Big-Headed Son declared, "Start!" Small-Headed Dad, blindfolded, roamed around the house with outstretched hands. Quietly, Big-Headed Son and Apron Mum slipped under his arms, eluding his touch. Small-Headed Dad decided to play tricks, arching his nose to make the silk scarf slide down a bit. He peeked and spotted Big-Headed Son hiding behind the curtains, swiftly moving to catch him.

Big-Headed Son hollered, "Not fair! Not fair! You peeked!"

Small-Headed Dad insisted stubbornly, "Show me the evidence!"

Big-Headed Son pointed to a small bench in front of him, accusing, "You didn't touch it when you walked by. You circled around like you could see it."

"Big-Headed Son's got a point," Apron Mum chimed in, coming over to support the argument. "You must have peeked; that's a penalty!" She turned around, grabbed another silk scarf, added it to the original one, and tied the whole bundle over Big-Headed Son's eyes. Big-Headed Son, not taking any chances, fetched some tape and secured it in place.

Alright, let's have another go. Mimicking a dazed man with a bashed head, Small-Headed Dad turned away once more, arms outstretched.

Seeing that Small-Headed Dad seemed unable to touch it, Big-Headed Son taunted, "You're useless! Watch me instead!"

The silk scarf was now tied around Big-Headed Son, who turned with his arms wide open, just as his father had done. He reached out and abruptly stopped, sniffing the air intently. Slowly and thoughtfully, he walked toward Apron Mum, who was discreetly hidden behind the bookcase. "Whoa! Gotcha! Gotcha!" he declared triumphantly.

Apron Mum playfully removed Big-Headed Son's silk scarf and placed it in front of her eyes, remarking, "This silk scarf is so thick; how did you manage to catch me?"

Big-Headed Son giggled mischievously, withholding the secret.

Feigning anger, Apron Mum declared, "If you don't

tell me, I won't play with you!"

Big-Headed Son relented, "Just lower your head and smell it yourself."

As soon as Apron Mum lowered her head, she realized, "So you're 'catching' the scent!"

Small-Headed Dad, patting Big-Headed Son on the side, admitted, "Oops, why didn't I think of that just now?"

A few days later, Big-Headed Son and Small-Headed Dad encountered many blind children disembarking from a vehicle. Some leaned on sticks, while others relied on adults for assistance, making their way toward a school for blind children.

Observing this, Big-Headed Son suggested, "Let's come here every morning to help them, okay?"

Small-Headed Dad considered and responded, "We can only assist two children a day, but there are so many blind children! We'd better think of a better way."

The two fell silent, pondering a solution. As they walked through the grocery market, Big-Headed Son sniffed and exclaimed, "It's the scent of white orchids, just like the ones Apron Mum wears."

Small-Headed Dad also took a whiff and said, "I smell it too. Let's find them; we'll buy a few for Apron Mum, and she'll be delighted!"

Picking four flowers each, they adorned their chests, striding along as if wearing medals. As Big-Headed Son walked, he sniffed vigorously, suddenly stopping in surprise and calling out, "Small-Headed Dad, I know the way!"

"Come on! "

"Blind children may not see with their eyes, but they can certainly smell with their noses. Remember the last time we played hide-and-seek, I caught Apron Mum with my nose, didn't I?" Big-Headed Son reminded Small-Headed Dad, who nodded in agreement.

Continuing his idea, Big-Headed Son proposed, "Why don't we plant a row of scented flowers and trees along the road in front of the school for blind children? That should work, right?"

Small-Headed Dad, with a delighted expression, nodded and lifted Big-Headed Son into the air, exclaiming, "What a brilliant idea!"

Without wasting time, Big-Headed Son and Small-Headed Dad headed to the flower and bird market to purchase seeds.

"Grandpa, we want to buy trees with a scent," Big-Headed Son informed the old man.

The elderly gentleman was a bit puzzled. Small-Headed Dad clarified, "Oh, Grandpa, we're looking for tree seeds that can bloom in all seasons and will eventually emit fragrance."

After a moment's thought, Grandpa said, "Alright, I'll give you four kinds of trees with flowers in spring, summer, fall, and winter."

With the seeds in hand, Big-Headed Son and Small-Headed Dad immediately headed to the School for Blind Children and got to work: tilling the soil, ploughing the ground, and sowing the seeds.

In just a few days, shoots emerged; within a few weeks, the little trees started to grow; and after half a year, the flowers on the trees blossomed.

Finally, one day, when the blind children descended from the car, they collectively exclaimed, "It smells amazing! What is it?" Some dropped their canes, while others let go of the adults' hands. Following the scent, they walked towards the entrance of the school.

Big-Headed Son and Small-Headed Dad jubilantly exclaimed, "Success! Success!"

Parents and teachers expressed their gratitude, acknowledging, "Thank you so much; this is a truly brilliant idea!"

Big-Headed Son proposed, "We'll teach them to play games with their noses in the future!"

Inspired by their success, the duo visited a store and bought various spices—apple, orange, banana. Upon returning home, they crafted headdresses shaped like fruits from cardboard and filled small cloth bags with the corresponding spices, hanging them next to each headdress.

Taking the headdresses to the playground of the School for Blind Children, Big-Headed Son and Small-Headed Dad first allowed each blind child to smell the spices individually and then distributed the headdresses.

"Now, do you remember the smell of each fruit?" inquired Big-Headed Son.

The blind children wearing the headdresses replied joyfully, "I remember!"

Taking over, Small-Headed Dad declared, "Now, we'll use our noses to play hide-and-seek. I'll count one, two, three, and start!"

The only blind child not wearing a headdress embraced the challenge, touching the air with outstretched arms and inhaling through his nose.

"Got it! Got it!" shouted the nose-sucking blind boy, successfully catching a little girl, "It's a banana doll!" The little girl was adorned with a banana headdress.

"That's right! That's right!" exclaimed Big-Headed Son and Small-Headed Dad in unison.

They were having such a good time, and lo and behold, white clouds gathered overhead; they were having such a good time that little birds flew overhead. They played so joyously that the dozing dog and kitten were awakened, stretching out their necks and staring with wide eyes.

When the game concluded, the Banana Doll wiped the sweat from her forehead and said, "I've never played hide-and-seek before; it was so much fun! Can we play again tomorrow? Can we play again tomorrow?"

"Okay," replied Big-Headed Son.

The Peach Doll, red-faced and already a big boy, ran over and grabbed Small-Headed Dad with both hands. He said, "I used to think I'd never be happy as a blind person. Now, I don't think so anymore ..."

Small-Headed Dad responded, "If you truly change your mindset, your happiness will grow!"

...

After school, Big-Headed Son and Small-Headed Dad stood in front of the school, observing the blind children strolling along the "Fragrant Road" with smiles on their faces. Big-Headed Son gazed at the scene and suddenly whispered, "Small-Headed Dad, why do I feel like I want to cry?"

"Why? Tell daddy quickly!" Small-Headed Dad responded gently.

Big-Headed Son's lips quivered, and he burst into tears, expressing, "They're just like me, but they can't see anything anymore – not the stars, not the moon, not the school, not daddy and mummy ..."

Small-Headed Dad enveloped Big-Headed Son in a tight embrace, saying, "Yes, they are very unfortunate. They don't have bright eyes. But we have eyes, and we should share with them everything we can see. That's how we can help." Big-Headed Son nodded, tears streaming down his face.

Later, Big-Headed Son and Small-Headed Dad adorned the trees with numerous colourful lights that sparkled in the evening. Though the blind children couldn't see the lights, Small-Headed Dad and Big-Headed Son described them, saying, "There are red lights, green lights, and yellow lights on the trees ... They twinkle and twinkle, just like ..."

"Just like the stars in the sky, right? That's what mummy told me!" interjected a blind child.

"Exactly!" exclaimed Big-Headed Son.

One by one, the blind children walked beneath the trees adorned with coloured lights, their noses inhaling the fragrance, and their ears absorbing Big-Headed Son's descriptions: "There are red lights, there are green lights, there are yellow lights ... They are like stars in the sky, twinkling, twinkling ..."

New Year's Eve Dinner

It's New Year's Eve, the excitement is palpable! Laughter and warmth fill every kitchen as people prepare egg dumplings and roll round rice balls.

In the kitchen, Small-Headed Dad is washing fish, while Apron Mum is frying sunflower seeds. Big-Headed Son looks at the spread of food and asks, "Why do we have to make so many delicious things for New Year? It's like you're getting married again!"

Apron Mum and Small-Headed Dad burst into laughter. Small-Headed Dad explains, "It's called saying goodbye to the old and welcoming the new, understand?"

Apron Mum adds, "After this, we are going to make glutinous rice cakes and sesame candies."

After a while, the glutinous rice cakes are ready and left to dry on the balcony with the fish. Similarly, the sesame candies are prepared and left to dry in the kitchen alongside the sunflower seeds.

The next morning, while Small-Headed Dad and Big-Headed Son are still sleeping, Apron Mum gets up. Suddenly, her shouts roll into the bedroom like thunder, forcefully opening the tightly closed eyelids of Small-Headed Dad and Big-Headed Son: "Oops! It's too bad! The mouse has come to steal the sunflower seeds! Sesame candies have also been bitten! It must be a white mouse that escaped from the institute next door!"

Big-Headed Son and Small-Headed Dad rushed in, each holding a slipper, making their way to the kitchen. To their surprise, they found a small pile of empty shells right next to the large plate of sunflower seeds, and the sesame seed candies were scattered and bitten in a chaotic mess.

Apron Mum noticed their arrival, ready to say something when she suddenly recalled something. She hurriedly dashed out of the kitchen, and from the balcony, a thunderous exclamation echoed, "Oops! This can't be! The fish tail is missing! It must have been stolen by a stray cat! Oh no! There's bird poop on the glutinous rice cake! Probably a damn sparrow!"

Big-Headed Son and Small-Headed Dad rushed back to the balcony, only to witness a tail-less fish dangling in the air and black spots tarnishing the snow-white glutinous rice cake. Apron Mum's face contorted in anger, "Tomorrow's New Year's Eve, and we nearly missed our New Year's Eve dinner tonight! Starting now, one of you will stand guard in the kitchen, and the other on the balcony." Having said that, she turned and walked away.

Big-Headed Son and Small-Headed Dad stood in disbelief, staring at Apron Mum's retreating figure, almost speechless.

Small-Headed Dad gasped, turning to Big-Headed Son, "Did you hear that? Apron Mum asked us to stand guard here."

Big-Headed Son responded cheerfully, "I heard! I've never stood guard before; it might be fun." Then he glanced around and couldn't see the kitchen. He added, "It's just a bit of a shame that we're so far away."

Small-Headed Dad contemplated, "Let me see what I can do ..."

"I have an idea!" exclaimed Big-Headed Son as he rushed into the house, returning with a red toy telephone. "Small-Headed Dad, it will come in handy this time!"

Small-Headed Dad happily took one handset and placed it on the balcony. Meanwhile, Big-Headed Son took the other handset and darted into the kitchen.

"Small-Head 007, Small-Head 007, any sign of the enemy? Please report, please report," came Big-Headed Son's voice through the earpiece.

Small-Headed Dad promptly responded, "Big Head 007, Big Head 007, no enemy detected, report over."

On the balcony, Small-Headed Dad surveyed the rows of big and small fish, occasionally glancing back at the drying glutinous rice cakes in the sun. Birds chirped in the trees, and Small-Headed Dad taunted them, saying, "Ha-ha! This time, you don't dare to come and eat it!"

The birds, frightened, hastily flew away. "Meow! Meow!" echoed the purr of a kitten from downstairs. Just as Small-Headed Dad peeked out, the kitten vanished in terror.

Small-Headed Dad yawned twice and stretched his legs before attempting to doze off. However, Big-Headed Son's voice emerged from the earpiece again, "Small-Head 007, Small-Head 007, have you found any enemy situation? Please report, please report."

Small-Headed Dad replied, "There won't be any hostiles today; are you still willing to stand down?"

"No, it's too dull without an adversary!"

"Then how do we slip away?"

"We'll just tell Apron Mum that we're going to buy rat

poison, bird poison, and feral cat poison ..."

The continuous chatter of Small-Headed Dad resonated through the earpiece, "Great idea! Great idea!"

Big-Headed Son and Small-Headed Dad successfully deceived Apron Mum and headed to the sunny grove. While walking, they noticed a line of small birds perched on the tree branches, chirping away, seemingly singing to them.

Big-Headed Son exclaimed, "The birds are singing; it's New Year! It's the New Year!"

Small-Headed Dad added, "The birds are saying, 'Your rice cakes taste good. Your rice cakes taste good!'"

They burst into laughter.

Continuing on their stroll, they encountered two cats basking in the warm sunshine, peacefully dozing with closed eyes. Approaching gently, the kittens woke up, fixing them with wide-eyed gazes.

"Don't be scared; we're not here to catch you!" Big-Headed Son reassured them.

Small-Headed Dad chimed in, "Ha-ha! You must be the cats that stole the fish's tail!" The moment he uttered those words, the two cats swiftly turned and dashed away.

Big-Headed Son scolded, "I blame you for scaring them off!"

As they continued their walk, they suddenly spotted something peculiar wriggling on the ground ahead. Drawing closer, they discovered a beautiful stocking twisting around like a little train.

"Hey, can a stocking walk too?" Big-Headed Son exclaimed in amazement.

Small-Headed Dad squatted down to take a look and noticed that the stocking still had a few small holes, resembling windows. Peeking through one of the holes, he chuckled as he discovered a little mouse's face. When the little mouse spotted them, it squeaked and scurried away.

Big-Headed Son delightedly remarked, "Look, the little train is going faster and faster; it's really fun! So much fun!"

Small-Headed Dad, pointing at the "window" where the little mouse had appeared, said, "Little rascal, tell me quickly, how many sunflower seeds did you eat?"

The "train" suddenly stopped and swiftly departed.

Big-Headed Son expressed disappointment, "It's all your fault for scaring them away again!"

Small-Headed Dad defended, "I didn't scare them; that was their mum calling them home for New Year's Eve dinner!"

Big-Headed Son suddenly remembered Apron Mum,

"Oh no, what are we going to tell Apron Mum when we get home?"

Small-Headed Dad suggested, "Just tell her the pesticides are sold out."

"But then she'll want us to stand guard again," Big-Headed Son protested, "and I don't want to."

Small-Headed Dad inquired, "So ... are we genuinely going to buy pesticide?"

Big-Headed Son replied with a sigh, "No, no, no. They are still quite adorable when they're not snatching food, especially those rats."

Small-Headed Dad noted, "And if we don't stand guard, and if we don't buy the pesticides, then we won't be able to have our New Year's Eve dinner today!"

Big-Headed Son said, "I have a great idea ..." and then whispered very softly.

Big-Headed Son and Small-Headed Dad rushed home with a large bag of items.

"Apron Mum, come and see!" exclaimed Big-Headed Son as he placed the items on the table one by one. "This is rat poison, this is bird poison, and this is feral cat poison."

Apron Mum scrutinized the bags of cakes, dried fish, and melon nuts, examining them carefully. "Is this pesticide?"

Big-Headed Son and Small-Headed Dad nodded in unison, proudly declaring, "Yes." When Apron Mum turned away, Big-Headed Son and Small-Headed Dad exchanged a triumphant, discreet high-five.

As darkness fell, firecrackers began to pop.

"It's New Year's Eve dinner! Let's have New Year's Eve dinner!" shouted Big-Headed Son joyfully, assisting his mum with setting the plates and bowls. Apron Mum was delighted, and Small-Headed Dad wore a contented smile.

They raised their glasses and wished each other a happy new year! However, as they enjoyed the meal, Big-Headed Son disappeared, and shortly after, Small-Headed Dad also vanished. In the living room during the New Year's Eve dinner, only Apron Mum remained, quietly savouring her food.

Feeling a bit puzzled, Apron Mum stood up and walked over to the balcony, where she found Small-Headed Dad leaning on the railing, contentedly watching something below.

"What are you looking at?" Apron Mum inquired.

Without turning back, Small-Headed Dad replied, "Watching them eat their New Year's Eve dinner."

Realizing it was Apron Mum, he suddenly covered his mouth in surprise. Apron Mum followed his gaze and saw a few cats and birds gathered under a street lamp, feasting on the "pesticide" that Big-Headed Son and Small-Headed Dad had brought back.

Apron Mum huffed, turned back to the kitchen, and noticed Big-Headed Son hiding in the corner of the doorway, peering out and laughing with wide eyes. Apron Mum followed his line of sight and spotted a few mice sharing a piece of cake.

As Apron Mum observed, her initial frown gradually turned into a smile.

"What did you buy? A bag of pesticide or a bag of New Year's Eve dinner?" she asked, chuckling.

Big-Headed Son, upon seeing Apron Mum, quickly spoke up, "Apron Mum, you won't scold us, right? You see, the mice don't come to steal from us when they have their New Year's Eve dinner!"

Apron Mum sighed, saying, "You guys can think of everything."

Small-Headed Dad, Apron Mum, and Big-Headed Son returned to the dining room to continue their New Year's Eve dinner. Big-Headed Son gleefully nibbled on a big chicken leg, proclaiming, "Now we can have a big New

Year's Eve dinner!"

Small-Headed Dad glanced at Apron Mum and added, "Anyway, the cat and the mouse are eating, eating ... their poison." Unexpectedly, as Small-Headed Dad said this, Apron Mum burst into laughter, spraying a mouthful of wine onto the table like red rain.

Downstairs, the wild cat continued to feast; in the kitchen, the mice were still enjoying their meal. At the table, Big-Headed Son, Small-Headed Dad, and Apron Mum ate, laughed, and toasted repeatedly, creating a joyful atmosphere for the New Year!

Writing and Reading Letters

In the morning, the little alarm clock went off, and as soon as Big-Headed Son opened his eyes, he asked, "Where's Small-Headed Dad?"

Apron Mum was making the bedspread on the big bed and said, "Small-Headed Dad has gone to work."

Big-Headed Son tilted his chin up as if addressing the ceiling, "No fun, Small-Headed Dad's gone off again!"

Apron Mum walked over, patted his big head, and said, "If he doesn't go to work, how can he earn money? If he can't earn money, how can he buy you toys?"

"I don't care," Big-Headed Son said angrily, "I'm going to see Small-Headed Dad when I get up in the morning anyway!"

In the evening, when Small-Headed Dad came back, and they all ate dinner together, Apron Mum told Small-

Headed Dad about it. Small-Headed Dad listened while nodding his head.

As soon as the little alarm clock rang the next morning, Apron Mum ran in and shook Big-Headed Son, "Come on, come on, Small-Headed Dad left you a letter!"

Big-Headed Son's eyes widened when he heard that, "Liar! Where is it?"

Apron Mum held the clothes out to Big-Headed Son and said, "It's better for you to get dressed and go get it yourself; Mum has taught you all the words on there."

Big-Headed Son hurriedly got up, put on his clothes in a rush, and ran into the living room. Ah, only to see the Transformer placed in the corner of the toy stood majestically, and under its iron arm, there really clamped a snow-white letter. Big-Headed Son cheered and ran over to take down the letter and carefully opened it. He saw four big words written in blue pen on a tiny letterhead: "Big-Headed Son, Goodbye!"

Big-Headed Son read the letter several times, raised his right hand, and moved his fingers, making the gesture of "goodbye."

Apron Mum kissed Big-Headed Son and said, "Are you happy now?"

Big-Headed Son smiled and kissed his mum.

The next morning, Big-Headed Son found the letter in the pocket of the big hairy monkey in the toy corner, and the letter was also written with these six big words, but this time with a red pen.

On the third morning, Big-Headed Son discovered the letter in the dumper in the Toy Corner, and the six words on the letter were written with a green pen.

On this day, Big-Headed Son received the letter and examined it carefully. He then hurried into the kitchen and addressed Apron Mum, "Small-Headed Dad wrote me a letter, and I want to write him back! Apron Mum, will you teach me how to write? I want to write ..."

In the evening, Small-Headed Dad returned from work.

"Where's Son?" Small-Headed Dad inquired, glancing towards the living room and bedroom. Usually, Big-Headed Son was the first to welcome him home.

Apron Mum simply smiled, offering no response.

Small-Headed Dad changed his shoes and headed towards the living room. "Big-Headed Son! Small-Headed Dad is back!"

The living room was empty, but the bedroom door was closed. Small-Headed Dad stroked his small head, growing increasingly puzzled. Just then, Big-Headed Son's voice emanated from the bedroom, "Small-Headed Dad, you have to read the letter I wrote to you first. Only then can you see me. You can't see the letter writer when you read the letter!"

Apron Mum entered and gestured towards the coffee table. There, a letter lay, adorned with a tiny plum deer sticky note on the envelope.

Small-Headed Dad swiftly picked it up and opened it. The letterhead, written in red crayon, bore four large letters: Hello Small-Headed Dad! Accompanying the greeting were comical drawings of father-son moments, unmistakably depicting the two of them.

Overjoyed, Small-Headed Dad read it aloud, then whispered, then went word by word: "Hello, Small-Headed Dad."

He planted a kiss on the letterhead and then addressed the closed bedroom door, "Come out, Big-Headed Son! I've read your letter."

The bedroom door swung open, and Big-Headed Son "flew" out, resembling an eager pigeon. He leaped into Small-Headed Dad's arms, wrapping his hands around his neck.

Every day after that, Big-Headed Son always received a letter from Small-Headed Dad when he got up in the morning, and Small-Headed Dad always received a letter from Big-Headed Son when he came home from work in the evening. They both thought it was the most pleasant thing in their day.

But soon, Small-Headed Dad had to go to another city on a business trip, and it would be a long time. When he was leaving, Small-Headed Dad said, "I can't write to you in the morning."

Big-Headed Son said, "I can't write to you in the evening either." They both felt a little sad.

Small-Headed Dad left with his suitcase, and Apron Mum and Big-Headed Son said to him at the door of the house, "Bye!"

That night, Big-Headed Son was watching TV alone. After the cartoon was over, Auntie Announcer came out and said, "Good news! Good news! We will soon hold a national children's poetry contest. The contest will be broadcast to the whole country; All kids are welcome to participate. The registration number is 1122334: 1122334. Broadcast it again ..."

Big-Headed Son stared as if he remembered something, then he stood up and took the phone, dialing without hesitation: 1122334.

On the day of the match, Apron Mum sent Big-

Headed Son to the TV broadcasting hall, and the match had already started. Big-Headed Son had just sat down when the host reported, "The following will come out is the No. 7 contestant. He recited a poem titled: 'I Miss My Dad'"

No.7 contestant was Big-Headed Son, who was wearing a long-sleeved shirt, short pants, and stockings. Big-Headed Son bowed to the audience and began to recite:

"My Dad,

Small head, big hands.

Tell me a joke every day,

Tell me a joke every day.

Now that Daddy's not home.

I miss him.

I miss him."

At that moment, Small-Headed Dad, staying in the hotel, sat on the sofa watching TV. Witnessing Big-Headed Son reciting the poem, he smiled through tears and hurriedly picked up the phone to call the live broadcast, saying, "Hello! I'm an off-camera audience member. Please convey to contestant #7 that the poem he recited touched the hearts of all the dads away on business ..."

The music began, and all the participating children

came out. The host announced the winners on the spot, "Three excellence awards. They are: contestant No. 1, contestant No. 5, and contestant No. 7 ..."

Contestant No. 7! That's me! Big-Headed Son was so excited that he forgot he was still on the stage. He jumped to his feet, clapped his big head, and cheered, "Wow! Wow!" The judges and the audience laughed at the sight. Several reporters aimed their cameras at Big-Headed Son, "click, click, click, click" ... The flashes were so intense that Big-Headed Son couldn't keep his eyes open. Quickly turning around, he presented the back of his head to the reporters.

Meanwhile, Small-Headed Dad strolled down the streets of another city. The newspaper seller called out all the way, "Evening News Today, see the latest news!" Small-Headed Dad purchased a copy, opened it, and saw Big-Headed Son's competition poem featured on the front page. Next to the poem was a large colourful photo of a peculiar big head from the back. The father chuckled and couldn't resist pushing his small head against the big head in the newspaper.

Turning to the newspaper seller, he asked, "How many copies do you have? I'll take them all!"

The newspaper seller said in surprise, "You want them

all? I have 300 copies!" Small-Headed Dad pulled out his wallet, still nodding.

Small-Headed Dad went home with his suitcase. As soon as he entered the house, he first closed his eyes, then fished out a letter from his coat pocket and handed it to Big-Headed Son. Big-Headed Son immediately caught it and ran into the bedroom.

Big-Headed Son opened the letter in the bedroom, read it, and then lay down on the table to write a reply. Small-Headed Dad sat in the living room with his eyes fixed on the bedroom door. A moment later, from under the door slowly drilled out a letter, the envelope attached to a small white rabbit sticky paper, eyes fixed on the small head of the father to see. Father Small-Headed jumped up and picked it up like a treasure ...

Alien Car

In the evening, a mass of dark clouds in the sky resembled the face of a monster. They twisted and turned, being pushed and squeezed, as if they were playing a game or quarrelling. The cinema had just finished showing "Super Monster," and it was letting out now, with many adults and children emerging, each face displaying either nervousness or excitement.

A girl exclaimed, "I don't want to see this kind of film ever again; it scares me to death!"

A boy chimed in, "Over the top, what a ride! That monster has hands coming out of its eyes!"

Big-Headed Son and Small-Headed Dad were also strolling in the crowd, and they didn't begin conversing until they turned onto a side street.

Big-Headed Son inquired, "Small-Headed Dad, is

there really that kind of monster?"

"No, that's imaginary."

"Anyway, I'm not afraid even if there is," Big-Headed Son said loftily. "So I am going to say to it, 'I am the king of monsters! You have to listen to me!'"

Small-Headed Dad listened and remarked, "Before you could finish, the monster would have thrown it to the stars."

Speaking of this, they looked up at the sky together. The dark clouds had covered the sky, and they gazed at the earth proudly, as if they were awaiting some mischief.

Big-Headed Son said, "The stars didn't come out tonight, so they've probably all been eaten by the dark clouds."

Small-Headed Dad responded, "It's going to storm; let's hurry and run!"

"Aye! Small-Headed Dad!" Big-Headed Son exclaimed and ran ahead.

Big-Headed Son took the lead, and Small-Headed Dad followed behind. As they were sprinting, a lightning bolt, akin to a colossal sword, crackled across the sky, followed by a resounding "boom," as if a massive stone in the heavens had been cleaved by the sword. Startled, Big-Headed Son swiftly crouched down, clutching his sizable head tightly with both hands. Right on his tail, Small-Headed Dad couldn't stop in time, stumbled over Big-Headed Son's prone form, and somersaulted. Small-Headed Dad's glasses were catapulted up onto a tree branch, where they swung merrily.

Fearing the "sword" and the deafening noise, Big-Headed Son lifted Small-Headed Dad and suggested, "Small-Headed Dad, you'd better run ahead; I'll trail behind you."

They resumed their dash, and as they did, the rain began to pour. Big-Headed Son exclaimed joyfully, "What fun! It's so much fun!" He tilted his face upward, allowing the rain to fall into his mouth.

Small-Headed Dad remarked, "Well? Apron Mum has never taken you out in this much rain before, has she?"

In just a few moments, their clothes were thoroughly soaked, as if they had been fished out of the washing machine without being wrung dry. Their hair was also drenched, adhering to their big and small heads, with the former appearing even larger and the latter smaller. The uneven ground soon formed puddles, and they merrily splashed through the large and small puddles, creating a lively scene as if running through a water fountain.

Running, Big-Headed Son, panting, exclaimed,

"Small-Headed Dad, I really can't run."

Without glancing back, Small-Headed Dad replied, "Just imagine that there are monsters chasing behind you."

Big-Headed Son turned his head to look behind him – dark, silent, only the "clattering" sound of rain on the ground. He was so frightened that he immediately rushed up and grabbed Small-Headed Dad's large hand.

The rain truly pursued them like a monster, "clatter, clatter, clatter," the sound growing louder and more urgent.

Small-Headed Dad commented as they ran, "If we keep running, we'll turn into two fish!"

"Great!" exclaimed Big-Headed Son, "I want to turn into a shark!"

"What about Apron Mum? She'll be lonely without us!" Small-Headed Dad reminded Big-Headed Son.

Big-Headed Son pondered, "Then ..." He suddenly spotted a substantial concrete pipe ahead, "Let's just be human and go in there!"

Small-Headed Dad took a look and suggested, "Yes, step up; inside, we can shelter from the rain and rest!"

They ran until they reached the concrete pipe, seeking refuge from the rain.

Removing their shirts, they wrung out two large puddles of water; taking off their shoes, they poured out four significant puddles. Tilting their heads left and right, they saw the water flowing out, cleansing their feet. Finally, Big-Headed Son forcefully sucked in his nose and sprayed the rainwater from his nose onto Small-Headed Dad's smaller head. Small-Headed Dad hastily dodged it. Unexpectedly, when he moved his feet, the concrete pipe shifted with him, turning in one direction. Big-Headed Son was jolted so vigorously that he nearly toppled over.

Small-Headed Dad's eyes lit up behind his eyeglass lenses: "Ha-ha! I've discovered the 'centre of gravity shifting method'; we can use this principle to avoid getting wet and get home at the same time."

"Really?" Big-Headed Son jumped for joy, and the cement pipe wobbled again.

Small-Headed Dad said, "You are guaranteed to succeed if you obey orders and follow directions."

The pipe slowly rolled in one direction, and Big-Headed Son and Small-Headed Dad each stood on one end of the pipe, moving their feet together at the same speed.

The cement pipe rolled faster and faster, and Big-Headed Son followed Small-Headed Dad's footsteps more rapidly.

As Big-Headed Son moved his feet, he exclaimed loudly: "Ah, happy! Happy! It's so much fun!"

Small-Headed Dad shouted, "Pay attention and focus your minds! You watch the cars on the left, I'll watch the cars on the right!"

Big-Headed Son replied quickly: "Yes! I will resolutely carry out the order!"

The cement pipe went straight down the street, rolling fast in the pouring rain. Big-Headed Son and Small-Headed Dad couldn't get wet anymore, and they triumphantly made up their own song as they watched the pavement:

We are men

Not afraid of dark skies

Rumble, rumble, rumble

Rumble, rumble, rumble

We'll leave the darkness

Behind us

At that moment, a lorry approached in the distance, driving straight towards them. The driver continued on his route, and suddenly his eyes widened as if he had seen a ghost. As the vehicle drew closer, he finally got a clear view of the concrete pipe rolling in the rain. He thought to himself that it had no doors or windows, yet it moved on its own, so it must be – "Ah! A UFO! A UFO!" He yelled, slammed on the brakes, executed a rapid U-turn, and fled without a trace.

Shortly after, another car approached from behind the concrete pipe. The driver slowed down, illuminated the cement pipe with the headlights, but couldn't discern anything. He rolled down the window for a closer look, and upon realizing it was a peculiar rolling object, his voice quivered, "It's the Devil's Car! The devil car!" He promptly turned left and took another side road.

"I never thought our 'car' would transform into a tiger car and scare away all the other cars!" exclaimed Small-Headed Dad triumphantly.

Big-Headed Son added, "This way, we can drive with our eyes closed, and there won't be any other cars anyway!"

As they conversed, ha! A group of young lads and lasses in a convertible pulled up at the junction, singing pop songs loudly, with the rain providing a rhythmic backdrop. Just as they were singing and bopping their heads, they spotted the concrete pipe and were so startled that they lost their tunes, leaving only the pattering rain. In a panic, they closed the car hood and sped away with more horsepower. They dared not speak until the cement pipe was out of sight:

"What kind of monster is that? Could it be a UFO?"

"We're still on Earth, right? How could we see something from an alien planet!"

"That's probably an alien car!"

"Let's ring up the television." ...

The cement pipe continued to roll down the street. The rain started to lighten as all the drivers were frightened away, and the street was empty. The cement pipe rolled faster and faster, and in no time, it rolled in front of their house.

"It's so boring!" said Big-Headed Son as he got out of the cement pipe. "I'd rather stay up tonight than stay in the cement pipe."

Small-Headed Dad said, "Then we're sure to be sent to the hospital in the morning for another week, and that's going to be tough."

As soon as he entered, Small-Headed Dad urged Big-Headed Son to take a shower first: "Soak hard in hot water." Small-Headed Dad turned on the TV, only to see the martial arts movie on the screen suddenly interrupted and turn into an announcer. The announcer said, "Viewers, we've just received a call from an enthusiastic viewer who said they saw an alien vehicle on Highway 7. All of our camera crews are now on their way to the scene, so please tune in to ..."

Big-Headed Son heard it too, and wrapped in a towel, he ran out of the bathroom to watch.

Many people appeared on the screen, as well as the police, and the TV station's car drove through the streets at night, finally arriving – and stopping – in front of a concrete pipe.

The announcer went on: "Look, behind us, this concrete pipe is the alien car ..."

Daddy and Son laughed and opened the window to see a sea of people surrounding the concrete pipe they had just left behind, with camera lights and searchlights like lightning.

Big-Headed Son said: "Small-Headed Dad, that makes us 'aliens'!"

Small-Headed Dad said: "Yes, the 'aliens' have to call the TV station now!"

Small-Headed Dad dialed the TV station hotline: "Hello! I'd like to come to the TV station to explain about the 'alien car' you're broadcasting. Okay, I'll be right there."

Big-Headed Son and Small-Headed Dad quickly

showered, quickly changed into clean clothes, and quickly walked out of the house toward the TV station. Along the way, they couldn't help but sing again:

We are men

Not afraid of dark skies

Rumble, rumble

Rumble, rumble, rumble

We'll leave the darkness

We'll leave the darkness behind

...

The Retrieved Swing

Big-Headed Son had a brilliant idea – he wanted to fashion a swing under the grand tree in front of his abode. This way, he could swing whenever the mood struck, eliminating the need to queue up at the distant children's playground. Moreover, the swings there were communal, belonging to everyone, but the one he crafted would be solely his – a prospect that delighted Big-Headed Son.

Armed with a lengthy rope, he aimed to toss it over the branches and secure a knot to create the swing. However, the tree proved too towering, and the rope consistently fell to the ground halfway through its ascent, leaving him quite frustrated!

Undeterred, Big-Headed Son persisted in his attempts to fling the rope upward. A kitten approached him, sparking an idea. Waving at the feline, he called, "Mimi, come here and help!" The kitten dutifully complied. Big-Headed Son fastened one end of the rope to the kitten's tail, then patted its rear, instructing, "Mimi, up the tree!"

However, the kitten hesitated, casting a reluctant glance at the rope on its tail. Big-Headed Son produced a bag of dried fish flakes from his pocket, tempting the feline by waving it before its eyes. He declared, "If you climb up from here and come down from there, I'll give you some dried fish flakes." The kitten purred, seemingly understanding, and began to ascend the tree.

From below, Big-Headed Son directed, "Yes, that's it, go up a little more!" Waving the dried fish in his hand, he encouraged the kitten. Seeing the treat, the kitten assumed it was for consumption and promptly descended using the same route.

Big-Headed Son, vexed, stamped his feet. "Go up! Quickly go up! I want you to come down that way!" Startled, the kitten swiftly retreated up the tree. Observing this, Big-Headed Son patted his ample head. This time, he moved to the other side of the tree before waving a dried fish fillet and shouting, "Come down!" Reluctantly, the kitten leapt down the tree along with the rope.

Big-Headed Son exclaimed, "Blimey! It worked!" Now the long rope can be seen hanging down like a snake through the branches of the tree. Big-Headed Son squatted down to untie the rope from the cat's tail and then chucked the bag of dried fish flakes all over the kitten. The kitten happily nabbed it with its front paws and lay down on its side to scoff it down.

Big-Headed Son tied a knot between the two ends of the rope, and the swing was ready. He just fancied a sit on it, but suddenly he stopped and looked at the rope with a worried expression, afraid that it might not be strong enough.

At that moment, the kitten finished munching on the dried fish and was happily circling around Big-Headed Son's feet. Big-Headed Son lowered his big head and had another idea: Yes, let the kitten try first.

The kitten seemed to have sussed out what Big-Headed Son was thinking and scarpered. Big-Headed Son chased after it and pounced on it before catching the kitten, declaring, "Now you can't leg it!" He plonked the kitten on the swing. The kitten was so scared that it "meowed" and grabbed the rope on both sides with its two front paws.

Big-Headed Son saw this and remarked, "Yes, the kitten is really smart; it will work." When he finished, he gave the swing a good shove. He observed the kitten closing its eyes tightly in fear, and the hairs on its body stood up, as if it were a hedgehog. Just as the swing reached its highest point, the kitten leaped up into the tree and never came down again.

Big-Headed Son cursed at the kitten, now high up in the tree, "You coward, you'd better watch me swing!"

Big-Headed Son turned around, plonked his backside on the rope, and then looked up, finding no change in the rope. So, he slowly raised his feet off the ground, then looked up again, and everything still appeared normal. He laughed and gave himself a pep talk, saying, "Not afraid! I am not afraid!" Son closed his eyes, pulled with his buttocks, but the swing had not swung up yet—only to hear a "bang" sound. Big-Headed Son sustained a heavy fall on the ground, and his buttocks felt so painful! He opened his eyes, only to see two ropes cut off in front of his eyes, swaying around as if intending to mock him. The kitten, witnessing everything from the tree, happily "meowed". Big-Headed Son was so angry that he swung his fist at it, saying, "Yeah, don't you dare laugh at me ..."

At that moment, Small-Headed Dad returned.

"Big-Headed Son, why are you sitting on the ground?" Small-Headed Dad inquired, puzzled.

Big-Headed Son rose with a rueful expression and

said, "Can you make me a swing under the big tree?"

In the afternoon, the duo of Big-Headed Son and Small-Headed Dad jointly rolled an old car tire and made their way to the grand tree.

Seated on the tire, Small-Headed Dad exclaimed, "I'm so tired!"

Big-Headed Son insisted, "Not tired, not tired! Hurry, make me a tire swing; I've never seen one before." He attempted to pull the seated Small-Headed Dad, but to no avail.

Still seated, Small-Headed Dad stated, "I don't have the strength."

Now, Big-Headed Son decided not to rely on strength alone but to use his wits. He tapped his big head, recalling that Small-Headed Dad often said, "Love is power." He promptly embraced Small-Headed Dad and planted five kisses in quick succession. Indeed, Small-Headed Dad extended his arms, regained his strength, and stood up.

Small-Headed Dad began constructing a frame with long wooden strips. Subsequently, he threaded a rope about as thick as Big-Headed Son's arm through the tire, hung it up, and voilà, the swing was ready. Big-Headed Son and the kitten joyfully circled the swing, their happiness evident.

Small-Headed Dad took the inaugural swing, with Big-Headed Son pushing vigorously – one, two, three ... Small-Headed Dad closed his eyes and reminisced, "Ah, I feel like I'm back in a happy childhood!"

Observing Small-Headed Dad with closed eyes, Big-Headed Son, anxious, interjected, "Small-Headed Dad, don't fall asleep! I haven't tried it yet!" To rouse him, he playfully tickled Small-Headed Dad, prompting him to jump down and make space for his son and the kitten to enjoy the swing.

Swing, oh, swing! Big-Headed Son sported a joyful smile, and the kitten emitted contented purrs. A little boy approached, observing with feet seemingly glued to the ground; a little girl, captivated, followed the swing's turns. Gradually, the swing attracted a cluster of small children who, in unison, expressed their delight: "Swings made out of tires are so much fun; I've never played on one before!"

A younger sister approached Big-Headed Son on the swing with fingers in her mouth, saying, "Big Head Brother, can I sit down for a while, please?"

Small-Headed Dad halted the swing, addressing Big-Headed Son, "You can come down now and let the other children have some fun too!"

Ignoring the suggestion, Big-Headed Son remained

aloft. The children watched and waited, but eventually, one by one, they departed. Small-Headed Dad reiterated the idea, waited once more, and eventually took the kitten away too.

Left alone beneath the tree, Big-Headed Son swung in solitude, exclaiming, "You all go away, just so I can play alone, ha-ha!" But without the audience, his enthusiasm waned. The swing gradually stilled, resembling a stool hanging in the air. With no children around, it felt akin to playing alone at home. Big-Headed Son's joy turned to a frown, and eventually, he hopped off the swing and headed home as darkness approached.

The following morning, before Small-Headed Dad woke up, Big-Headed Son rushed into the house, shouting, "Small-Headed Dad! Small-Headed Dad! The tire swing is gone!"

Small-Headed Dad, now awakened by the commotion, inquired, "What? The swing is gone?"

Big-Headed Son, visibly upset, pulled Small-Headed Dad outside. His cries drew the children from the previous day. Learning that the swing had been stolen, they rallied around Big-Headed Son, expressing their concern, "Big head brother, don't worry; we'll help you look for it together."

Wiping away tears, Big-Headed Son admitted in embarrassment, "I'm sorry I didn't let you play on the swing yesterday."

A young lass remarked, "It's alright; we'll play together once we retrieve the swings."

Small-Headed Dad observed from the side, nodding his head non-stop, and said, "Right then, all of you go and search for it together!" After saying this, he chuckled and turned around to head back to the house.

Everyone started searching individually. A wee lad got down on the ground to take a closer look, and as he observed, he exclaimed, "You lot, have a gander at this! There are marks here where the tyres rolled over!"

The kids all crouched down to have a look and said, "I see it!" "I see it too! It was going in that direction!"

So, they all dashed forward along the tyre tracks, turned left, then right, to find ... or at least attempt to find, as the tyre tracks vanished in a patch of weeds.

Big-Headed Son started to cry again, "The clue is broken ..."

The young lady took his hand and reassured, "Don't fret, there's strength in numbers."

The little brother also took his hand and suggested, "Now let's split up into five groups and head straight into the weeds; we're guaranteed to find it." With that, the little brother waved his hand, and one by one, everyone courageously delved into the weeds.

They burrowed through and felt their way amidst the weeds, with Big-Headed Son trailing closely behind. Suddenly, he stumbled over something and fell to the ground with a loud cry of "ouch." Initially wanting to inspect his arm, injured from the fall, he suddenly seemed to recall something. He turned his head to look and laughed, "I found it! I found it! Here are the tyres!" When the children heard this, they all cheered and rushed over. Each of them had grass all over their faces, heads, and bodies, as if they had rolled in the grass together.

They all exclaimed, "Oh! Oh!" as they rolled the tires back. In the distance, Small-Headed Dad stood beneath a grand tree. Big-Headed Son kicked the tire, and it soared through the air, shooting straight towards the swing frame. Small-Headed Dad swiftly opened his arms, akin to a goalkeeper, rushing to intercept the tire.

The children clapped and leapt in joy, proclaiming, "Great! Small-Headed Dad is really good!" They surrounded Small-Headed Dad, expressing their admiration.

Small-Headed Dad affectionately touched the

children's heads and remarked, "You guys are great, not only helping Big-Headed Son find the swing but also discovering the friendship between you all." Turning to Big-Headed Son, he asked, "Isn't that right?" Big-Headed Son rubbed his ample head, smiling sheepishly.

Promptly, Small-Headed Dad reconstructed the swing set. The children queued up, taking turns to swing. Their laughter, echoing as the swings swayed up and down, brought joy to Small-Headed Dad. Watching from the sidelines, he mused, "Looks like I haven't been a 'thief' for nothing ..."

"Hee hee hee ..."

"Ha ha ha ..."

The laughter enveloped the latter words of Small-Headed Dad.

Animal Inn

Small-Headed Dad took Big-Headed Son to a vast forest, planning to live there for a few days. Isn't it magnificent?

"Small-Headed Dad, can we spot little squirrels today in the big forest?" inquired Big-Headed Son eagerly as they walked.

"We surely can," responded Small-Headed Dad.

"And what about the plum deer, woodpecker, and the big bear?"

"They'll all make an appearance, as long as we don't harm them."

Big-Headed Son dashed ahead, exclaiming, "Fantastic! I get to live with lots of little animals tonight!"

Deep within the woods, they halted. The birds observed them, chirping as if expressing a mixed welcome.

Surveying the surroundings, Big-Headed Son remarked, "Why aren't there any other animals besides the birds?"

While setting up the tent, Small-Headed Dad reassured him, "Don't worry, let's set up the tent together first."

"Alright!" agreed Big-Headed Son, rushing to assist his father in inserting sticks, tying ropes, and performing other tasks. Before long, a beautiful tent stood amidst the forest, resembling a large, colourful mushroom.

Big-Headed Son swiftly climbed inside, then poked his head out, calling to the big tree, "Little bird, little bird, come down and live with me; it's warm and beautiful in this tent!" The birds, however, fluttered away with a flutter of wings.

The forest fell silent, devoid of any sound.

Big-Headed Son scratched his head, expressing disappointment, "The birds are afraid of us; the deer, the bear must also be afraid of us ..."

Small-Headed Dad strolled over and patted Big-Headed Son's oversized noggin, saying, "As long as we're patient, we'll surely regain the animals' trust in us. Come on, it's getting late; let's go pick some mushrooms!" Big-Headed Son and Small-Headed Dad hoisted a hefty basket and ambled together toward the distance.

There was no one in the vicinity of the tent, and suddenly, a squirrel leaped down from a tree. It circled around the tent twice, and upon seeing the little door ajar, it stuck its head in first to inspect, then gradually slid its body inside.

Another deer appeared seemingly out of nowhere, studying the tent for a while. It pricked up its ears and listened intently before passing through the door.

A flock of small birds swooped in. They halted at the tent, beneath it, "chirping" away until the squirrels and deer from the tent window stuck out their heads to see. The birds stopped chirping, one by one, lined up and confidently entered the tent.

As the sun began to set, the white clouds grew darker and darker. Just then, from the forest along the dirt road emerged a slightly pudgy bear. It poked its head, as if searching for something. Ah, the bear spotted the tent and clapped its hands like a child. The bear rushed over to the tent, giving it a bump with its rear end before raising its hefty paw to clap. The tent shook, and there were alarmed cries from the animals, ready to escape through the door. However, upon realizing it was the bear, they withdrew again.

The bear also wanted to enter, but its head couldn't fit with its buttocks in, and vice versa. The bear grew anxious, ending up with its upper body inside the tent and its lower body outside.

As the sun descended, the stars and moon emerged, and Big-Headed Son and Small-Headed Dad returned with a basket full of mushrooms. When they neared the tent, they halted in amazement, hearing a loud snoring sound emanating from within, as if the animals were engaged in a snoring competition. Setting down the basket, they peeked through the window, witnessing the animals lying comfortably inside, sound asleep.

"Hee hee!" Big-Headed Son was bursting with joy, ready to burst into laughter, but Small-Headed Dad promptly covered his mouth with large hands.

Moving to the tent's door, they found the bear's hindquarters blocking the entrance. Big-Headed Son extended his hand to touch it, but once again, Small-Headed Dad intervened, whispering, "Don't wake them up."

"They look so funny when they sleep!" whispered Big-Headed Son, secretly yearning to join the animals in the tent for a peaceful slumber.

Small-Headed Dad remarked, "I never expected the

animals would fancy our tent too!"

They observed for a while, until they yawned, and then quietly departed, strolling casually toward the woods.

"It seems we won't be able to stay in the tent tonight unless we shoo away the animals," Small-Headed Dad expressed concern.

"Nah! I'd rather not live in a tent," grumbled Big-Headed Son.

Small-Headed Dad pondered, "Then where shall we live?"

Big-Headed Son hopped from stump to stump like a rabbit, proposing, "We can live in a tree hole like bears!"

Agreeing, Small-Headed Dad nodded, "Good idea, let's split up and search for a tree hole!"

Small-Headed Dad headed east, and Big-Headed Son ventured west. In the end, Small-Headed Dad found a tree hole, but it was too small for his body to fit. Fearing wolves might attack if he protruded, he abandoned the idea. Meanwhile, Big-Headed Son discovered a hole where his body could enter but not his big head. Apprehensive about his head being vulnerable to tiger attacks, he too gave up on the notion.

They searched and searched, eventually making a big circle and reconvening at a section of dead wood. Big-

Headed Son displayed his empty hands, stating he hadn't found it. Small-Headed Dad shrugged his shoulders, indicating he had no luck either. They stood at one end of the dead wood, then at the other end of the dead wood ... Suddenly, both of them bent down together, sticking their buttocks out from the two ends of a hole in the tree to peer inside: Hee hee, one eye on this side, one eye on that side.

Looking in, Big-Headed Son suddenly raised his hands and exclaimed, "Let's disguise ourselves as monsters and nap; then no one will dare to eat us." To avoid the tiger hearing, Big-Headed Son whispered the dressing-up method into Small-Headed Dad's ear so the tiger wouldn't catch on that it was a fake monster and no longer be frightened.

This is how they dressed up as a monster: Big-Headed Son concealed his feet and body in the withered tree, only revealing his big head; Small-Headed Dad concealed his small head and body in the withered tree, with only his feet showing. The dead tree turned the two into one entity, a monster, sprawled across the ground.

It was pitch dark, and fireflies floated up and down in the air, illuminating the monster on the ground.

A tiger approached. It ran to one end to inspect, then to the other end to observe, and suddenly turned and fled.

Another wolf appeared. It stuck out its tongue, stood at a distance, gazing at the monster. It looked and looked, slowly retreated, and vanished in a flash.

"Hullo – hullo –" Big-Headed Son was sleeping soundly. "Hullo – hullo –" Small-Headed Dad's snores were muted since his head was in a hole in the tree. They slept like this, with one audible sound and one muffled sound, until morning.

The sun emerged, and the birds roused Big-Headed Son with their twittering. He opened his eyes and froze, only to see the animals that slept in the tent the previous night standing in a row, watching them from a distance – monsters.

Big-Headed Son swiftly climbed out of the dead tree and approached them, saying "Good morning." However, the animals scattered and ran away as if Big-Headed Son was a genuine monster.

Big-Headed Son chased after them, shouting, "Don't run away! I won't hurt you!" But the animals ran faster and faster. As he pursued them, he gradually disappeared.

The muffled purring continued, and Small-Headed Dad remained undisturbed. A rabbit joined in from the other side of the tree, causing the snoring to cease abruptly, replaced by an "ouch." Small-Headed Dad withdrew from the tree, discovering a lock of his hair had been yanked out from the top of his head like a blade of grass.

Small-Headed Dad ran his hands through his hair, looking around, "Huh, where's Big-Headed Son? Big-Headed Son! Big-Headed Son!" Small-Headed Dad, almost stumbling, called out while rushing to the east and west, the forest echoing with "Big-Headed Son."

Climbing the tallest poplar tree, Small-Headed Dad finally spotted Big-Headed Son running.

Panting, Small-Headed Dad caught up with him, only to find Big-Headed Son in tears and perspiring.

"What's wrong, Big-Headed Son? Have you been bitten?" asked Small-Headed Dad anxiously.

"No, it's not ..." Big-Headed Son sobbed, "Why don't they believe me ..."

"Because people have hurt them," Small-Headed Dad uttered softly.

Carrying Big-Headed Son on his back, Small-Headed Dad traversed highs and lows. Big-Headed Son, perched on his father's shoulder, pondered something. They arrived at the tent, and Small-Headed Dad suggested, "Let's close up the tent and go home!"

"No way, I haven't lived in a tent yet!" objected Big-

Headed Son.

Small-Headed Dad contemplated and proposed, "Alright, we won't take it down. We'll stay in the tent by ourselves tonight."

"But, but if we live in the tent, where will the animals stay when they come?" inquired Big-Headed Son.

Pointing to a distant tree hole, Small-Headed Dad replied, "Birds can live in birdhouses." Then, gesturing to a nearby hole in a tree, he continued, "Bears can live in tree holes ..."

Interrupting, Big-Headed Son remarked, "Then why did the animals come to the tent last night? It must be that the bird's nest leaks, and the tree hole is not warm ..."

Listening attentively, Small-Headed Dad nodded and suggested, "Let's try this – tonight, we'll build an inn for the animals. We'll use these dead branches and leaves to ensure it's not leaky and warm."

Upon hearing this, Big-Headed Son was so chuffed that he dashed over and embraced his dad, planting a hearty kiss on him! The animal inn was complete. It was a small pointed house, its walls crafted from withered branches and trees, the roof composed of dried leaves and grass. It featured doors and windows, with wildflowers adorning the windows and pine cones hanging from them.

Big-Headed Son squatted down for a while, stood up for a while, scrutinised the little house, and couldn't contain his joy: "Oh, I really wish I could become a little animal so I could find out whether they like this little house or not."

"Tonight we can hide in the tent to observe, watch, and then we can find out ..." suggested Small-Headed Dad, inscribing two significant words on a board—Animal Inn.

As the sun descended, and the stars and the moon emerged, Big-Headed Son and Small-Headed Dad concealed themselves in the tent, eagerly awaiting the arrival of the animals. Big-Headed Son carefully closed the tent door and remarked, "We gotta keep the door closed; if the animals spot us, they'll be scared off again."

They waited, and waited until it was dark. The squirrel was the first to glide down from the tree, the deer approached leaping from a distance, the bear ambled over, and there were woodpeckers and owls ... but one by one, they still circled the tent and wandered around it several times, as if searching for the entrance.

They hadn't noticed the Animal Inn yet.

"I'll go out and tell them," Big-Headed Son suggested anxiously.

Small-Headed Dad pulled him back, "No, they'll be

scared off; let's wait."

Finally, a fawn spotted the Animal Inn. It sniffed with its nose and entered confidently. Witnessing the deer's courage, the other animals followed suit, one by one.

"Ah, the animals are finally residing in the little house we built!" exclaimed Big-Headed Son softly and joyfully.

Small-Headed Dad added, "Even though we don't share the same house as the animals, we've become neighbours!"

The moon cast its glow upon the tents and the animal inn. Meteors streaked through the air, and fireflies twirled in circles. Soon after, there were assorted snores resonating through the quiet, high and low, emanating from both the tent and the animal inn ...

Surprising Apron Mum

It's August 7th, Apron Mum's birthday. She rose early, donned her favourite purple dress and a pair of matching shoes, and then informed the still-sleepy Small-Headed Dad: "I'm going to get my hair permed, and I'll bring back the birthday cake. I'll also get a new sweatshirt for Big-Headed Son, and I plan to capture a video during dinner tonight. I might be a little late ..."

With that, Apron Mum departed. Small-Headed Dad glanced at the still-sleeping Big-Headed Son and promptly returned to slumber.

At some point, both Big-Headed Son and Small-Headed Dad opened their eyes simultaneously and locked gazes.

Big-Headed Son leapt off the crib, rushed to Small-Headed Dad's bed, and buried his head in the blanket, causing the bed to echo with laughter.

After the laughter subsided, Small-Headed Dad inquired, "Big-Headed Son, it's Apron Mum's birthday today. What kind of gift should we give her?"

Big-Headed Son patted his big head and suggested, "Let me think of a gift that will amaze her. We can brainstorm by tapping our heads together."

They both leaned in and started tapping their heads on the bed, going back and forth without a clear winner. Amidst the tapping, Big-Headed Son suddenly exclaimed, "There! I've got an idea! Apron Mum loves the colour purple, so let's give her a purple home!" Big-Headed Son leaned in and whispered something into Small-Headed Dad's ear, prompting more laughter.

Quickly, they got up, purchased a large bucket of purple paint, and started brushing it onto the white door. As they painted, the original white door transformed into a radiant purple one. What a splendid, new look for their home!

They admired their handiwork with great satisfaction.

Big-Headed Son remarked, "Apron Mum will be amazed."

Small-Headed Dad added, "Apron Mum will surely thank us for the gift."

They returned to the closet, found purple waxed glossy paper, and crafted numerous large and small flowers. They hung them on the closet, draped them over the bed, and particularly adorned Apron Mum's dresser, which was practically overflowing!

Big-Headed Son and Small-Headed Dad even pinned one each to their chests.

They eagerly awaited Apron Mum.

The sun had ascended, and birds chirped in the trees while catching bugs. The clock on the wall pointed to twelve o'clock, but Apron Mum had not returned.

Big-Headed Son and Small-Headed Dad anxiously rushed to the balcony to check, and as they gazed, their stomachs growled.

"Why hasn't Apron Mum returned yet?" said Big-Headed Son, rubbing his belly. "I'm famished!"

"I'm going to waste away from hunger!" said Small-Headed Dad, grabbing a tube full of cookies, which the two of them devoured.

The clock on the wall reached 4:00 pm. Big-Headed Son and Small-Headed Dad didn't utter a word, just stared at the empty cracker barrel. Suddenly, the phone rang, causing both of them to jump.

Big-Headed Son seized the phone, "Hello, hello, are

you Apron Mum? What? The police station? Hello ..." The call abruptly ended. Big-Headed Son froze for a moment with the handset in his hands, then exclaimed, "Something bad happened; Apron Mum is at the police station."

Small-Headed Dad was shocked, "What?" He grabbed the phone, "Hello! Hello!" Still, no response.

Big-Headed Son and Small-Headed Dad hailed a cab and hurried to the police station.

Apron Mum sits in the reception room, her newly permed hair slightly tousled, the purple dress was stained with the black and white marks. She clutched an oversized birthday cake tightly in her hands. Spotting Small-Headed Dad, she stood up, tears in her eyes, cake in her arms, and limped towards him. It turned out that one of the heels on her left purple shoe had fallen off.

Small-Headed Dad hurried to meet her, supporting Apron Mum. Big-Headed Son, quick to react, joked, "You ... you robbed the bank?"

Apron Mum neither shook her head nor nodded, simply saying, "I can't find home."

"Do grown-ups get lost too?" wondered Big-Headed Son.

A policeman discreetly pulled Small-Headed Dad aside and inquired, "Isn't there something ... wrong with your wife's brain?"

Small-Headed Dad responded indignantly, "You're the one with problems!"

Big-Headed Son and Small-Headed Dad assisted Apron Mum in walking home. Along the way, Apron Mum explained, "I searched and searched; how could I not find the white door of our house ..."

Big-Headed Son laughed, "Ha-ha! What a silly mum. The white door has turned into a purple door – that's our birthday present to you."

Apron Mum froze, questioning, "Purple door? A birthday present? That purple door is our home?"

Big-Headed Son and Small-Headed Dad smiled in unison and nod.

Saying that, they approached the purple door. Small-Headed Dad tossed the key into the air, caught it, and then gently inserted it into the lock, turning it to open the purple door. Apron Mum seemed slightly disbelieving, first peering inside to examine the furniture, then following Small-Headed Dad through the door.

Apron Mum headed for the couch and expressed her frustration, "I don't like the present you gave me at all! It made it impossible for me to find my home and almost broke my legs running." Apron Mum said this and straightened her legs. Small-Headed Dad and Big-Headed Son quickly squatted down to help Apron Mum take off her shoes.

However, when they stood up, they forgot that Apron Mum was holding a big cake. A "bang" was heard as the big head of Big-Headed Son caused the cake box to flip into the air like a ball. Ah! The cake fell out. "Splat" fell right on Small-Headed Dad's small head, and the cream smeared his hair and face.

Small-Headed Dad blinked, and his eyes bulged out;

Small-Headed Dad opened his mouth, and his mouth hung wide;

Small-Headed Dad sniffed his nose, and his nostrils flared.

At that moment, the doorbell rang. Big-Headed Son rushed to open the door, only to see a hefty uncle carrying a camera, whistling as he entered. The moment he saw Small-Headed Dad, he exclaimed, "Awesome!" He aimed the camera at Small-Headed Dad's small head and snapped away.

Small-Headed Dad was flustered, repeatedly saying, "Don't, don't shoot me ..." He used his hands to block left and right, but couldn't prevent it; he even tried to hide under the sofa, but it proved futile. Finally, he resorted to opening the refrigerator and sticking his face in it.

Apron Mum laughed so hard that she toppled onto the sofa and couldn't sit up. Big-Headed Son clapped and jumped, shouting, "Come on! Come on!"

"Huh?" Small-Headed Dad leaned into the refrigerator and suddenly froze in place. Apron Mum approached, pulling his face out of the freezer, only to discover that it had solidified, along with the cream.

Big-Headed Son broke off a piece of cream from Small-Headed Dad's frozen face and eats it. Apron Mum followed suit, breaking off a piece of cream with an "ah-oh-ah." Even the cameraman couldn't resist, breaking off the biggest piece of cream from Small-Headed Dad's face and eating it.

Suddenly, Small-Headed Dad raised his hand, and broke off the entire cream into his mouth along his face ...

The melody of "Happy Birthday to You" started, and the birthday dinner commenced. The table was adorned with small and large purple flowers, and a candle was lit, creating a beautiful setting.

Apron Mum sat between Big-Headed Son and Small-Headed Dad. She delicately picked up a small lit candle and placed it on Small-Headed Dad's small head. She then grabbed another and put it on Big-Headed Son's big head. Turning to the camera, she said, "These are my two favourite birthday cakes!"

With that, she blew out the two candles.

Green Frog by the Pond

A toy frog was leaping on an open ground, but it wasn't jumping on its own; instead, Big-Headed Son was making it jump. You see, a long and thin plastic tube was attached to the toy frog, and the other end of the tube was connected to a small box held in Big-Headed Son's hand. When he pressed it, the frog jumped.

The frog leaped whenever Big-Headed Son pressed the box. Big-Headed Son also jumped like the frog, but he was always a step behind when he jumped. Big-Headed Son looked at the frog in front of him and said, "When we get to the pond later, you can't outdo a real frog."

Small-Headed Dad observed from behind and couldn't resist joining in, jumping up like them.

The toy frog first, Big-Headed Son second, Small-Headed Dad third; they leapt and leapt, almost reaching the pond. Suddenly, a big sack jumped out from the bushes. The sack was bulging, and its mouth was tightly tied. It hopped and jumped after Small-Headed Dad.

Small-Headed Dad heard the noise and gradually halted, raising his hands as if surrendering, "Big-Headed Son, stop, there's a situation!" Big-Headed Son also stopped, as if surrendering, and the toy frog dropped to the ground, not moving a muscle.

"Boom! Boom!" The big bag continued to jump forward, reaching the front of Small-Headed Dad, then Big-Headed Son, and finally the toy frog.

Big-Headed Son and Small-Headed Dad, now fully awake, shouted in unison, "Catch it!" and lunged toward the mysterious bag. However, they hesitated, retracting their hands in fear, uncertain about the contents of the bag. Could it be a demon? Perhaps a devil? Small-Headed Dad had an idea: he moved a large rock to block the bag, preventing it from jumping away.

Big-Headed Son cautiously extended a finger to touch the bag and remarked, "It's soft, not like a demon, more like a rabbit." Small-Headed Dad squatted down, brought his ear close to the bag, and heard the sound of "coo coo! Gu Gu." He patted his thighs, stood up, and exclaimed, "Oh, it's a sack of frogs!" He then loosened the mouth of the sack.

Upon inspection, the sack was indeed filled with lively frogs. Big-Headed Son, hands on his waist, declared indignantly, "Frogs are helpful in controlling pests, so we shouldn't catch them. I'm going to report this to the police!"

Small-Headed Dad quickly covered Big-Headed Son's mouth and gestured toward the pond. There, they observed a man in black struggling to catch frogs with a fork, resembling a genuine devil.

In a hushed tone, Small-Headed Dad explained something to Big-Headed Son, who grinned and agreed, saying, "Good, let's do it!"

They dragged the sack to the left side of the pond, hidden behind a tree. Releasing the sack, the frogs jumped out one by one, joyfully leaping into the pond. Excitedly, Big-Headed Son remarked, "I told you, real frogs can jump so far; they can reach the centre of the pool in a single bound!" The frogs continued to jump, and the sack gradually deflated.

Finally, they carried the empty sack into the woods, laughing softly. They gathered dead branches, leaves, mud, stones, and more, stuffing them into the sack. The once-deflated sack was now bulging again.

Big-Headed Son chuckled and remarked, "When he opens the sack later, he'll be fuming!" After saying this, he tumbled backward on the ground, acting as if he were "enraged."

Small-Headed Dad added, "This is the punishment the bad guy deserves."

On the other side of the pond, the man in black was still busy catching frogs. Upon noticing the disappearance of the sack, he stretched and twisted his head, asking, "Hey, where did the sack go?" He hastily dropped the fork, causing it to knock over the bamboo basket. The frogs in the basket scattered, hastily jumping back into the pond. The man in black paid little attention, shouting repeatedly, "Where is my sack? Who stole it? If you don't hand it over, I'll beat you up!" He continued to shout and curse before heading into the woods.

Searching in all directions, tired and sweaty, the man in black finally spotted his sack next to a large tree. He hurriedly ran over, tightly embraced the bag, akin to hugging his own child, and then proceeded to take the bag to the market for selling.

As soon as the man in black departed, a big head and a small head peeked out from behind a small tree. They observed the man's back, stifling laughter, and then stealthily followed him.

The man in black, laden with a big bag and drenched in sweat, entered the market. Gasping for breath, he announced, "Selling frogs! The freshest frogs! Come and buy!"

A crowd gathered upon hearing the announcement, some peering to get a glimpse, others rushing forward to declare, "Quick, I'll take ten!"

The man in black, still bewildered by the empty sack, decided to continue his frog-catching mission. This time, he brought two big boxes secured with large locks. Confidently, he threw the captured frogs into the boxes, asserting, "Where are you going to run away this time?"

Not far away, behind a small house, two figures emerged—Big-Headed Son and Small-Headed Dad. Observing the man in black with clenched fists, they were clearly frustrated.

Big-Headed Son voiced his concern, "What can we do? The man in black is catching frogs again!"

Small-Headed Dad pondered the situation, replying, "Yes, this time he isn't using sacks; he's using boxes with locks. It's going to be harder for us to deal with him."

Determined, Big-Headed Son urged, "Then we have to think of something!"

Small-Headed Dad patted his small head, swiftly pulled up Big-Headed Son, and they hurriedly ran to the market. Finding the man in black's stall, they found a wooden sign, scribbled a few words on it, and discreetly inserted it in the middle of the stall. They then concealed themselves in a fast-food restaurant across the street, eagerly awaiting the unfolding events.

A moment later, the man in black grabbed two big boxes and hurriedly ran. He walked and yelled, "Frogs for sale! The freshest big frogs!" However, as he proceeded, he couldn't spot a single person. Particularly around his stall, it was deserted. The man in black curiously set down the boxes and stepped into the middle of the road, shouting, "The frogs have arrived! Come and buy frogs." He shouted for quite a while, but still, no one appeared. Disappointed, the man in black turned around to check his stall and froze instantly. The big wooden sign inserted in front of the stall read: "Frogs can catch pests, here will never sell frogs!" The man in black screamed wildly, lunging over to the wooden sign, forcefully throwing it on the ground, and then stood up, stomping on it. Consequently, the wooden sign split into two and slid to the left and right, and the man in black fell heavily to the ground.

At that very moment, behind the glass of the fast-food restaurant across the street, two heads were reflected— a large one and a small one. Their noses were flattened against the glass, and their mouths were wide open in laughter!

Big-Headed Son and Small-Headed Dad emerged from the fast-food restaurant.

Big-Headed Son exclaimed happily, "It's so funny, I'm laughing my head off!"

Small-Headed Dad remarked, "It's called outsmarting the man in black."

Big-Headed Son suggested, "Let's outwit the man in black once more, so that he'll never dare to catch frogs again."

Small-Headed Dad agreed, "Then we have to combine your wisdom and my wisdom, so we can completely outsmart the man in black!"

A few days later, the chap in black headed down to the pond to nab some frogs again. This time, he ditched the fork and opted for a hand net – a far more efficient tool, mind you. In no time, two out of three bamboo baskets were brimming with frogs. Grinning widely, the man in black muttered to himself, "Haha! This time, I'm sending all of you to large restaurants, and I'm not afraid of folks mocking me anymore!"

With a cheerful "hi yo hi yo," the man in black hoisted up a hefty net, revealing countless frogs within it, limbs flailing in desperate resistance. Swaggering proudly, he declared, "Now, even your old ancestor can't save you!" As he was about to reclaim the net, his eyes seemed to bulge out, fixating directly ahead with his mouth half open, incessantly trembling. There, floating slowly in front, was a lotus leaf bearing a colossal frog, motionless, its two eyes bulging with anger, glaring at the man in black.

Startled, the man in black's hands shook, causing him to lose grip on the net. With a resounding "snap," the net plummeted into the pond, and the frogs swam off, one by one, to the depths of the water. The lotus leaf, with the large frog, steadily approached, and the man in black abruptly dropped to his knees, hands clasped in reverence and kowtowing. "Frog father, oh, no, frog grandfather, spare me! I'll never dare to capture your offspring again, spare me!" he pleaded, delivering a hearty slap to his own face. Turning his head, he scurried away, desperately seeking escape.

Suddenly emerging from the nearby weeds, Big-Headed Son jubilantly shouted, "Victory! Victory!" He rushed over, plucking the big frog from the lotus leaf, giving it a gentle squeeze, and the frog emitted a distinctive "croak! croak." It turned out to be an inflatable toy frog.

Small-Headed Dad also joined in, snatching the frog and pulling out a plug from its stomach, then compressing it vigorously. The inflatable frog deflated, and a rush of air escaped from underneath, causing Big-Headed Son's hair to stand on end like a gusty wind, rendering him unable to open his eyes. Nonetheless, Big-Headed Son chuckled and exclaimed, "The big frog has farted! Big Frog farts! Big Frog farts!"

At this moment, numerous frogs emerged from the water, climbing onto lotus leaves and facing the shore while emitting their distinctive "croak." Small-Headed Dad turned around and observed, realizing behind him were three large bamboo baskets, brimming with frogs.

"Look, the pond frogs are calling their partners on the shore," quipped Small-Headed Dad! And with that, Small-Headed Dad, together with Big-Headed Son, tipped the three large baskets of frogs back into the pond.

Not Afraid of the Real Tiger

At night, Big-Headed Son slept in his little bed, and Small-Headed Dad rested in his big bed. A long rope stretched between the two beds, with one end pressed under Big-Headed Son's pillow and the other tied to Small-Headed Dad's wrist. This arrangement allowed Big-Headed Son to pull the rope when he needed to get up in the middle of the night to pee, and Small-Headed Dad would wake up to accompany him, ensuring the tiger wouldn't dare to come out and bite Big-Headed Son.

However, on this particular night, Big-Headed Son pulled the rope one, two, three ... more than a dozen times, but Small-Headed Dad remained sound asleep, with his snoring growing louder: "Hoo – hoo –" Anxious, Big-Headed Son jumped up and rushed to the big bed, shaking Small-Headed Dad's hands. Despite the effort, Small-Headed Dad just rolled over, continuing to snore: "Hoo – hoo."

Unable to wake up Small-Headed Dad, Big-Headed Son had no choice but to venture out on his own, though he was hesitant. The room was shrouded in darkness, with only a sliver of moonlight filtering in through the curtains. Scanning the room, Big-Headed Son finally spotted his toy submachine gun hanging on the wall, the moonlight casting a fierce shadow. He hastily took down the submachine gun and clutched it to his chest as he approached the door.

Upon opening the door, the dark corridor loomed like a giant tiger about to pounce on him, prompting Big-Headed Son to slam the door shut with a bang. The urgency to pee grew stronger, and Big-Headed Son paced around the room. Ouch! He stepped on something, and it hurt! Reaching down, Big-Headed Son realized it was his new toy sword. Quickly picking it up, he headed towards the door, brandishing both his new sword and submachine gun. However, as he opened the door, a sense of unease swept over him, feeling as if hundreds of demons were watching in the dark corridor. Fearful, Big-Headed Son closed the door again with a bang.

What should he do now? If he didn't go out to pee, he risked wetting his pants, and that would be embarrassing!

At that moment, Small-Headed Dad's snores reverberated once more. Big-Headed Son turned his head to glance at it and suddenly got an idea. Setting aside his submachine gun and dropping his sword, he sauntered towards the door with arms outstretched. Swinging the door open, he proclaimed loudly, "I'm Small-Headed Dad! I'm Small-Headed Dad!" Then he ambled all the way to the toilet. Perhaps the big tiger believed this was indeed Small-Headed Dad and was too intimidated to emerge.

After finishing his business, Big-Headed Son exited the toilet, shook his large head in contentment, patted his belly with both hands, and gave it a more forceful press, declaring, "No more."

Standing before the toilet, Big-Headed Son surveyed his surroundings. Where was the big tiger? Nowhere to be found. Fear no longer gripped Big-Headed Son, prompting him to dash to the living room door and press his ear against it, straining to detect any sounds of the tiger outside. But, alas, there was no sign of the tiger's roar. He peered out the door but, after what felt like an eternity, not a single tuft of tiger fur was in sight.

Feeling daring, Big-Headed Son flung the door open,

announcing, "I am Small-Headed Dad! I am Small-Headed Dad!" and boldly ventured outside.

Oh, how tranquil the night was! The moon hung high like a lantern, casting its glow on the serene houses, trees, and streets ...

"Wha-wha-wha-" Just then, the cry of a child echoed from a nearby window. Big-Headed Son hurried over and spoke through the window crack, "Don't cry, little boy, there are no big tigers out there!"

The little boy truly ceased crying, and Big-Headed Son chuckled softly in triumph.

Walking towards the street, Big-Headed Son declared, "I am Small-Headed Dad! I am Small-Headed Dad," only to discover the street was deserted. Big-Headed Son could move freely without bumping into people or cars. What a relief! Holding his big head, he vigorously shook it in excitement.

Suddenly, a breeze swept through, rustling the leaves on the trees with a soft sound. A bit scared, Big-Headed Son instinctively shrunk his neck, crouching down to observe.

He then noticed a significant movement not far to the left—there was a big black tiger on the ground, seemingly shifting and shifting. Terrified, Big-Headed Son hastily turned around and fled, shouting, "Help! The tiger is coming to get me!" However, in his panic, he tripped and fell to the ground, struggling to get back up.

It seemed like the end—being devoured by the big tiger and never returning! Big-Headed Son lay on the ground, anticipating the tiger's bite. After waiting for a while without feeling the sharp teeth, he curiously turned his head. To his surprise, the tiger was still lying on the ground, unmoving.

Big-Headed Son slowly raised his head and noticed a large dark shadow above the "big tiger." It dawned on him—it was the shadow of a big tree!

Big-Headed Son burst into laughter. He climbed to his feet, dusted himself off, and said, "That was so scary!"

Big-Headed Son strolled back across the street, proclaiming, "I'm Small-Headed Dad! I am Small-Headed Dad!" A stray cat, napping under a holly tree, startled awake and scampered away with a meow. Undeterred, Big-Headed Son shouted, "Don't run away! There's no genuine big tiger!" However, the cat fled even faster, and Big-Headed Son gave chase.

When Small-Headed Dad awoke, he realized Big-Headed Son was no longer in his cot and leapt up in anxiety. Observing the bedroom door ajar and the living room door wide open, he suspected Big-Headed Son might be sleepwalking. Hastily donning his shoes, he dashed outside.

In the dead of night, Small-Headed Dad couldn't shout, so he circled the neighbourhood frantically searching for his son. Unintentionally, his footsteps roused the elderly gentleman guarding the bicycles. In the moonlight, the old grandpa peered towards the wall, noting the clock hands pointing at 3 o'clock.

This must be a bicycle thief! Swiftly, the old grandpa picked up the phone and discreetly called the patrolman.

Small-Headed Dad continued his search tirelessly. Eventually, he spotted Big-Headed Son darting across the street and hurriedly pursued him. Just in the nick of time, two patrolmen arrived, assuming Small-Headed Dad was attempting to slip away. They joined the pursuit. What followed was quite amusing: Big-Headed Son was after the stray cat; Small-Headed Dad was chasing his son; the patrolmen were pursuing Small-Headed Dad. Unbeknownst to them, the wind playfully rolled up a can, an empty cardboard box, and numerous fallen leaves behind the patrolmen, as if engaged in their pursuit.

Small-Headed Dad was swiftly apprehended by the patrolmen. Thinking they were coming to his aid, he pointed urgently at Big-Headed Son and exclaimed, "It's him! It's him!" Perplexed, the policeman released Small-Headed Dad and pursued Big-Headed Son instead.

But Big-Headed Son came to a halt, as did the cat, finding itself in a dead end.

Addressing the approaching patrolman, Big-Headed Son said, "Uncle, please go and inform the kitten that there's no real tiger, and tell it not to be afraid to come out to pee in the middle of the night in the future."

A portly patrolman scoffed, "What? You stayed up late at night just for this cat!"

A slender patrolman suggested, "Maybe it's an unusual cat. Come on, let's go catch it."

The patrolmen quickly apprehended the feral cat. The slender patrolman carried the cat, glancing around and remarking, "Nothing special!" He then handed the cat over to Big-Headed Son.

Taking the kitten, Big-Headed Son cradled it in his arms. While walking back home, he whispered reassuringly to the cat, "Don't be afraid, don't be afraid, there is no real tiger ..."

Returning to his little bed, Big-Headed Son drifted off to sleep. Similarly, Small-Headed Dad went back to his big bed and fell asleep. In place of the long rope between the crib and the big bed, there was now an additional cardboard box for shoes—the newfound home of the former stray cat.

Searching for the Alien

At noon, the sun was high up in the sky. Apron Mum tidied up the lunch table, instructing Big-Headed Son, "Go and have a nap to freshen up. Once Small-Headed Dad returns this afternoon, we'll head to 'Cosmic City' for some fun."

As Big-Headed Son crawled under the table, he chimed in, "Only if you tell me a story ..."

Apron Mum agreed, "Alright."

So, Big-Headed Son and Apron Mum settled on the large bed for a nap together.

"Once upon a time, there was a Monkey King ..." Apron Mum began her story but was abruptly interrupted as Big-Headed Son covered her mouth with his hand, declaring, "I don't want to hear about the Monkey King or his colleague, Monk Pig. I want a story about the aliens and Transformers!"

Apron Mum responded, "I won't be telling any of those peculiar tales!"

"But I will. Today, I'll share a story about aliens, alright?"

Curiously, Apron Mum asked, "Do they eat children?"

Indignantly, Big-Headed Son replied, "They aren't like Granny Wolf; they don't eat children!"

"Then what do they eat?"

Sitting up, Big-Headed Son gestured with his hands, saying, "Aliens don't eat anything. They have electricity in them, 'whoosh,' shooting light onto houses ..."

Suddenly, a light streamed in through the window, stinging Big-Headed Son's eyes. He screamed and dove under the covers. Apron Mum, sitting up in surprise, asked, "What's wrong? What's wrong?" Another light entered, stinging her eyes, and she too yelped before hiding under the covers.

In the darkness of the quilt, Big-Headed Son and Apron Mum huddled together.

Whispering, Big-Headed Son said, "I guess the alien is really here!"

Complaining, Apron Mum retorted, "It's all your

fault, talking about the aliens! He probably thought we liked him and came running."

Intermittently, the blinding light continued to filter in through the window, illuminating the wall, the bed, the chair ... Following the light outside, it turned out to be a kitten playing with a broken lens using its paw downstairs. The broken lens reflected the sun's rays in all directions, creating a dazzling play of light.

The kitten was having a ball, and the bright light flickered and flashed. Small-Headed Dad, walking on the street, was stung in the eye and exclaimed, "Ouch," quickly shielding it with his hand. Upon realizing it was the kitten's broken lens causing the discomfort, he scolded the kitten, "Purr-purr." The kitten paused to glance at him, then scampered away with the broken lens in its mouth.

Small-Headed Dad ascended the stairs to his front door and knocked twice, receiving no response from within.

"Knock! Knock!" he tried twice more, still met with silence.

Undeterred, Small-Headed Dad knocked three times, but the house remained unresponsive. Perplexed, he pressed his ear to the door, extending his hands in a puzzled gesture.

Inside, Big-Headed Son and Apron Mum were still concealed under the covers. Big-Headed Son nervously remarked, "Apron Mum, did you hear that knocking?"

Apron Mum, hearing the knocks, whispered, "Oh no, the aliens are coming in."

Finally stopped knocking, Small-Headed Dad placed a large ladder outside the door and climbed through the closed window to peer inside. Seeing the quilt on the big bed arched high, he smiled, thinking that Big-Headed Son and Apron Mum were fast asleep.

Descending the ladder, Small-Headed Dad strolled down the street. In a hushed voice, he muttered, "I'll go buy something, maybe play in 'Cosmic City' later ..." He wandered through the streets, purchasing a couple of cakes and cans of coke. Carrying these goodies, he noticed a sign outside a sporting goods store proclaiming, "Unbelievable price inside! Full Cosmic Suit for only 50 yuan." Amused, Small-Headed Dad chuckled and entered the store.

Side by side on the counter stood three sets of spacesuits: Large, Medium, and Small. They gleamed in silver and came complete with shoes, gloves, and sunglasses – truly exquisite! Small-Headed Dad, reaching for his money, addressed the sales clerk, "Miss, please fetch me three cosmic suits."

"Which size?" inquired the clerk.

Small-Headed Dad pointed towards the three sets of hanging samples, stating, "I'll take these three sets, please hurry."

Meanwhile, Big-Headed Son and Apron Mum were still concealed under the covers.

"I'm boiling in here!" panted Big-Headed Son.

"Why hasn't Small-Headed Dad returned yet?" Apron Mum was at a loss.

Big-Headed Son remarked, "What if Small-Headed Dad comes back just in time to encounter the alien and gets captured?"

"Could that happen?" Apron Mum suddenly felt anxious.

Deciding to investigate, they emerged from under the covers and walked together to the door, listening for any signs of movement. They then dashed to the window and peered outside. All was quiet – no sounds, no one in sight.

They approached the door, scanning the little alley and calling out, "Small-Headed Dad! Small-Headed Dad!" As they turned around from a dead end, they spotted a figure glittering with silver at the other end of the alley. This person wore a peculiar hat, sunglasses with colourful circles painted on the lenses cover most of their face, and they carried two large bags. Their feet were clad in black, oversized shoes.

Big-Headed Son, in a sudden burst of fear, screamed, "The alien is coming!" He grabbed Apron Mum and turned into a side alley, running wildly. The mysterious figure, apparently an "alien," froze momentarily before chasing after them. Big-Headed Son and Apron Mum sprinted desperately towards their home.

Reaching their door, they rushed upstairs to get the key, hearing the approaching footsteps with a rhythmic "thud, thud, thud." Looking down the stairs, they realized, "The Cosmonauts are catching up!"

The Cosmic Man arrived just as they entered and turned to slam the door. He pounded on the door, insisting, "What are you doing? I'm Small-Headed Dad! Let me in!"

Big-Headed Son, still skeptical, said to Apron Mum, "How dare he pretend to be Small-Headed Dad?"

Apron Mum shouted at the door, "Do you think we don't know that you're posing as Small-Headed Dad?"

"I'm not pretending, I'm really Small-Headed Dad," insisted the alien from outside.

Big-Headed Son, remaining unconvinced, told Apron

Mum, "Let's not believe him. Let's not believe him."

Apron Mum called out again, "We don't believe you! Please give us the real Small-Headed Dad!"

Surprisingly, the "alien" laughed and responded, "What? You think I'm an 'alien'? No wonder you see me like a ghost! It's all because of this cosmic suit. I'll go return them ..."

"The alien thundered downstairs. Big-Headed Son and Apron Mum hurried to the window to witness the "Cosmonaut" striding, panting, towards the street.

Big-Headed Son suggested, "Come on, let's follow him. We'll find out whether he's a real alien or just a pretender."

They rushed downstairs to closely tail the "space visitor."

Once inside the sporting goods store, the "alien" angrily removed his spacesuit, exclaiming, "I don't want this suit anymore. I can't go home because of it."

Curious, the salesman asked, "Why?"

"Because my son and even my wife don't recognize me," retorted Small-Headed Dad, growing more agitated as customers gathered around. "It's not because of this cursed cosmic suit! They mistook me for a real 'extraterrestrial being'!" The customers chuckled as Small-

Headed Dad, having shed his full cosmic attire, returned to his original appearance.

Realizing the truth, Big-Headed Son couldn't wait any longer, exclaiming, "So you really are Small-Headed Dad! This cosmic suit is incredible; it looks like a genuine alien when you wear it!"

Apron Mum joined the crowd, informing the sales clerk, "We won't be returning this spacesuit!"

Big-Headed Son echoed, "No return, no return!" He then grabbed the smallest set and put it on, while Apron Mum also donned her set.

Small-Headed Dad, looking anything but "angry," remarked, "Fantastic! That's brilliant! I guess I'll have to put it on again!"

Embracing their newfound "space visitor" identity, the trio, surrounded by curious customers, felt like models in their cosmic suits.

"This dress looks so cool!"

"It's like a real alien!"

"I'll buy a set too!"

"I'll buy two sets, it's only 50 yuan anyway ..."

The enthusiastic customers rushed to the counter, forming a long line that snaked around the store. The salesman, delighted with the unexpected success, announced, "Please line up, one by one ..." The line extended all the way to the store door.

Exiting the store, the three "cosmopolitans" ventured to the "Cosmic City." Boarding a spaceship, they felt as though they had truly entered the starry sky.

Inquisitive, Big-Headed Son asked, "Small-Headed Dad, are you serious about there being outer-space people?"

Small-Headed Dad replied, "If there really are, humans must be able to find them."

"Then am I considered a human?"

"Of course! We all belong to the human race," Apron Mum reassured with a smile.

Contemplating the idea, Big-Headed Son declared, "Then I must find the real Cosmic Man in the future!"

With a "wow-" sound, the spaceship propelled them into another mysterious place.

Magic Hat

Big-Headed Son and Small-Headed Dad were engrossed in watching a magic show together. The magician, clad in a black suit, was skillfully pulling out a seemingly endless string of handkerchiefs from the sleeve of another figure who only revealed half of its body.

Quietly, Big-Headed Son stood up, leaving Small-Headed Dad behind. He bowed, retreated from the seats, and then crawled on the ground to slip through a side door adjacent to the stage.

Meanwhile, the magician continued triumphantly pulling handkerchiefs to the music.

As soon as Big-Headed Son entered through the side door, he stood up and glanced towards the top of the stage. He quickly realized it was a scarecrow-like dummy, and beneath the dummy, inside the stage, handkerchiefs tied together were coiled like ropes and piled on the floor. They went from one cuff of the dummy to the other, and the magician skillfully pulled them out again.

Ah, that's the trick!

With a sly grin, Big-Headed Son quietly approached and gathered the handkerchiefs from the floor. The magician continued to pull and pull until he could pull no more, becoming frantic and screaming. In his haste, he shouted, "Alas!" and exerted too much force, causing the tied-together handkerchiefs to break, and he tumbled backward with a thud. The audience burst into laughter, and the curtain hastily closed.

Amidst the laughter, Small-Headed Dad was joyous, nodding his head. However, as he shook his head, he suddenly realized that Big-Headed Son had vanished. Anxiously, he stood up and looked around, calling out, "Big-Headed Son! Big-Headed Son!"

The crowd at the rear yelled, "Sit down! Sit down!"

Small-headed Dad had to stoop down and leave his seat, heading towards the aisle. Glancing behind him to check the situation, he straightened up and waved his hand while calling out, "Big-headed Son! Big-headed Son!"

At that moment, the curtain was drawn, and the magician positioned himself beside a large wardrobe, announcing, "Now we need a member of the audience to come up to the stage to participate ..." As he uttered these words, he noticed Small-headed Dad approaching with a raised hand, pointing towards him. "Very well, this gentleman has voluntarily come up to the stage." The two assistants hurriedly left the stage to welcome Small-headed Dad.

Believing they knew the whereabouts of Big-headed Son, Small-headed Dad quickly followed them onto the stage.

The magician grinned and addressed the audience, "I am now going to conceal this audience member inside the cupboard ..."

However, Small-headed Dad, anxious to locate his son, misinterpreted the magician's words, exclaiming, "In the closet? You're saying Big-headed Son is in the cupboard?" He approached the large wardrobe, meticulously searching for the handle on the cupboard door but found none. Small-headed Dad, in his anxiety, tapped the top with his small head. Voila! The door swung open, and Small-headed Dad hastily entered.

The magician continued, "This gentleman is very cooperative, and he has stepped into the cupboard. Please watch; in three minutes, he will disappear ..."

Small-Headed Dad entered the cupboard and peered down to discover a hole in the floor with a ladder beneath it. Descending the ladder, he reached the bottom, finding his head flattened just like the bottom of the cupboard. Suddenly, with a "wow," the hole sealed shut. Small-Headed Dad, now anxious, pounded his fists against the board above his head, shouting, "Hey! Open the door! Don't lock me in here! I still need to find my Big-Headed Son!"

From the stage, the magician continued, "Alright, three minutes are up; please open the door." The assistant swung the door open, revealing an empty cupboard, eliciting amazed applause from the audience. The magician gestured for silence and declared, "Certainly, I'll bring him back in another two minutes ..."

Unable to knock on the top board, Small-Headed Dad turned a corner and descended further. It seemed like a dark tunnel down there, with seven turns. Small-Headed Dad continued, twisting and turning until he reached a bright spot – the basement exit.

Unexpectedly, Small-headed Dad emerged, and Big-headed Son peeped in, saying, "Hey, what's this place? Let me check it out!" With curiosity, Big-headed Son entered, following the path Small-headed Dad had just walked out of. He also stumbled upon the ladder, turned a corner, and ascended.

Meanwhile, the magician continued on stage, declaring, "Ah, two minutes are up, the most exciting moment is approaching. Five, four, three, two, one, open the door!" The door swung open. The magician's eyes widened in surprise, then he looked down, only to find Big-headed Son. He was so astonished that his mouth hung open, seemingly unable to close.

The audience erupted in excitement, rising from their seats and converging towards the stage, repeatedly exclaiming, "It's divine, transforming adults into children." "It's incredible!" "It's marvelous, turning a small head into a big one!" The audience swarmed onto the stage, lifting the magician into the air and chanting, "Perform another one! Perform another one!"

Big-headed Son, frightened and overwhelmed by the enthusiastic audience, cried out, "Small-headed Dad! Small-headed Dad!" as he dodged through the surrounding people.

Small-headed Dad circled around and re-entered the theater. Spotting Big-headed Son on the stage, he rushed over. Big-headed Son, upon seeing Small-headed Dad, was overjoyed. He wiped away his tears and embraced Small-headed Dad tightly.

Assisting Big-headed Son off the stage, Small-headed Dad remarked, "They're in a frenzy, aren't they? Come on, let's just find a good seat." They made their way to the first row and comfortably took the two center chairs.

As the curtain closed, the audience gradually returned to their seats.

As the magician continued with his performance, Small-Headed Dad whispered to Big-Headed Son, "Let's enjoy the show, and later we'll have a good laugh about this magical experience!" And so, the father and son duo settled back into their seats, savouring the enchantment of the moment.

The second half of the show commenced, and a magician in a white suit took the stage. He announced, "I am now going to perform a magic hat." Taking a colour-striped clown hat from his assistant, he continued, "This is an obedient hat. When I tell it to become bigger, it becomes bigger; when I tell it to become smaller, it becomes smaller. It's just right for grown-ups and just right for kids. Okay, now let's pick a father and son to come up on stage and participate in the performance."

Scanning the front rows, the magician spotted Big-Headed Son and Small-Headed Dad. Happily, he gestured for them to come up, and the father and son looked at each other before joining him on stage.

The magician, rotating the hat, chanted, "Become big, become big, become big ..." The hat indeed expanded slightly. Just as he was about to place it on the small head of the father, he froze and then put it on the big head of the son, earning warm applause from the audience.

Rotating the hat again, he recited, "Become small, become small, become small ..." The hat slightly diminished. As he moved to put it on the big head of the son, he froze for a moment and then placed it on the small head of Small-Headed Dad.

At this point, an audience member stood up and exclaimed, "Mr. Magician, the previous magician turned the adult into a child. Can you turn this child's big head into a small one and the adult's small head into a big one? That would be truly impressive!"

Hearing this, Big-Headed Son and Small-Headed Dad were initially nervous, clutching their respective heads. Then, they shouted in unison, "No!" before hastily jumping off the stage and fleeing the theatre. The audience, momentarily stunned, quickly recovered, and a cry rang out, "Quickly, chase them! Don't let them get away!"

Big-headed Son and Small-headed Dad raced ahead, holding their heads, with groups of spectators chasing from behind. As they ran, they spotted two sets of diving suit samples in front of a store. They hastily climbed into them, posing as models standing in the diving suits. Only when the pursuing spectators passed the diving suits did they emerge and continue running in the direction of their home.

In the distance, their hut was illuminated.

Big-headed Son pounded on the door, exclaiming, "Apron Mother! Apron Mother! Open the door!" The door swung open, but instead of Apron Mother, it was the magician in the white suit.

"Help!" yelled Big-headed Son and Small-headed Dad as they darted straight into the bedroom, nearly colliding with the magician.

Apron Mother, surprised, asked, "What's going on? Aren't you welcoming the magician?"

Big-headed Son and Small-headed Dad emerged from the bedroom, their heads concealed in pillowcases that extended all the way to their shoulders.

The magician reassured them, saying, "Don't be afraid, I am here specifically to give you magic hats." He then presented the hats he had just used in his performance. "For you are a very unique father and son!"

After the magician left, Small-headed Dad and Big-headed Son donned their magic hats and put on a show for Apron Mother. She sat on the couch with a cat on her left and a dog on her right. Next to the cat were a cloth bear and a stuffed elephant, and next to the dog were an Altman and a robot. They resembled the audience in the theater.

Big-Headed Son's Disappearance

A friend of Small-Headed Dad and Apron Mum is getting married and has invited the whole family to a wedding banquet tonight. The car halted in front of a hotel, where numerous brides and grooms stood on the steps, all dressed in identical wedding attire – the bride in a white wedding dress and the groom in a black suit.

Big-Headed Son trailed his mom and dad, quietly counting: "One, two, three, four, five ... so many, I have to eat at so many wedding banquets!"

Apron Mum chided, "Silly son! We only dine with one pair of brides and grooms, who are friends of mom and dad." Walking towards a specific couple, she offered them flowers.

Big-Headed Son continued to turn his big head, looking around until Apron Mum firmly restrained him, saying, "Stop looking around, just greet uncle and auntie."

Momentarily frozen, Big-Headed Son then called out, "Auntie and uncle, how are you!" Pointing to their matching clothes, he added, "You and the other brides and grooms all wear the same clothes; I can't distinguish!"

Laughter erupted, and the bride reassured him, "It's okay, just eat more while you're drinking the wedding banquet."

The groom playfully pulled Big-Headed Son over and suggested, "You're so cute; why don't you be our little pageboy?"

"No problem!" Big-Headed Son agreed, stepping into the middle of the bride and groom. Small-Headed Dad and Apron Mum entered the hotel with smiles on their faces.

Outside the hotel, cars and vans continued to arrive, all carrying people coming to partake in the wedding festivities. Some carried flower baskets, while others held flowers and approached the brides and grooms. Big-Headed Son wondered, how can they recognise the specific bride and groom they are looking for?

At this moment, there were two really old grandparents making their way up the steps, and the bride and groom, who were standing with their Big-Headed Son, hurriedly went to greet them because they're their elders. But Big-Headed Son wasn't aware; he was still lost in thought and unintentionally followed another couple of bride and groom who walked ahead of him, leading up to a wedding car adorned with flowers.

The groom gave Big-Headed Son a quizzical look and asked, "Who are you? Your head is massive!"

Big-Headed Son also gave him a strange look and replied, "I'm Big-Headed Son! Have you forgotten? I'm here to toast at your wedding!"

The bride chuckled and invited her Big-Headed Son to sit beside her, then said to the groom, "Having Big-Headed Son as our companion will surely bring us joy!"

As the car set off, Big-Headed Son suddenly exclaimed, "But Small-Headed Dad and Apron Mum are still at the hotel!"

The groom exclaimed, "What? Small-Headed Dad? Apron Mum? Haha ... We've got a truly big and peculiar guest today."

The bride reassured her Big-Headed Son gently, saying, "Don't worry, your mummy and daddy will come on the big bus at the back."

The wedding car arrived at the beach, revealing golden sand awaiting many people. Big-Headed Son immediately noticed, amidst the crowd, a hot air balloon parked in the middle. The bride, in excitement, pointed to the two words on the hot air balloon and said to Big-Headed Son, "Do you recognise it? Let me read it for you – Skyward, Nuptials."

"What? Getting married in the sky?" exclaimed Big-Headed Son with enthusiasm, "Then I'll be toasting in heaven? That's brilliant!"

Small-Headed Dad and Apron Mum were seated, beaming, at the reception table, with an empty chair between them reserved for Big-Headed Son. Most of the guests had arrived when the groom, accompanied by his bride, entered through the door. Small-Headed Dad, standing up promptly, boomed, "Hey, where's Big-Headed Son?" In front of the bride and groom, empty spaces surrounded them.

The bride and groom, sharing a moment of realization, exchanged glances before dashing out of the door together. Small-Headed Dad and Apron Mum hastily got up and followed suit. Outside the hotel, there were few guests remaining, just a parked car and a van. The bystanders, not in any rush, patiently awaited the return of those enjoying the wedding festivities.

Small-Headed Dad assured the couple, "Carry on with your celebration, the guests are waiting; we'll find him ourselves." He hailed a cab, and with Apron Mum, they sped away.

Driving through the city centre, Apron Mum peered out of the left window, and Small-Headed Dad shouted from the right, "Big-Headed Son! Where are you?" Pedestrians on the road gazed with curiosity; some even stopped to inquire about the commotion.

An elderly lady selling cold drinks heard the commotion and ran towards the cab with arms outstretched, exclaiming, "Do you fancy a big head brand ice cream? I've got it here!"

Small-Headed Dad hurriedly responded, "No, no, I'm not buying ice cream; I'm looking for my Big-Headed Son!" He then withdrew his head into the car window as the cab sped off.

The old lady, watching the receding cab, muttered to herself, "Big-Headed Son? What kind of cold drink is that?"

As the car approached a kindergarten's entrance, Apron Mum spotted a large group of Big-Headed Sons through binoculars. Excitedly, she exclaimed, "Look at that! Look at that!" She eagerly handed the binoculars to Small-Headed Dad. However, as the car drew nearer, they realised it was just a group of children wearing oversized doll props for a performance.

Apron Mum and Small-Headed Dad let out a collective sigh of disappointment, "Whew—"

Apron Mum exclaimed, "We'd better ring up the police sharpish!" So, they promptly directed the car straight to the Police Headquarters. As they strolled through the reception area inside the Police Headquarters, they caught sight of a bride and groom in wedding attire on the television screen, set against the backdrop of the azure sea. At that very moment, the host declared, "Today, we're hosting a wedding in the air over this beautiful sea. First, let's interview ..." Suddenly, the camera zoomed in and focused on none other than Big-Headed Son: "May I ask the young one, are you the special guest of the bride and groom?"

Big-Headed Son responded loudly, "No, I'm here for the wedding banquet!"

"Big-Headed Son!"

"Big-Headed Son!" echoed Small-Headed Dad and Apron Mum as they descended in front of the television set, their four hands reaching up high, as if attempting to embrace the TV ...

Big-Headed Son joined the bride and groom on the hot air balloon, which slowly ascended higher and higher.

Big-Headed Son joyfully exclaimed, "Oh! I'm in the sky! I'm in the sky!" A flock of birds flew by, and Big-Headed Son extended his hand; indeed, the birds halted at the top and then flew away.

The bride remarked, "Look, the birds have come to congratulate us too!"

Big-Headed Son remarked, "But the little bird can't join us for a sip of the wedding wine!"

As the balloon ascended, it headed towards a small island named "Happy Island." When Big-Headed Son reached the happy island, he suddenly froze, neither speaking nor smiling.

The bride inquired, "Big-Headed Son, what's the matter? What's the matter with you?"

The groom questioned, "Did you misplace some treasure?"

Big-Headed Son suddenly let out a loud cry, "Yes, it's a lost treasure ... I've lost Small-Headed Dad ... Lost Apron Mum ... Wooo ... You're happy, but I'm not happy anymore ... Wooo ..." At that moment, Small-Headed Dad and Apron Mum had just arrived at the beach. However, it was deserted, nearly no one around, except for an elderly man dismantling the large balloons in the air. Small-Headed Dad hurried over and asked, "Excuse me, may I inquire where the couples who've come here for an aerial wedding are?"

The old man pointed, "Took a hot air balloon ride to Happy Island in the ocean!"

"What? To the Happy Island?" Small-Headed Dad exclaimed. He grabbed the old man's hands holding the big balloon rope, and from the sand, he yanked out the ropes tethering several other balloons in the air. He secured seven or eight ropes together, and then stomped hard; seven or eight balloons, along with Small-Headed Dad, soared into the air ...

The elderly man was visibly agitated, exclaiming, "You there, what on earth are you up to?" Apron Mum, even more distressed, implored, "Why didn't you take me with you?"

The old man, in a hurry, asked Apron Mum, "Are you two together?" Apron Mum nodded vigorously. The old man chuckled, seizing Apron Mum, and remarked, "Don't think about escaping; I'll release you only when he returns the balloon!"

Meanwhile, Small-Headed Dad was suspended in the air with the balloon, oscillating between moments of ascent and descent, speed and slowness. Terrified, he alternated between closed and open eyes, adopting various poses resembling a bird flapping its wings or a fish finning its tail. Finally, he clasped his hands in front, extended them towards the rope, and used his legs like paddles, stabilizing the balloon's flight towards the happy island.

Proudly, Small-Headed Dad peered through binoculars towards the happy island, observing upright trees, clusters of flowers, and turquoise-hued vegetation. He spotted the bride and groom and, notably, Big-Headed Son crying loudly.

"Big-Headed Son! Small-Headed Dad is here!" he shouted, propelling himself forward in a freestyle motion. Hovering above Happy Island, he released the balloons one by one, gradually descending.

Big-Headed Son, upon witnessing this, beamed and ran towards him, exclaiming, "Small-Headed Dad! Big-Headed Son is here!"

As Small-Headed Dad let go of the final balloon, he gently descended to meet Big-Headed Son. Looking up, they saw the balloons gracefully floating above the happy island – a vibrant display of red, yellow, and green that enhanced the island's beauty.

Small-Headed Dad embraced Big-Headed Son tightly and declared, "We are the happiest folks on Happy Island!"

Football Oasis: Arena of Big & Little Heads

There's a clearing near the new village, surrounded by both large and small poplar trees that form a natural football field. Big-Headed Son, Small-Headed Dad, and other kids frequently gather here to play football and have a jolly good time!

One afternoon, amidst a spirited game, Big-Headed Son scored a goal into the opposing team's brick net. Ecstatic, he exclaimed, "Oh! Oh!" while waving his arms like a proper footballer, darting around the field.

However, the revelry was interrupted by the arrival of a large truck that rolled to a stop at the edge of the clearing. It carried construction workers armed with tools to fell trees. Big-Headed Son abruptly halted and nervously shouted, "Small-Headed Dad, it's no good – they're planning to build a house here too." Small-Headed Dad and the other children gathered around to observe.

The workers disembarked from the truck, wielding their tools. A burly man in hiking pants held up a sizable wooden sign and planted it prominently in the clearing. Four words adorned the sign.

Big-Headed Son anxiously shook Small-Headed Dad and urged, "Small-Headed Dad, what's written on the wooden sign?"

Small-Headed Dad read aloud, "'Moon Hotel Construction Site.' What a disappointment – we're getting a building on our football pitch!"

"Then we've no place to play football!"

"We won't let them build it here!"

The collective mood turned anxious and irate. Big-Headed Son suggested, "Let's keep playing so they can't cut down the trees." With that, he took the lead and resumed playing.

The burly man raised his whistle, blowing it vigorously and shouted, "Hey, please get out of here! We're about to cut down a tree – danger!"

Undeterred, no one paid him any attention; they all continued kicking away.

The hefty chap blew his whistle once more and hollered, "Can't you hear me? We're about to fell the tree!"

Still, no one paid any heed, and the football was kicked with increasing gusto, accompanied by cheers and shouts repeatedly.

The burly man blew a sharp whistle, then hunkered down, gasping for breath. He remarked to the workers, "Seems we'll have to resort to felling the trees under the cover of night; they have to head home and get some shut-eye sometime."

The substantial lorry, laden with men and machinery, rumbled away.

As everyone gazed at the distant lorry, cheers erupted as if they had just scored a goal. "Oh! We've triumphed!"

Small-Headed Dad commented, "It's a victory for now, but what about tonight? We can't play football here after dark," he said with a mysterious grin, motioning for everyone to gather and listen to his "bright idea." With a cryptic smile, Small-Headed Dad beckoned to everyone, and they leaned in to hear Small-Headed Dad's "bright idea" ...

It was a dark night, the silence accentuating the emptiness around, when the anticipated big truck arrived. Its two large headlights stared into the quiet surroundings. As the truck came to a halt, the workers swiftly disembarked. The burly man surveyed the scene triumphantly, proclaiming, "They're playing football in their dreams right now!"

With that, he approached a tree, gazing upward. The moon, filtering through the branches, illuminated the tree trunk, revealing a startling sight – a horrifying human face! The big man recoiled, exclaiming, "Good Lord! Tree monster! I saw the tree monster!"

The other two workers, witnessing ghostly faces on different tree trunks, were petrified and hastily clambered into the big truck, declaring, "We can't cut down this tree; God will punish us! God will punish us!" The truck sped away.

Early the next morning, Big-Headed Son and Small-Headed Dad hurried to the clearing, finding everything intact, and joyously exclaimed, "We've triumphed again!" Other children joined, and together they wiped the ghostly faces off the tree trunks before resuming their energetic football game.

As everyone revelled in their game, not far away, in the window of a small building, the big man peered through binoculars towards the clearing, remarking,

"They're playing football again. There's no tree monster at all; perhaps we misunderstood." He concluded with a shrug.

That night, the big truck returned. The workers, cautious and vigilant, approached each tree methodically, inspecting from every angle. Suddenly, a gust of wind rustled through the branches, and with a clattering of leaves, two or three massive hands emerged from each tree, as if poised to strike. The big man was the first to flee, shouting, "Help! We won't cut it down!"

In a frenzy of panic, the big truck sped away, echoing with the shouts and screams of the terrified workers.

As dawn broke, Big-Headed Son and Small-Headed Dad joined the other children in the clearing, shouting and dancing: "Victory! Victory! The football pitch is saved." They ascended the tree, took down the giant inflatable hands, and commenced a game of football.

Unbeknownst to them, a substantial figure in sunglasses lurked behind the tree, surveying the scene and muttering to himself: "Still nothing in the tree," he exclaimed! As he spoke, he noticed the giant inflatable hands piled beneath the tree and suddenly grasped, "So, they're the ones who deceived us, eh?" He removed his sunglasses and turned around.

Once the football game was over, everyone wiped their sweat while nervously discussing, "How do we handle them tonight? Any new ideas?"

Big-Headed Son proposed, "Tonight, we'll sleep here!"

A slightly chubby lad chimed in, "Alright, I've got a sleeping bag anyway."

Another boy added, "I have my tent!"

Small-Headed Dad interjected, "That won't work; your mums and dads will worry. Let's consider something else."

Big-Headed Son suddenly exclaimed, "I've got an idea

– I'll let my rag bear keep watch at night."

Other children followed suit: "I'll have the robot dinosaur stand guard."

They huddled together again, whispering and plotting, then joyfully bounded home.

In the evening, the large truck arrived unusually early, speeding to a stop. The burly man was the first to leap out, declaring, "Brothers, it's been the kids causing a ruckus for the past two days, so don't fret, let's get on with it!" They flicked on all the lights, instantly illuminating the night, unveiling the clearing and exposing the aspens.

Approaching one of the grandest trees, the big man looked up and suddenly froze. Perched on a branch was an endearing rag bear, grinning at him. Swiftly dropping his tools, the big man gently retrieved the little rag bear.

Gazing at the cloth bear, the big man's expression softened, and he turned around, shouting, "Hold on, everyone! Check and see what's in the trees first!"

"There's a dinosaur toy here!"

"A watermelon ball here!"

"Here's a trumpet!"

Voices of the workers echoed from all directions.

"Captain, there's a rag doll here, and it's holding a letter!"

The big man approached, opened the letter, and read aloud, "Uncle, please leave this open space for us to play football!"

A worker with a solemn expression remarked, "Seeing these toys reminds me of my childhood, when I loved playing football!"

A bearded worker added, "Indeed, with houses springing up everywhere, children have no place to play!"

The burly man nodded repeatedly and remarked, "I'll convey the children's wishes to the general manager and ask him to reconsider ..."

Another sunny morning, Big-Headed Son, Small-Headed Dad, and the children continued playing football in the open space.

"Small-Headed Dad, go after them!"

"Big-Headed Son, pass it!"

"Tubby, shoot!"

"Oh ... scored!"

...

The toys sat quietly in the tree, resembling an audience.

As the game reached its climax, a limousine pulled up with a "ga" sound, parking beside them. From the car, the first to step out was the burly man, who grinned and approached them, saying, "Our general manager has something to say to you."

Following him, a portly uncle emerged from the car, wearing gold-rimmed glasses and appearing quite composed. He announced, "I've come here today to inform you that I've had a change of heart. Instead of constructing the Moon Hotel here, I've decided to build a football field ... for the children."

Big-Headed Son leaped up immediately, embraced the uncle, and exclaimed, "You're truly a splendid uncle!"

The other children gathered their toys and eagerly presented them to Uncle. With joy, Uncle affectionately patted each child's head. However, when he reached Small-Headed Dad, instead of a pat on the head, he shook his hand.

In no time, the football field was genuinely constructed, complete with proper goals, nets, and sun umbrellas on one side, along with newly transplanted fruit trees on the other. Adjacent to the field stood a large wooden sign that proudly proclaimed: "Football Oasis: Arena of Big & Little Heads."

Candy Dentist

In the morning, Small-Headed Dad was diligently brushing his teeth in the bathroom. Between foamy mouthfuls, he hollered, "Big-Headed Son, come and brush your teeth! If they rot, the dentist will pull them out with those big pincers, which really hurts a lot."

Responding promptly, Big-Headed Son, clad in his pyjamas, made a swift "Duk Duk Duk Duk" dash to the bathroom to brush his teeth.

After lunch, Apron Mum's voice echoed once again, "Big-Headed Son, come and rinse your mouth! If your teeth rot, it can be quite daunting for the dentist to use those big pliers."

Upon hearing the call, Big-Headed Son rushed to rinse his mouth with the familiar "Duk Duk Duk Duk" sound.

In the afternoon, as Big-Headed Son popped a piece of chocolate into his mouth, Small-Headed Dad and Apron Mum, alarmed, shouted in unison, "Big-Headed Son, cut down on the sweets! If your teeth rot, the dentist will be using those big pliers to pull out a significant hole!"

Startled, Big-Headed Son promptly spat out the chocolate, covering his mouth tightly with his hand.

During dinner, Apron Mum remarked to Small-Headed Dad, "It's quite peculiar. My colleague's children are all experiencing tooth changes, but Big-Headed Son's teeth haven't budged."

Small-Headed Dad suggested, "He might be lacking calcium. Tomorrow, I'll take him to the dentist to get it checked."

Before Small-Headed Dad could finish his sentence, Big-Headed Son's face turned red, and he exclaimed loudly, "No! I'm not going to the dentist! NO!!!"

That night, Big-Headed Son had nightmares, repeatedly waking up Small-Headed Dad and Apron Mum. Each time, he described dreaming of the dentist approaching with raised big pliers.

In their bedroom, Small-Headed Dad expressed regret, "We really shouldn't have scared him like that."

Apron Mum concurred, "We frightened the poor kid

into having nightmares!"

The following morning, Small-Headed Dad went alone to the Children's Dental Clinic. The petite dentist scrutinised him and remarked, "Your head looks rather childlike, but your size is that of an adult. You ..."

Small-Headed Dad hastily intervened and said, "No, no, you've got it all wrong. I'm here to see the dentist for my son ..."

The doctor looked around and inquired with curiosity, "Where's the kid?"

Small-Headed Dad sat down and stood up again, displaying visible uncertainty. "Oh yes, we usually avoid scaring him with you."

The dentist dropped the pen in his hand in frustration. "What? You used me to scare your child? Am I a ghost?" He stood up.

Quickly, Small-Headed Dad said, "No, no, no," while using both hands to gently guide the dentist back into the chair. "I mean, scare him with your substantial pincers ..."

Hearing this, the dentist raised his own hand to inspect it and asked, "Big forceps? You call my hands big pincers? Am I a crab?" He was so agitated that he couldn't sit down again.

Small-Headed Dad restrained him again, then pointed

a finger at the surgical forceps on one side and clarified, "It's not that your hands are big forceps, it's the tool you use to pull teeth."

The dentist sighed, clasped his hands to his chest, reclined in his chair, and said, "You parents, you can't manage your children yourselves, so you scare them with us doctors. No wonder the children nowadays cry as soon as they step into the hospital, as if the doctors are wolves, tigers, and demons ... Do you think this is fair?"

Small-Headed Dad spoke softly, lowering his small head, "Yes, that's why my child wouldn't come to see you today, so I had to come alone. If you could do me a favour and visit my house yourself, I'm sure your presence would help my child overcome his fear of the dentist."

The dentist listened silently and said nothing.

On that day, Big-Headed Son was painting alone at home when the doorbell rang. He dropped his brush and hurried to the door. He peered through the cat's eye and saw a stranger.

Big-Headed Son inquired, "Who are you?"

The stranger responded, "I'm a dentist."

Instinctively, Big-Headed Son craned his neck in fear, then turned his body and pressed his backside against the door, apprehensive that the dentist might forcefully open it with his substantial pincers.

"Don't be afraid," reassured the stranger through the door. "I'm the candy dentist, whether you believe it or not."

Upon hearing this, Big-Headed Son cautiously turned back, peering through the keyhole. He noticed the stranger holding a small bottle filled with colourful candies. Still a bit uneasy, he insisted, "Turn around and let me see if you have a big pincer hidden behind your back!"

The stranger complied, making three consecutive turns and shaking off his sleeves and trouser-tubes. "There, that's a relief!"

Overjoyed, Big-Headed Son opened the door, exclaiming, "You really are the Candy Dentist! Truly a candy dentist!"

...

When Small-Headed Dad and Apron Mum returned, they found Big-Headed Son with his mouth wide open, as the dentist examined his teeth.

The dentist opened a small glass bottle, poured out tiny candy grains, and handed them to Big-Headed Son, saying, "These are calcium candies. Remember, take five every day. Once you finish this bottle of calcium candy, your teeth will start changing. Make sure to let me know when it's time for the tooth transformation."

Big-Headed Son took the calcium tablet candy, nodded repeatedly, and declared, "I know, and I'll save my teeth for you to inspect!"

Three weeks elapsed, and the calcium tablets were all consumed, yet Big-Headed Son's teeth stubbornly clung on. Apron Mum reassured, "Don't worry, they will fall out."

One day, Son and Father engaged in martial arts play on the lawn. Big-Headed Son threw punches, while Small-Headed Dad showcased his kicks. Amidst their enjoyment, shouts of "Hey, hey!" filled the air. In the midst of their play, Big-Headed Son accidentally tumbled with his mouth chewing mud and grass, resembling a big sheep. Spitting out the grass, he suddenly cried out in a rush, "Daddy, I've spat out my teeth. I've spat out my tooth!"

Small-Headed Dad rushed over, laughing heartily, "Silly son, this tooth wasn't spat out by you; it fell out on its own."

"Really? Oh, I'm getting a new tooth! I got new teeth! I'm growing up!" Big-Headed Son jumped with his hands in the air, but then stopped suddenly, lowering his head to search for something. "There it is, my tooth!" He spotted his lost incisor hiding in the green grass, rushing over to pick it up. "I said I would save it for Candy Dentist to see."

The next day, Big-Headed Son and Small-Headed Dad visited the Children's Dental Clinic.

Small-Headed Dad greeted, "Hello, Mr. Dentist!"

Big-Head said, "Hello Candy Dentist!"

Big-Headed Son hastily took out a paper ball from his pocket, carefully unfolding it layer by layer. A small snow-white tooth emerged, resembling a jewel in Big-Headed Son's hands. "Candy Dentist, I really changed my teeth! Look, this is my tooth!"

Candy Dentist took Big-Headed Son's hand and asked, "Are you still afraid of the dentist?"

Big-Headed Son confidently declared, shaking his substantial head, "Not afraid, not afraid at all."

"Would you like to take some pictures with me to show the children?" asked the Candy Dentist.

"Willing! I like my candy dentist the best!" exclaimed Big-Headed Son.

A few days later, at the entrance of the Children's Dental Clinic, several pictures adorned the wall. Among them were snapshots of Big-Headed Son and the Candy Dentist embracing, another capturing Big-Headed Son with his mouth wide open for a dental check, and a third featuring Big-Headed Son proudly holding a calcium candy bar. Four prominent words adorned the display: Candy Dentist.

As parents observed the pictures, some commented, "My son is usually terrified of dentists, but now with a candy dentist, he'll happily come." Another parent said, "My daughter has already been scared by me; now, if I tell her about a candy dentist, I wonder if she'll believe me."

Early the next morning, a long line formed outside the Children's Dental Clinic, comprising parents with their children. One girl pointed to the picture and remarked, "Candy dentists surely don't use big pliers!"

A boy chimed in, pointing to the image, "This little child isn't afraid, and neither am I."

When the clinic door opened, everyone rushed in, eagerly inquiring, "Where's Dr. Candy Dentist? Is Dr. Candy Dentist open today?"

The bustling nurses directed everyone toward a particular door. Before the crowd reached it, out stepped Big-Headed Son and a small dentist adorned in a white coat and hat, bearing four prominent words on the front, identical to those on the door: Candy dentist.

The children joyfully screamed, "Oh, there's the candy dentist! Candy Dentist, come and check my teeth!"

Big-Headed Son proudly proclaimed, "Candy Dentist

doesn't need big pliers to treat children's teeth!"

A plump little boy voiced his concern, "But my mom always says dentists use big pliers to pull out teeth, and it hurts a lot!"

A bespectacled girl added, "My dad says that too. He also mentions that if they can't pull it out, the dentist uses a small hammer. 'Knock! Knock! Knock!' I get so scared I can't sleep at night!"

Dr. Candy Dentist furrowed his brow as he listened, "So you lot would rather have rotten teeth than come to the dentist, eh?"

The children chorused, "Yes!"

The candy dentist continued, "Now, please open your mouths wide so I can check your teeth." The children obediently opened their mouths wide. The dentist examined the first child and remarked, "You eat too many sweets." He glanced at the second child and added, "You didn't brush your teeth this morning, did you?" Then, turning to the third child, he commented, "You didn't use toothpaste to brush your teeth."

The dentist turned around, retrieving bottles of candy medicine in various colours and distributed them to everyone while saying, "From today onwards, you have to brush your teeth twice a day, in the morning and evening, and rinse your mouths after meals. The candy pills will then be effective. Can you all do that?"

"We can!" The children answered in unison.

At that moment, Small-Headed Dad barged in, "Dentist, did you want to see me?"

Candy Dentist replied, "Yes. For any parents who have scared their children, I'm going to pull their teeth out with big pliers today ..."

Small-Headed Dad hastily covered his mouth, "Don't, don't do that." Afterward, he slammed the door shut and disappeared.

The children laughed, and some remarked, "My mum scares me too!"

Others chimed in, "My dad scared me too!"

The candy dentist chuckled, "Are they outside the door? I'll fetch the big pincers ..."

This time, the kids weren't keen on it. They crowded together towards the door, exclaiming loudly, "No-" They located their parents and fled far away with them.

The Candy Dentist leaned against the hospital gate with his big pincers in hand, shaking them as he laughed with joy. The ones who escaped the furthest were, of course, Big-Headed Son and his Small-Headed Dad!

The Trouble of Being a Celebrity

Today, Big-Headed Son and Small-Headed Dad were all set to participate in the "Father and Son Performance Competition." Apron Mum dressed them up and saw them off at the door, saying, "Bye! Wish you success! May you become famous!"

Small-Headed Dad assured, "Don't worry, just wait to hear our good news."

Big-Headed Son waved his hands, bidding, "Bye-bye Apron Mum!"

Small-Headed Dad checked his watch and suddenly dashed forward, with Big-Headed Son closely following.

In front of the Oriental Pearl Tower, a crowd had gathered, with balloons soaring high, colourful flags fluttering, and a vast banner reading "Father and Son Performance Competition." Various pairs of sons and fathers, of different heights, sizes, and appearances, hurriedly rehearsed their performances.

Big-Headed Son looked nervous and suggested, "Small-Headed Dad, let's quickly practice the Big Head tipping Small Head too!" And so, they began their rehearsal.

The competition commenced, and a pair of hosts, dressed as a father bear and his cub, took the stage, announcing, "Father and Son Performance Competition now begins!"

The first act featured a hefty father and son performing a boxing routine, resembling a big and a small boxer.

Following them were a slender father and son who swiftly inflated balloons, reminiscent of a crab blowing bubbles, creating an impressive string of balloons in no time.

Big-Headed Son and Small-Headed Dad stepped onto the stage. Before their performance, the audience erupted in applause, saying, "This is the father and son who just tipped their heads!" "Those with such two peculiar heads must be skilled!" "They are sure to be the champions of the day!"

Big-Headed Son and Small-Headed Dad stood facing

each other, ready for their game. Big-Headed Son held numerous plastic rings in his hands as music played. He tossed the rings, one by one, onto Small-Headed Dad's small head. The rings slid down from the small head to the shoulders and continued down to the top of the feet. In a short while, a towering stack covered Small-Headed Dad.

The audience erupted in wild applause and cheers, nearly overwhelming the police attempting to maintain order. The noise persisted until the whistle sounded, bringing a momentary hush.

With the music playing again, it was now Small-Headed Dad's turn to throw rings on Big-Headed Son. However, the rings got stuck on the big head, forming a high hat in a short while. The crowd screamed in delight, unable to contain their excitement. They pushed past the police, squeezing through any available space, and reached the stage. They pulled Big-Headed Son off the field, lifting him into the air, and shouted, "Big head, Small head! Small head, big head!"

Big-Headed Son and Small-Headed Dad had indeed won the championship. They proudly held the certificate of award, faced press interviews, posed for photographers, and enthusiastically signed autographs for the fans.

Meanwhile, Apron Mum sat at home, eagerly watching the live broadcast on TV.

The following day, as Father and Son prepared to go out, Apron Mum hurriedly brought a large bottle of styling mousse. She applied it to their disheveled hair, saying, "Now that you're celebrities, pay attention to your image. Don't disappoint your fans!"

Small-Headed Dad assured her, "Don't worry, I'll always maintain my celebrity status."

However, Big-Headed Son, looking at his oily head in the mirror, remarked, "I just want to be a celebrity for a while and then return to being the original Big-Headed Son!"

Apron Mum responded urgently, "Silly big head, there are music fans and football fans and then there are Big-Headed and Small-Headed fans. I'm really proud of you, and you should cherish it."

Big-Headed Son and Small-Headed Dad donned their suits and ties, striding out of the house with heads held high and chests puffed out, as if the entire world had its eyes on them. They hadn't gone far when a child caught up, extending a chubby arm for Big-Headed Son to sign. With a crooked scrawl, Big-Headed Son wrote: "Big-Headed and Small-Headed." The child beamed with satisfaction and happily went on his way. A lady approached next, dividing a bouquet of flowers into two bunches and presenting them to Big-Headed Son and Small-Headed Dad. Then, a mother and daughter hurried over, removing their chest pendants and giving them to the duo.

Moments later, a large group of people trailed behind them, showering flowers upon them. As they received the blossoms and turned their heads to look, Father and Son started to feel uneasy. They couldn't help but quicken their pace. Upon turning their heads again, they realised the crowd had almost taken up half of the street. Flowers flew like erratic arrows, "shooting" towards them. Big-Headed Son and Small-Headed Dad began jogging, and the crowd jogged with them. In a hasty move, they turned a corner and spotted a truck with a trailer parked at a four-way intersection, waiting for the green light. Acting on impulse, they rushed over and climbed aboard. As the crowd turned the corner and caught up, the green light came on, and the truck started moving.

The people went wild, chasing the truck and hurling bouquets of flowers at it. The impact was so intense that Big-Headed Son could only shield his face with his hands, avoiding looking at it. After a while, the truck became a flower-filled spectacle, burying them beneath a cascade of blossoms.

Big-Headed Son managed to reveal his prominent head and exclaimed, "Small-Headed Dad, I never want to be a celebrity again!"

Small-Headed Dad nodded his petite head vigorously, "Being a celebrity is too miserable!"

Adding to the sentiment, Big-Headed Son remarked, "We could have been playing football, going swimming, or doing something else fun right now. Instead, we have to hide in the flowers."

Small-Headed Dad reassured him, "Don't worry, I'll take you to play football this afternoon."

Suddenly, the truck halted in front of a building. They stretched out their heads to see, only to find the driver getting off the front of the truck, looking at them both in surprise, then glancing at the bucket as if he understood something. "Great, you guys are using my truck to transport flowers, and you didn't even inform me in advance," he exclaimed.

Small-Headed Dad hurriedly spoke, "It's not ... it's ..." He was too flustered to articulate.

The driver interrupted him, saying, "Don't explain. Let's do this – my wife likes flowers. You send half of the flowers to her, and I promise to deliver the rest to your home."

Small-Headed Dad nodded repeatedly, "Good, good, all the flowers can be given to your wife."

Just then, a voice exclaimed, "Ah, if it isn't the Big-Headed and Small-Headed Champions! Quickly give me your autograph!"

A woman yelled from a balcony, disappearing briefly before rushing out of the door with pots and pans in her hands. "I'm the biggest fan of your work, please make sure you sign a few more autographs for me, just sign this ..." She handed an item upwards.

The driver froze, walked over to touch her forehead, and said, "Are you sick?" He then crossed to the driver's side and drove his truck away.

The woman jumped in place and shouted, "I'm not sick, it's you who are sick! You don't even recognise famous people!" She then threw all the pots and pans on the ground and burst into tears.

After the car had driven for a while, the driver stuck his head out and shouted to the back, "I reckon you don't want these flowers; it's a shame to throw them away. Why not just take them to the flower shop?"

Upon hearing this, Small-Headed Dad exclaimed,

"Great! What a fantastic idea!"

The car came to a halt in front of a flower store, and the driver called out to the owner, "You're in luck, ma'am! Look at all these beautiful flowers I've brought you. You're going to be rich!"

The owner, adorned in grease paint, hurried out, expressing her gratitude to the driver. She eagerly examined the car's bucket and, to her surprise, discovered Big-Headed and Small-Headed nestled among the flowers. Overwhelmed with excitement, she exclaimed, "Ah, I finally see you, father and son, with my own eyes ... oh ..." She cried tears of joy and even showered Big-Headed and Small-Headed with a handful of flowers from her store, instantly emptying the bucket.

The driver shook his head, muttering, "What's wrong with these women? All following the devil ..." He stepped on the gas, and the car resumed its journey.

At noon, Apron Mum hummed her way home. However, she froze at the door, as flowers blocked her path, and Father and Son lay fast asleep on the sofa. Perplexed, Apron Mum wondered, "What's going on here?"

In the afternoon, Apron Mum cautiously poked her head out of the shed, surveyed the scene, and then retreated back inside. Moments later, a large and a small man, both clad in trench coats and sunglasses, emerged from the door, the small man holding a football. They moved stealthily forward like thieves, quick and silent.

Pedestrians coming from the opposite direction stared at them in surprise and murmured, "Strange, wearing trench coats on a hot day!" Those who approached from behind came to a sudden halt, waiting until Big-Headed Son and Small-Headed Dad had moved farther away before daring to comment, "They probably escaped from the madhouse!"

Undeterred by the curious onlookers, Big-Headed Son and Small-Headed Dad strolled through the woods, navigated through a supermarket, and walked through an underpass until they reached a vacant piece of land. There, they swiftly shed their trench coats and sunglasses, revealing only sweatshirts and shorts. They resumed their familiar routine, kicking up a football.

Big-Headed Son joyfully exclaimed as he kicked, "Oh! We are the original Big-Headed Son and Small-Headed Dad again."

The football spun in the air repeatedly, seemingly sharing in the happiness of Big-Headed Son and Small-Headed Dad!

Apron Mum's Weight Loss

At dawn, Big-Headed Son woke up and reached for a whistle beneath his pillow. Gently approaching his parents' bed, he blew a few notes, shouting, "Get up and run! Get up and run!" Small-Headed Dad promptly sat up, but Apron Mum, unimpressed, covered her head and returned to sleep.

Undeterred, Big-Headed Son climbed onto the big bed and blew on Mommy's covered head, saying, "Duh-duh, no lazybones!"

Angrily, Apron Mum lifted the blanket and declared, "I'm not going. I'm going to sleep." She covered her head again and dozed off.

Slightly annoyed, Big-Headed Son, with a little encouragement from Small-Headed Dad, decided to let it go and run together. As they left the house, they sprinted, with Big-Headed Son leading and Small-Headed Dad following, chanting, "Left, right, left, right ..."

They traversed the woods with elderlies engaged in Tai Chi physical exercise, crossed the river where older kids practiced sword dances, and ran through the square filled with many people participating in morning exercises.

Big-Headed Son remarked while running, "Everyone is exercising, except Apron Mum."

Small-Headed Dad, catching up, suggested, "We need to find a way to ensure that Apron Mum gets up every morning and runs with us."

Just then, a plump mom with her chubby kid strolled down the street. Big-Headed Son abruptly stopped and exclaimed, "I have an idea!" He looked at the plump mom passing by and whispered to Small-Headed Dad, "From now on, let's call her Fat Mom and get her to run with us. She's probably terrified of gaining weight!"

Small-Headed Dad paused and remarked, "But Apron Mum is not fat at all; you see, she proudly stands in front of the mirror every day!"

Big-Headed Son's excitement waned, but Small-Headed Dad resumed running, and Big-Headed Son followed suit.

They sprinted up the street and spotted an open-air "distorting mirror showroom" on the roadside. Big-Headed Son dashed straight towards it, exclaiming, "Small-Headed Dad, hurry, let's take a picture in front of the mirror."

Small-Headed Dad intended to run, but Big-Headed Son used his substantial head to gently push Small-Headed Dad towards the mirror. Small-Headed Dad chuckled happily when he saw the reflection, "Haha, I've become you, and you've become me!"

They cavorted around the mirror, transforming from a stout person to a slender one, from a short figure to a tall one, at times sporting long legs and a short body like a heron, and at others, having short legs and a long body like a short-legged dog. They laughed and laughed, with Big-Headed Son's large head emitting a hearty "giggle," almost touching the ground.

Suddenly, Big-Headed Son positioned himself in front of the mirror, which made him appear as a super-sized man. He turned to Small-Headed Dad and remarked, "If only we had this mirror at home. Apron Mum would be alarmed when she sees herself in it. Maybe then, she would willingly join us for a morning run every day to shed some weight."

Small-Headed Dad's eyes gleamed with excitement, "Exactly! Later, when Apron Mum is not at home, we'll transform the dressing mirror into a double-sided distorting mirror. One side will show her as a larger person, and after a week of morning runs, we'll switch it to the thin version. That way, she'll gain confidence."

At noon, a truck arrived in front of their house. Workers lifted down a special double-sided distorting mirror, carried it into the house, and then removed the original mirror, placing it in the truck to be taken away.

In front of them was a double-sided distorting mirror that distorted the reflection both horizontally and vertically. Although the curves on the front and back of the mirror were not the same, the cleverly done border made it not immediately apparent. Big-Headed Son caught a kitten and carried it to the distorting mirror. In an instant, the kitten's image transformed into a "tiger," then a "mouse," frightening the little creature with a "meow" as it tried to escape.

Meanwhile, Apron Mum finished work and entered a fashion store. After joyfully browsing, she ultimately purchased two dresses. Upon arriving home, she happily announced to Big-Headed Son and Small-Headed Dad, "I received my bonus today and bought two dresses.

I'm going to have a fashion show later!" She proceeded straight into the bedroom.

As soon as Apron Mum closed the bedroom door, Big-Headed Son and Small-Headed Dad exchanged amused glances and rushed over, putting their ears close to the door.

Inside the bedroom, Apron Mum tried on the new dress and hummed a song as she walked to the mirror for comparison. Suddenly, her expression turned to one of bewilderment, and the song came to an abrupt halt. Nervously looking left and right, front and back, she realised that no matter how she examined herself in the mirror, she appeared to be a plump woman!

In a flurry, Apron Mum pulled open the bedroom door and ran out, exclaiming, "I look like this in the mirror, and I'm supposed to wear new clothes? What are you two doing at the door?" She asked, puzzled by their presence.

Small-Headed Dad hastily interjected, "We're here to buy you dinner."

Big-Headed Son quickly added, "Yes, absolutely!"

Apron Mum declared, "I'm not eating anything from today!"

Big-Headed Son countered, "If you don't eat anything,

you'll turn into a little ant. I don't want little ants to be my mommy!"

Despite their pleas, Apron Mum remained standing and refused to sit at the table.

At that moment, Small-Headed Dad winked at Big-Headed Son and said to Apron Mum, "All you have to do is run with us every morning, and you're guaranteed to lose weight."

Relieved, Apron Mum exclaimed, "Really? Then I'll start running with you every morning from tomorrow." Saying this, she picked up a piece of fish and stuffed it into her mouth.

In the morning, all three of the family ran together, shouting "left, right, left, right." Three birds in the sky seemed to be flying after them, and three puppies on the ground seemed to be running after them.

As they ran, Apron Mum commented, "The air is so nice in the morning, it seems to have a scent!"

Big-Headed Son remarked, "That's why we like running in the morning. Now you like it too!"

Running through a grove, they felt as if they were running under a green sky.

One afternoon, when Big-Headed Son and Small-Headed Dad were not at home, Apron Mum returned from work early. Entering the bedroom, she spotted the kitten playing on the big bed. Playfully, she lifted one of the coat hangers and pretended to strike the mischievous kitten, saying, "You naughty thing, how dare you crawl into bed and play! Let me teach you a lesson!"

The kitten, startled, meowed and darted around. It leaped onto the dressing mirror, causing it to tilt. The kitten jumped again, tumbled to the ground, and swiftly scampered away from Apron Mum's feet.

Apron Mum glanced up at the mirror, now facing her. To her surprise, the reflection showed a very slim Apron Mum! Excitedly, she tossed away the hanger and began dancing a disco in front of the mirror.

Hearing the song and dance, the kitten entered the room, noticing that its owner wasn't upset. It once again jumped on the mirror to play. This time, the kitten wasn't scared and patiently waited for the mirror to turn downward before gracefully leaping to the ground. Apron Mum, unaware of this, reached out to pick up the kitten, gently saying, "Baby, be careful. Did you hurt yourself from the fall?" She kissed the kitten, held its face to the mirror, and remarked, "Look, I exercise every day, and I'm getting slimmer ..." As she spoke, she raised her head to look in the mirror with the kitten, only to unexpectedly see a plump woman holding a "tiger."

"Ah!"

"Meow!"

They both screamed simultaneously, and the frightened kitten fled again, leaving Apron Mum collapsing on the bed in fear.

After a moment, she opened her eyes and stared at the ceiling, as if recalling something. Suddenly, she sprang up and rushed to the mirror, scrutinizing the border carefully. Then, with a gentle push, the mirror turned up, and Apron Mum looked towards it, reverting to her slim appearance.

Meanwhile, Big-Headed Son and Small-Headed Dad returned, noticing Apron Mum's bag and shoes, indicating her return. They headed for the bedroom, pushed open the door, and were met with the sight of ... a very thin and slender Big-Headed Son and Small-Headed Dad, who were also walking towards them. Perplexed, they realised that Apron Mum had positioned the dressing mirror against the door.

Now, Big-Head and Small-Headed exchanged glances, hesitant to meet Apron Mum's gaze. Apron Mum, with a cold tone, walked past them, saying, "Well, it seems that you father and son teamed up to play a trick on me!"

Small-Headed Dad quickly rushed out after him, wearing a smile, "We're doing this for the sake of your health, truly!"

Big-Headed Son also joined in, adding, "If we didn't do this, how would you know that the morning air is good?"

Suddenly, Apron Mum paused for a moment, turned around, laughed, and said, "What two great fools; I was pretending to be angry. I couldn't be happier that you love me so much." With those words, she put one arm around Big-Headed Son and the other around Small-Headed Dad, kissing them gently and warmly.

Meanwhile, back in the bedroom, the kitten returned to play with the turning mirror!

Subway Circus

Small-Headed Dad held Big-Headed Son's hand as they walked towards the subway station.

Big-Headed Son exclaimed happily, "It's my first time riding the subway!"

The subway station was bright and spacious, featuring a counter with food, toys, and books.

Curious, Big-Headed Son asked, "Why are there things for sale here?" He promptly pulled Small-Headed Dad towards the toy counter.

Small-Headed Dad explained, "This is called a subway store."

Intrigued, Big-Headed Son inquired further, "Apart from the subway store, are there other stores?"

After a moment's thought, Small-Headed Dad replied, "There's also the Subway Fast Food, the Subway

Supermarket, and the Subway Circus ..."

Excited, Big-Headed Son turned to Small-Headed Dad, exclaiming, "What? There's a subway circus? Take me there! Hurry, take me there!"

Small-Headed Dad grabbed Big-Headed Son's hand and headed towards the ticket office, saying, "Yes, yes."

The ticket booth window was high, so Small-Headed Dad stood on tiptoes to hand over the money, saying, "One ticket please."

Meanwhile, Big-Headed Son, unable to see inside the ticket office, climbed onto a nearby garbage can for a better view. Anxiously, he told the ticket agent, "Buy two tickets, there's still me!"

Small-Headed Dad interjected, "You're under 1.2 metres, you don't need to buy."

However, the conductor, after glancing at Big-Headed Son, remarked to Small-Headed Dad, "You're not as honest as the kid. With such a big head, how could he be less than 1.2 metres?" Taking the money, he quickly issued two tickets, tossed them out of the window, and added with a final jab, "How does such a man deserve to be a father!"

Small-Headed Dad intended to reason with the conductor, but the people behind had already occupied the window, leaving him unable to squeeze in, resulting in furrowed eyebrows and mounting frustration. In the midst of this, Big-Headed Son jumped down from the dumpster, snatched a ticket from Small-Headed Dad's hands, and dashed away. As he ran, he turned back, declaring, "I did it on purpose; you can't really ride the subway without buying a ticket."

Enraged, Small-Headed Dad shouted, "Fooled!" while pointing at his Big-Headed Son, "You stinky big head! Sneaky big head! Big Head!" He scolded and chased after him.

When the train arrived, Big-Headed Son looked around and inquired, "Small-Headed Dad, where is the train going?"

Small-Headed Dad responded, "Big-Headed Son, you'll find out later."

The surrounding passengers observed the peculiar duo in amazement and whispered, "What a funny father and son pair— one with such a big head, the other with such a small one." "Could the boy be his actual son? The big head must have been adopted by the small head, haha …"

Feeling a bit self-conscious about the comments, they quickly changed carriages. The second carriage had fewer passengers, where Big-Headed Son sat for a while, occasionally jumping and tugging at his collar. He then announced, "I'm going to the third car to take another look."

In the third carriage, Big-Headed Son couldn't help but cover his mouth and burst into laughter. It turned out that the passengers in this carriage were all dressed in costumes, adorned with painted large faces, creating a comical scene.

An uncle in a clown suit, upon hearing the laughter, turned his head and stared at the substantial head of Big-Headed Son in surprise. He then looked at him quizzically, asking, "Hey, kid, is your big head real or fake?"

Big-Headed Son tilted his big head regally and declared, "Of course, it's real. If you don't believe it, you should touch it."

The clown touched it, and so did the other actors. Excitedly, the clown shouted to the other end of the carriage, "Director Li, come over here!"

A middle-aged man ran from that end of the carriage, and upon seeing Big-Headed Son, his gaze mirrored surprise. He patted Big-Headed Son's big head and asked, "Are you here to see the circus show?"

Big-Headed Son nodded, saying, "Well, I know you are the Subway Circus."

Director Lee said, "It's better to act in a circus than to watch one. How about it, would you like to?"

Big-Headed Son jumped up at once, knocking the clown's fake nose out of place, exclaiming, "Really? Willing to—willing to—"

Now, all the actors came to life and surrounded Big-Headed Son.

A "grandfather" wiped off his beard, revealing himself as a young man. He said to Big-Headed Son, "Hey!"

A sturdy man walked up to Big-Headed Son and suddenly turned around, revealing two faces—one with the uncle's face and the other with a lady's face. He said to Big-Headed Son, "Welcome!"

A magician took the black bowler hat off his head, placed it in the palm of his hand, and said, "One, two, three, change!" The bowler hat transformed into a small monkey, dressed in a black suit with a red bow tie. Big-Headed Son cheered and clapped enthusiastically.

The actors disembarked, retrieving their respective props from the car door. Big-Headed Son hurriedly followed; small hand clasped in the big hand of the director.

Small-Headed Dad rushed to their carriage, spotting Big-Headed Son already off the train. He smiled reassuringly and followed suit, maneuvring through the crowd. Suddenly, he observed Big-Headed Son holding someone else's hand. Small-Headed Dad took a step over, pulled up Big-Headed Son's other hand, and exclaimed, "Big-Headed Son, you're with the wrong person!"

Big-Headed Son looked at him, retracted his hand, and continued to follow the director. Perplexed, Small-Headed Dad touched his small head, rushed up to pull him again, and said, "What's wrong with you, Big-Headed Son? I am your Small-Headed Dad, ah!"

The director stopped and asked Big-Headed Son, "Is he your dad? I don't see how it looks like that at all. Could it be an impostor?"

Big-Headed Son hastily nodded and said, "He's an impostor. My father's head is even bigger than mine." As he spoke, he gestured with his hand to illustrate.

The director then turned to Small-Headed Dad and remarked, "Seeing that your head is so small, you still want to pretend to be this boy's father, no way! Please stop pestering the boy; he will join us in the circus." With that, he assisted Big-Headed Son in walking away quickly.

Frustrated, Small-Headed Dad hit his small head

again, sighed, and squatted down, muttering, "This mischievous son! Instead of watching the circus with me, he ran away to act in the circus!"

The audience at the subway square was eagerly awaiting, and as the actors arrived, a round of applause erupted.

The show kicked off with music, featuring a unicycle performance followed by a magic act and, finally, a big head show.

Four big heads leaped and dashed onto the stage, identical in size and showcasing synchronised Shaolin martial arts. During a somersault, three smaller actors' big heads tumbled off, eliciting laughter from the audience. However, a big-headed kid continued to roll and spin, defying gravity to the amazement of the spectators, who cheered and clapped repeatedly.

An audience member exclaimed, "Wow, that's a real big-headed kid!"

Small-Headed Dad also joined the crowd to watch, proudly declaring, "Of course it's real; he's my son!"

Another spectator glanced at Small-Headed Dad and remarked, "What? Your son? Look at your small head! Where did you get such a big-headed son?" Laughter erupted around Small-Headed Dad's diminutive head.

At that moment, a group of "small heads" prepared to take the stage for a stilt-walking performance. A member of the audience pointed and said, "I think you could join the stilt walkers. Why pretend to be someone's father here?"

Small-Headed Dad heard this, glanced at the "Small-Headed" sign, rolled his eyes, and quickly withdrew from the crowd.

The stilt show began, featuring five individuals with small heads donned in uniform green clothes, creating a comical spectacle that left the audience grinning. Suddenly, another Small-Headed figure appeared, wearing ordinary clothes with no makeup on his face. The audience started murmuring, "What's wrong with this actor? He didn't even wear a costume!"

Behind the scenes, the director and the rest of the cast were in a panic, asking, "Who is this? What's going on!"

Observing the nervous glances towards the stage, Big-Headed Son pushed his way out of the crowd to see what was happening. Upon witnessing the scene, Big-Headed Son froze!

Spotting Big-Headed Son, Small-Headed Dad quickly stepped on stilts and made his way over. However, as he approached Big-Headed Son, he suddenly twisted and fell on the stage.

Big-Headed Son exclaimed, "Small-Headed Dad! Small-Headed Dad!" He rushed over, shaking him as hard as he could, "Small-Headed Dad, did you hurt yourself?"

The director ran onto the stage, looking at Big-Headed Son in surprise, "What? Is he really your father?"

Big-Headed Son nodded enthusiastically, "Yes, he's my Small-Headed Dad. I lied to you just now because ... because I wanted to go to the circus with you." He admitted, lowering his big head in embarrassment.

Suddenly, Small-Headed Dad stood up and addressed the director with anger, "Now you hear me!" After that, he grabbed Big-Headed Son and left, and surprisingly, his waist didn't hurt.

The director was momentarily stunned and then shouted, "Please wait a moment."

Hurrying over, the director said, "You father and son are a pair of talented circus performers. You are welcome to come to our Subway Circus program as often as you can for guest appearances!"

Big-Headed Son and Small-Headed Dad, hearing this, exclaimed, "That's a really good idea!"

They shook hands with the director and bid him farewell.

Rugby Ball

Big-Headed Son, Small-Headed Dad, and Apron Mum continued playing football in the field, taking turns being the goalkeeper.

Small-Headed Dad decided, "I'll be the goalkeeper first." He bent down and positioned himself between two trees.

As Big-Headed Son prepared for his shot, he suddenly heard Apron Mum exclaim, "Look quickly, a helicopter!" Small-Headed Dad, distracted by the excitement, looked up, allowing the ball to roll into the "goal."

Big-Headed Son jumped up and celebrated, "Oh! It's in! Into the goal!"

Small-Headed Dad expressed regret, saying, "That's cheating, Apron Mum distracted me ..."

Apron Mum teased, "It's your own lack of

concentration, and you're blaming me? Well, now it's my turn to shoot. Get ready." Apron Mum took her shot, and this time, Big-Headed Son pretended to fall to the side, exclaiming, "Wow!" Small-Headed Dad rushed over to help, and in the meantime, Apron Mum's shot rolled into the "goal."

"Goal! Another point!" Apron Mum cheered.

Big-Headed Son couldn't contain his laughter, and Small-Headed Dad realised that he had been tricked. Furious, he exclaimed, "I quit! You've teamed up to tease me!" He kicked the ball far away in frustration.

They had to run into the grass together to find it. Small-Headed Dad went to the right, Apron Mum to the left, and Big-Headed Son to the centre. The weeds were full of beautiful wildflowers, dandelions, and dogwoods.

A little while later, Big-Headed Son called out from a distance, "I've found it! I've found it!" But what he held up was a rugby ball.

Small-Headed Dad ran over and remarked, "Strange, a football turned into a rugby ball."

Apron Mum added, "And it's not even our ball!"

Big-Headed Son couldn't bring himself to throw it away and said, "But we can't find our ball! We'll just take a new one …"

"Wouldn't others be as anxious as you are when they can't find their ball?" Apron Mum questioned, looking at Big-Headed Son.

After a moment of contemplation, Big-Headed Son and Small-Headed Dad both nodded in agreement.

Apron Mum continued, "Let's write a note and hang it on the tree, asking the person who lost the rugby ball to come to our house and get it."

Big-Headed Son and Small-Headed Dad nodded together as they listened, saying, "Good idea!"

The following day, just before dawn, a knock echoed through the door. Small-Headed Dad rose from his bed, opened the door, and found a portly man standing there. He declared, "I've come to retrieve the rugby ball."

Small-Headed Dad, squinting, inquired, "Where did you misplace your rugby ball?"

After a brief pause, the rotund man responded, "By the tree."

"Wrong," Small-Headed Dad rebuked, staring at him. "That ball isn't yours!"

The portly man scratched his head and departed. Small-Headed Dad closed the door and had barely settled down when another knock resounded.

"It's your turn," Small-Headed Dad nudged Apron

Mum. She yawned and hurried to open the door, revealing a slender man who stated, "I'm here to claim the rugby ball."

Apron Mum yawned again and inquired, "Where did you lose your rugby ball?"

After a moment of contemplation, the slender man replied, "On the ground."

"Ah ... very sorry," Apron Mum interjected mid-yawn, "that ball wasn't yours."

The slender man was about to respond when Apron Mum shut the door. Just as she lay back down, another knock interrupted the quiet.

Small-Headed Dad and Apron Mum feigned slumber, pretending not to hear it.

"This time it's my turn!" Unexpectedly, Big-Headed Son leaped from his cot to the floor, donned one of Daddy's oversized sweaters, and shrouded his turtleneck up to the tip of his nose, revealing only his two eyes.

Big-Headed Son opened the door, and outside stood an elderly woman who declared, "I'm here to claim the rugby."

Big-Headed Son scrutinised her and asked, "You play rugby too?"

"Yes ... yes," the granny stammered, "I use it to lose

weight ... yes, to lose weight."

Big-Headed Son rolled his eyes and queried, "Are rugby balls edible?"

The old woman was delighted and exclaimed with a slap, "Of course, it's edible! Rugby is also known as olive ball in this country. Why else would it have this name?"

Big-Headed Son heard this and burst into laughter, laughing so hard that his sweater slipped down from the tip of his nose, revealing his big head. The old lady, upon seeing this, got scared and turned to run.

Big-Headed Son returned to his cot, lay down, and remarked, "How strange that three people would come to claim a rugby ball." No sooner had he said this than yet another knock was heard. This time, they jumped up together and went to open the door.

The door swung open, and outside stood a little boy, approximately the same height as Big-Headed Son. Seeing the three people rushing out, the boy took a step back, looking a little afraid, lowering his head and not knowing what to do.

Apron Mum gently took his hand and asked, "You're here to claim your rugby ball, aren't you?"

The boy nodded and said softly, "I put it in the grass so it would wait for Daddy."

Small-Headed Dad wondered, "Why do you need a ball to wait for Daddy?"

The boy looked at Small-Headed Dad and said, "Daddy and Mommy are divorced. I miss Daddy ..."

Apron Mum quickly pulled the boy into the house. Big-Headed Son brought the rugby ball and placed it in the boy's hands. The boy held the ball and smiled, saying, "Dad used to take me to play rugby on that field. Dad was so strong that he threw the ball so hard up into the sky that it was almost touching the airplane!"

"Really?" Big-Headed Son said enviously, "I really want to watch your dad throw the ball sometime."

The boy's smile faded for a moment, and he said softly, "Daddy's gone, no one to play with me ..."

"We'll play with you, okay?" Small-Headed Dad offered from the sidelines.

The boy smiled and nodded.

During dinner, Apron Mum wore a perpetual frown. Small-Headed Dad inquired, "What's the matter? Not feeling well?"

Apron Mum shook her head, pushed aside her half-eaten meal, and remarked, "I can't stop thinking about that boy; it's heartbreaking."

Big-Headed Son sighed, suggesting, "Perhaps if we

write a few more notes and hang them up, many dads might come to claim the boy, and he'll have a dad."

Big-Headed Son's suggestion resonated with the two adults. They exchanged glances, nodded approvingly, and rushed to shower Big-Headed Son with praise. "How clever! So smart!"

Early the following morning, Big-Headed Son, Small-Headed Dad, Apron Mum, and the boy gathered on the field. They adorned every tree with yellow ribbons, the vibrant strands fluttering in the wind, as if beckoning their loved ones back.

Small-Headed Dad said to the boy, "If your father sees these yellow ribbons, he'll surely understand that you're calling out to him."

Listening intently, the boy tied one of the remaining yellow ribbons around his chest.

From that day onward, Small-Headed Dad consistently brought Big-Headed Son and the boy to the field to play rugby. Small-Headed Dad caught the ball thrown by Big-Headed Son and launched it high into the air. The boy gleefully exclaimed, "Wow! The ball is going to hit the aeroplane!"

The boy caught the ball and threw it back to Big-Headed Son. Yellow ribbons adorned the trees around them, and the boy tightly wrapped his arms around Big-Headed Son's neck, placing his face on his shoulder.

In silence, they walked out of the field.

On another day at the field, as they played ball, the beautiful yellow ribbons had been carried away by the wind. The boy untied the one on his chest and stood on tiptoe to secure it to the trunk of a tree.

Only one yellow ribbon floated above the field!

As they played, the ball flew towards Big-Headed Son, who caught it and threw it hard. The ball took an unexpected path, soaring into the weeds. Suddenly, a grown-up emerged from the foliage, nimble as an arrow, catching the rugby ball with both hands.

Big-Headed Son began to express his gratitude but was interrupted by the boy, who opened his arms and shouted, "Dad!" He ran towards the adult and embraced him tightly.

"Dad ... Dad ..."

Big-Headed Son and Small-Headed Dad seemed to hear an echo reverberating across the open ground. They smiled, watching the boy with his dad and then gazing at the yellow ribbons floating above their heads.

Welcome the New Year

It would soon be the year 2001, and the streets bustled with activity. Fruit sellers, firecracker vendors, clothes merchants, and furniture sellers filled the thoroughfares. Small-Headed Dad and Big-Headed Son, eager to spruce up their home before New Year's Day, purchased four buckets of paint and five brushes, navigating through the lively crowd.

As they neared home, passing a green house, a kitten darted out, "meowing" and rubbing against Big-Headed Son's legs. Big-Headed Son paused and addressed the kitten, "I don't have time to play with you today." He continued walking, and the disappointed kitten followed for a few steps before halting.

Upon arriving home, Apron Mum sat on the couch, engrossed in her phone calls:

"Hello! I'd like to order a set of Italian furniture. Thanks!"

"Hello! Tulips for me, please, in purple and white. Thanks!"

"Hello! Do you have any Mickey Mouse children's bedding? Yes, one set please. Bye!"

...

While Apron Mum made her calls, Small-Headed Dad had already commenced painting the room. When Apron Mum noticed the absence of Big-Headed Son, she inquired, "Huh? Where's Big-Headed Son from the year 2000?"

Small-Headed Dad turned his small head around with a "2001" written on his forehead in paint. "He's probably rushing ahead to 2001, just like me."

After a thorough search, Apron Mum discovered Big-Headed Son in his room, tears streaming down his face. Anxious, she asked, "What's wrong, Big-Headed Son? Are you unwell?" She reached out to touch his large head.

Big-Headed Son pushed away his mother's hand and declared, "I'm not sick! I am angry!"

Apron Mum wondered, "It's about to be 2001, everyone is eager to be happy. Do you really have time to be angry?"

Angrily, Big-Headed Son responded, "You're happily decorating your room, but my room is still the same as it was in 2000!"

Apron Mum hurriedly brought the advertisement and pointed it out to Big-Headed Son: "I've ordered you a set of your favourite Mickey Mouse bedding ..."

Big-Headed Son stood up at once and said, "I used to like it, but now I don't, I've grown up!"

At this time, Small-Headed Dad came running, and he asked, "Then you say, what do you like?"

Big-Headed Son put his hands behind his back, spun around, looked, and suddenly pointed to the ceiling and said, "I'm going to build an attic!"

Father and mother looked at each other face to face at the same time, the father didn't stand still, his body rushed forward, his forehead hit the mother's forehead, and printed "2001" on the mother's forehead.

Small-Headed Dad said, "Don't you have your own room now?"

Apron Mum said, "Who else do you want the attic for?"

Big-Headed Son said, "It's no fun for you guys to always just walk into my room and throw away all the treasures I pick up like they're garbage. If I had an attic, I could hide them."

Small-Headed Dad looked at Apron Mum, thought for a moment and said, "Let's talk it over." They exited the small room.

Big-Headed Son waited in the room. A moment later, he heard the combined voices of Small-Headed Dad and Apron Mum coming from outside the room: "Big-Headed Son! We've agreed to build you an attic!"

Big-Headed Son dashed out, jumped up and hugged his mom and dad, and kissed hard. Afterwards, Big-Headed Son's head and face were everywhere printed with "2001".

The attic was complete, situated diagonally across from Big-Headed Son's crib. Overflowing with excitement, Big-Headed Son couldn't wait. Small-Headed Dad, matching his son's enthusiasm, hoisted him up, as if trying to place something into the attic.

Big-Headed Son poked his large head out of the attic and gleefully announced to his parents, "This is my room, and you have no way to come in; just like my clothes, my socks, you can't wear them. Haha! I have my own room!"

Mom and Dad stood below the attic, perplexed expressions on their faces. Apron Mum questioned, "There's no door, so why can't we go in?"

Small-Headed Dad replied, "When we buy the ladder, we can go in whenever we want!"

Turning around triumphantly, Big-Headed Son lay down in the attic with his mouth facing the sky, revealing the back of his head. "You've been fooled!" he declared.

Big-Headed Son and Small-Headed Dad headed to a hardware store together. Small-Headed Dad carried a ladder to the checkout counter, while Big-Headed Son dragged a thick rope to the same counter.

Curious, Small-Headed Dad asked, "What do you want this for?"

Big-Headed Son responded earnestly, "To hang it in my attic, of course! How else can I get up there?"

Shaking his head, Small-Headed Dad remarked, "No, that's an attic, not a boat. How can you hang such a thick rope?"

Big-Headed Son stomped his foot and insisted, "I can! I can! This is my attic, you should listen to me!"

Later, the rope was hung in the attic, one end on the top, one end on the bottom.

Big-Headed Son holding the rope "giggle" climbed up, "giggle" slipped down, like a monkey; Small-Headed Dad holding the rope to climb up, only to hear "cluck cluck ...", the rope almost broke, he hurriedly let go of his hand; Apron Mum holding the rope to climb up, she just force, "flopping", fell to sit on the ground.

Big-Headed Son stuck his head out of the attic and said, "I told you, didn't I, there's no way you can get in this 'room.'"

Look, Big-Headed Son throws the scrap iron bars and batteries he has found into the attic;

Look, Big-Headed Son loads up a basket with broken pieces of wood, slingshots, various cardboard boxes, broken alarm clocks, and whatnot, and hangs them on a rope up to the attic;

Look, Big-Headed Son rolled happily in the attic ...

That morning Big-Headed Son walked past the green house again, and the kitten ran out again, meowing.

Big-Headed Son said, "Come on, I'll take you up to my attic to play!"

The kitten ran happily after Big-Headed Son and ran into Big-Headed Son's house.

Big-Headed Son taught the kitten to climb the rope, but the kitten just couldn't learn.

Big-Headed Son had to use a thin rope to tie one of the kitten's legs, and then hang it up like a basket. This scared the kitten, it was in the air "meow" screaming, as if it was going to be eaten by someone. When the kitten was

Big-Headed Son and Small-Headed Dad

hoisted up to the attic, Big-Headed Son hastened to untie it, but the kitten jumped down from the attic and escaped like a madman.

There were already firecrackers going off in the evening: "Bang—pop—"

Small-Headed Dad carried the roasted chicken, and Apron Mum held the roasted duck, arranging them on the table as if preparing for a banquet. Big-Headed Son joyfully placed his chopsticks and wine glasses on the table, exclaiming, "Oh, it's the New Year! It's the year 2001!"

Small-Headed Dad announced, "This is the last dinner of the year 2000. After this, we will go to the Bund to watch the fireworks."

Suddenly, strange cries emanated from outside, escalating in pitch: "Whoa! Wow Wow! Meow wow ..."

Small-Headed Dad peered out the window and remarked, "Sounds like a crazy cat!"

Upon hearing this, Big-Headed Son dropped his chopsticks and wine glass, sprinted into his hut, ascended to the attic, and stowed away the rope.

Alarmed, Small-Headed Dad and Apron Mum rushed into the hut, only to find it empty. They raised their heads to look up at the attic.

Small-Headed Dad inquired, "What's the matter, Big-Headed Son? What happened?"

Big-Headed Son's voice echoed from the attic, "it's... it's...really...scary ..."

Anxious, Apron Mum slapped the bed and urged, "Tell us quickly! Don't scare yourself silly!"

Big-Headed Son's voice responded, "It's me who scared that, that kitten out of its mind, and it came back to revenge on me ..."

Small-Headed Dad and Apron Mum listened carefully, then shook their heads and walked away, left with no better options. Alas, the last dinner of the year 2000 was not shared by Big-Headed Son, but only by Small-Headed Dad and Apron Mum.

The Puppies

In the evening, Big-Headed Son and Small-Headed Dad emerged from the subway station, finding a crowd gathered by the roadside, all peering down at something.

The air was chilly, and the cold wind danced through the bare branches of the trees. Big-Headed Son pulled his hat down, and Small-Headed Dad followed suit to stay warm.

Big-Headed Son declared, "I'll go and see!" He made his way into the crowd, and as he did, his hat was accidentally pushed off and landed right on a fire hose.

Small-Headed Dad hurriedly joined the crowd, wearing glasses that hindered his sight. Patting the hat on the fire hose, he exclaimed, "Why haven't you gone to see?"

Upon seeing no reaction, he took a closer look and

shouted in bewilderment, "Huh, how did my Big-Headed Son turn into a fire hose?" Small-Headed Dad urgently cried out, "It's not good! There's a devil on the loose! My son has been turned into a fire hose!"

The commotion attracted the attention of the crowd gathered there.

"What's happening? What's going on?"

"What's the matter?"

"Where's the devil?"

...

The crowd dispersed a bit, allowing Big-Headed Son to get a better view. To his surprise, the people had gathered around three newly-born puppies: one white, one yellow, and one black. The puppies huddled together in a basket, covered by a tattered shirt, shivering in the cold. They looked at Big-Headed Son and let out soft barks.

Big-Headed Son was about to reach out to touch them when the owner sternly warned, "Children should not touch. If you like them, get an adult to buy!"

Big-Headed Son stared at the puppies and suddenly let out a loud cry, "Wow—"

Hearing Big-Headed Son's cries from the crowd, Small-Headed Dad rushed over, reassuring, "Don't be afraid, Big-Headed Son, Small-Headed Dad is here!"

Putting the hat back on Big-Headed Son's head, Small-Headed Dad exclaimed, "You scared me to death!" and happily led Big-Headed Son away.

However, Big-Headed Son quickly yanked off the hat and stood still, crying even more, saying, "You take off your hat too, oooh ..." he cried to Small-Headed Dad.

Puzzled, Small-Headed Dad removed his hat, only to feel a gust of cold wind that seemed to pour ice water onto his head.

"No, it's too cold! Why do you want me to take off my hat?" Small-Headed Dad protested.

Big-Headed Son replied, "Look, the puppies are even colder; they don't even have hats. They're just out here on the street ..."

Another gust of wind lifted the puppies' fur, and they huddled together, visibly shivering from the cold.

Small-Headed Dad inquired, "Do you want to give your hat to the puppies?"

Big-Headed Son answered, "No, I want to take the puppies home ..."

Small-Headed Dad's glasses slid to the tip of his nose. "What? Don't you know that Apron Mum hate critters?"

Big-Headed Son insisted, "I'll hide them in my attic!"

Small-Headed Dad chuckled, "Good idea!"

And so, they purchased three puppies. Small-Headed Dad wrapped one puppy in his little hat, while Big-Headed Son bundled two puppies in his big hat. Big-Headed Son and Small-Headed Dad pulled up their shoulders as they headed for home.

Big-Headed Son swiftly placed the puppies into the basket and used the rope to hoist it up to the attic. However, halfway up, the three puppies stood up, grabbed the basket, and swung joyfully in the air.

Anxiously lying in the attic, Big-Headed Son shouted, "Don't move! Apron Mum is coming back!"

Despite his plea, the puppies swung even more vigorously. Thinking quickly, Big-Headed Son took out three cookies and offered them to the puppies. Now, with their cookies in hand, the three puppies sat in the basket, eating obediently and no longer wiggling around.

As this scene unfolded, Apron Mum returned. Upon entering, she noticed the basket in the air and questioned, "Big-Headed Son, what kind of junk are you hoisting up into the attic again?"

One of the puppies sneezed, catching Apron Mum's attention. Standing on tiptoe, she peered at the basket and asked, "What's in there? Why did it sneeze?"

Quickly, Big-Headed Son responded, "It's me who

sneezed, I ... I think I have a cold!"

Apron Mum, slightly relieved, stopped scrutinizing the basket, instructing, "You have a cold? Come down and take your medicine!"

Puppies grow up day by day in the attic. Big-Headed Son taught them to stand, taught them to get down, taught them to climb the rope to the attic.

One day, Apron Mum came into the cabin, and she suddenly sniffled and asked, "Why does it smell so bad?" Saying this, she pulled over a stool to stand up to the attic to see.

Big-Headed Son was anxious and used his big head to push his mom out: "How rude of you to walk in without knocking!"

Big-Headed Son locked the door from the inside, then cut out a marker for the men's restroom from a book: "Haha! Now Apron Mum can never come in; this is the 'Men's Room.'" He went out and stuck the mark hard on the door.

After a moment, Apron Mum stood outside the door with a steaming bowl of pork broth and shouted, "Big-Headed Son, pork soup is here!"

Big-Headed Son opened the door and looked: "It's too hot, so bring it in for me!"

Apron Mum said, "What? I get to go in the men's room?"

Big-Headed Son thought about it and said, "It's break time; the men's room isn't open yet, so it's okay for women to come in."

Apron Mum walked into the room, and a delightful aroma wafted from the bowl, reaching all the way up to the attic. The three puppies stretched out their heads to smell, found the pork soup, and even jumped down from the attic. "Dang! Dang! Knock!" spilled the soup, broke the bowl, and startled Apron Mum with a shriek: "Whoa! Where did you get those three pups! Get them out of here!"

Big-Headed Son cried and pounced on them: "No, Apron Mum, the puppies are so poor, just keep them!"

Apron Mum insisted: "Make sure you get them out!"

"Well," said Big-Headed Son sadly, "then you wait until I find someone who will take them in ..."

One night, Apron Mum found herself home alone, and as she gazed at the darkening sky, a sense of fear crept over her.

In that moment, a bicycle salesman came running and knocked on the door, announcing, "Duh-duh-duh! I'm a salesman ..." The three puppies heard the knock and erupted into barking, "Woof! Woof! Woof," startling the salesman.

The salesman exclaimed, "Ah, there's a wolf-dog!" He was so frightened that he swiftly turned and fled.

Shortly after, another salesman arrived, holding pots of various sizes. "Duk Duk Duk, I'm a salesman ..." The three puppies barked loudly, causing the salesman to panic as he ran away, repeatedly saying, "I am not a thief! Don't, don't bite me!"

Inside the house, Apron Mum cowered on the bed, and it took a while before she dared to peek out from under the covers. To her relief, she saw the three puppies standing side by side in front of her bed, softly barking. Apron Mum quickly reached out, lifted the puppies onto the bed, and cradled them in her arms. "Ah, thanks to you guys, or they would have scared me to death!" The three puppies received affection, happily sticking out their tongues to lick Apron Mum's face.

When Big-Headed Son and Small-Headed Dad returned home that night, they were surprised to find Apron Mum cradling the three puppies, who were peacefully asleep in the quilt.

Big-Headed Son asked gently, "So, do I still need to find new owners for the puppies?"

Small-Headed Dad replied softly, "I think you've already found them!"

"Who is it?"

"It's her!"

Small-Headed Dad pointed to Apron Mum, who was "huffing and puffing" in her sleep.

Every evening after that, people would see Big-Headed Son, Small-Headed Dad, and Apron Mum, together with the three puppies—white, black, and yellow—taking a walk outside the house. The three puppies often hid behind the bushes. Only when their owners stopped and looked for them anxiously did they suddenly pop out—one running to Big-Headed Son, one to Small-Headed Dad, and one to Apron Mum. The sight of the happy family, along with their three adorable companions, became a familiar and heartwarming scene in the neighbourhood.

Toy Hospital

At night, Big-Headed Son was engrossed in playing with his toy cars, while Small-Headed Dad watched the news on TV.

Several of Big-Headed Son's toy cars were in disrepair: wheels falling off, doors coming loose, and some refusing to move. Undeterred, Big-Headed Son fetched his toolbox and diligently set to work fixing them.

While Big-Headed Son was immersed in his repairs, he overheard the news announcer saying, "A new auto hospital has opened on Rose Road in this city, specializing in repairing all kinds of cars."

Immediately, Big-Headed Son sat down in Small-Headed Dad's arms, pointing excitedly at the TV. "The TV said there's an automobile hospital! You must take me there tomorrow!"

Curious, Small-Headed Dad asked, "Why do you want to go to the automobile hospital?"

"I've got a lot of cars that are sick, look here." He gestured towards a pile of broken toy cars on the ground.

Small-Headed Dad chuckled and walked over, picking one up. "My silly son! That automobile hospital repairs real cars that drive on the road, and these are just toy cars that people don't usually fix."

Angrily, Big-Headed Son stomped his foot. "I don't believe it. If it's an automobile hospital, they should be fixing cars."

Smirking, Small-Headed Dad shook his head. "Well, believe it or not, I'll take you there tomorrow!"

Early the next morning, Big-Headed Son accompanied Small-Headed Dad to the automobile hospital on Rose Road.

However, as they reached the entrance, Small-Headed Dad suddenly stopped and said, "I don't think it's appropriate for me to go in. It's better for you to go in and ask yourself."

Perplexed, Big-Headed Son asked, "Why?"

Squatting down, Small-Headed Dad explained, "Because I'm an adult, and people might laugh at me."

Unfazed, Big-Headed Son declared, "I'm not afraid

of being laughed at! Well, you just wait for me here." And with that, he entered the automobile hospital alone.

Inside, he marveled at the spaciousness and saw car parts scattered everywhere—tyres, seats, windows, engines, and more. Several uncles were busy putting new tyres on a car that had its tyres removed.

Suddenly, a tall uncle with a black beard emerged and inquired, "Little friend, who are you looking for?"

Big-Headed Son shook his head, saying, "I'm not looking for anyone."

"Then what do you want?"

"I'm here at the auto hospital to get my car fixed!" Big-Headed Son declared, pulling out nearly a dozen toy cars from various pockets and lining them up on the ground.

A few uncles repairing cars nearby burst into laughter, but Big-Headed Son was undeterred. He continued, "You opened a car hospital, so you should repair all the cars! We kids have lots and lots of broken cars that we can't play with!"

Scratching his scalp, the tall uncle pondered and said, "It makes sense. You're right. Let me think about it ... How about this? We'll open a special 'toy car clinic' in the car hospital, specializing in children's cars, just like a pediatrics clinic in a hospital ..."

Before the uncle could finish, Big-Headed Son was so delighted that he shook his big head and rushed at the uncle to give him a hug. However, the uncle, fearing the impact of Big-Headed Son's large head, quickly blocked him with outstretched hands, exclaiming, "Don't, don't touch me! Your big head ... can run over people!"

Big-Headed Son, as he distanced himself from that man, remarked, "I'm chuffed, not attempting to bop you, don't be fretting! " He then darted towards the door, halting midway to declare, "I'm off to inform Small-Headed Dad post-haste!"

Before reaching the flowerbed, Big-Headed Son hollered to the awaiting Small-Headed Dad, "The motorcar hospital is gearing up for a 'toy car clinic', meaning our youngsters' cars can soon consult a doctor at the motorcar hospital if they're under the weather!"

A few days later, at the motorcar hospital entrance, two lengthy queues formed on either side: one comprised assorted real automobiles, and the other featured an array of toy cars. The drivers of the real cars sat in their respective cabs, observing the children and toy cars on one side, each chuckling at them in turn.

"Ah, are they here for car repairs as well? Just like the

genuine ones!"

"Where's the steering wheel, you reckon?"

"See, we're the actual drivers!"

...

They bantered, even honking at the kids. The children grew irate.

"What sort of drivers are you? One person, one car!"

"Exactly, I've got twenty cars all to myself!"

Big-Headed Son rushed to the forefront and proclaimed, "All my cars are top-notch! Behold, Ferrari, Porsche, Cadillac, Mercedes-Benz ... any in your possession? Hmm!"

The drivers erupted in laughter. Shortly after, the children emerged joyfully, clutching their mended cars, coincidentally encountering a girl cradling a doll.

The girl observed them and thought to herself, "Wow, having a toy repairer here is fantastic!"

Excitedly, she turned and sprinted towards the complex.

Soon, a multitude of girls rushed towards the automobile hospital. Some clutched rag dolls with missing arms, others carried shaggy rabbits with absent ears, and a few dragged little wooden carts with missing wheels, among other toys in need of repair.

Uncle Big Guy expressed concern, exclaiming, "Gee whiz, we're not a toy repair store here."

A girl with pigtails retorted, "Uncle, you're biased. You repair toys for boys, not for girls."

The girls gathered around the uncle and chanted, "Uncle is biased! Uncle is biased!"

With a laugh, the uncle scratched his scalp again. "Well, well, let me think about it again. You guys have a point. Let's do it this way: tomorrow and the day after tomorrow are the weekend. You won't be going to kindergarten, and your moms and dads won't be going to work. Let's all come together and build a house. We'll specialise in opening a 'toy hospital.' Do you agree?"

The girls cheered in agreement, shouting, "Agree! Agree!"

On Saturday morning, with the sun yet to rise, numerous mothers, fathers, and children gathered. Some pushed carts, some pulled carts, some laid bricks, some wielded spades, and others mixed cement. Everyone happily engaged in their tasks, and the big uncle, now resembling a chief commander, blew his whistle to coordinate the efforts.

As the day progressed, the house took shape, transforming into a beautiful castle-like structure.

Small-Headed Dad proudly lifted Big-Headed Son and affixed a large wooden sign on the door that proudly declared "Toy Hospital." The children and parents gathered outside applauded, cheered, and released balloons into the air, celebrating the new establishment.

Inside the "toy hospital," numerous huts were set up, each adorned with a small, exquisite sign. These signs identified the specific clinics within, such as the Ragdoll Clinic, Car Clinic, Pistol Clinic, Building Blocks Clinic, Animal Toys Clinic, and more.

A few days later, one evening, Big-Headed Son and Small-Headed Dad sat together to watch the news. The TV broadcast announced, "Following the automobile hospital on Rose Road in this city, a new toy hospital has recently opened. It was built by the workers of the automobile hospital together with the children in the neighbourhood and their parents during the weekend."

Upon hearing this news, Big-Headed Son and Small-Headed Dad were so overjoyed that they tumbled off the couch and onto the floor, with Big Head topping Little Head in their elation.

Mama Bear's Hotel

In the autumn, Big-Headed Son and Small-Headed Dad were preparing for a trip, packing their belongings. Three puppies came out, circling around their owners' legs, barking as if they wanted to join the adventure.

Big-Headed Son squatted down, petting the puppies, and then looked up at his dad. "Let's take the puppies with us on our trip."

Small-Headed Dad shook his head repeatedly, saying, "No, no, animals are not allowed in the hotel!"

Undeterred, Big-Headed Son picked up the three puppies and asserted, "They all have names; they can't be considered as animals. I must take them!"

"Alright then," conceded Small-Headed Dad, "just be prepared if we can't find accommodation in a hotel."

The three puppies were adorned with bows and little

vests, accompanying them as they went out, wagging their tails. The trio of puppies ran ahead for a while, lagged behind for a while, and even rolled around in a row, bringing laughter to Big-Headed Son and Small-Headed Dad.

As they sat on a tree stump to rest and enjoyed some bread, Big-Headed Son remarked, "The puppies seem to enjoy traveling as much as we do."

Small-Head Father agreed, saying, "That's for sure. All living beings love nature."

Curious, Big-Headed Son asked, "Then why were you reluctant to bring them along?"

"It's not that I won't; it's just that there might be accommodation issues," explained Small-Headed Dad.

As darkness fell, they headed towards an inn. As expected, the doorman stopped them and politely informed, "I'm sorry, dogs aren't allowed in the hotel."

Quickly, Big-Headed Son exclaimed, "But they all have names! One is called Black Doughnut, one is called White Doughnut, and one is called Yellow Doughnut. They can't be considered as just dogs!"

Amused, the doorman responded, "But they can't talk, so they can only be counted as dogs."

Disappointed, Big-Headed Son and Small-Headed

Dad had to leave the hotel with the puppies. With the sky turning dark, Big-Headed Son asked anxiously, "What should we do, Small-Headed Dad?"

Small-Headed Dad exclaimed in annoyance, "It's all your fault for not heeding my advice!"

As they strolled along, they came across a small family-run hotel with a courtyard.

"Hey, there's a homestay here; let's go and inquire!" Small-Headed Dad perked up.

Big-Headed Son looked at the prominent letters on the sign and inquired, "What's a homestay?"

"It's a privately owned hotel, and they still have rooms," explained Small-Headed Dad.

They entered the family hotel, where an amiable older woman warmly welcomed them, "We have various rooms here, big and small, and we also provide breakfast ..."

Big-Headed Son promptly spread his legs apart, revealing the three puppies nestled behind him, "And what about them?"

The woman hesitated. Big-Headed Son and Small-Headed Dad exchanged concerned glances.

After a moment's thought, the woman guided them towards the yard, "There's an extra chicken nest in the yard; let's see if we can find a place for your puppies." In the yard, they indeed found two brick chicken coops next to each other across a wall.

"Alright, this house is just perfect for three puppies," Big-Headed Son exclaimed.

Small-Headed Dad informed the lady, "We'll settle the accommodation fees when we depart."

Unexpectedly, during the night, just as Big-Headed Son and Small-Headed Dad had settled into bed, the dogs and chickens in the yard began barking, as if engaged in a dispute.

Big-Headed Son commented, "Perhaps the mother hens aren't keen on lending their space to the puppies."

Small-Headed Dad sighed, "Looks like we won't enjoy a peaceful night's sleep tonight."

"Bark, bark, bark ..." The canine and poultry uproar continued until the break of dawn.

Before they could rise the next morning, the landlady knocked on the door, expressing, "I'm sorry, but I can't let you stay here any longer! I can't let you stay here anymore!"

Small-Headed Dad rubbed his eyes and rose to open the door, saying, "Understood, we'll leave immediately."

Big-Headed Son, Small-Headed Dad, and the three puppies departed the homestay with a lackluster demeanor.

"Daddy, where are we spending the night?"

"I don't know."

Big-Headed Son, with a yawn, suggested, "How about

spending the night in the woods."

Small-Headed Dad yawned twice in succession, replying, "Like a little bird? Alright then!"

As darkness settled in, they decided to spend the night in a small forest. Big-Headed Son leaned against a big tree, Small-Headed Dad against another, and the three puppies nestled against smaller trees. The woods were quiet, and soon, all of them fell asleep, snoring softly.

During the night, a bear appeared from a distance. It cautiously approached the three puppies, lowering its head to gently kiss them and using its front paws to stroke them. The puppies, feeling the touch, rolled over in contentment and continued to sleep. When a cold wind blew, the bear noticed, and it carefully lifted the puppies in its front paws, carrying them away in the direction they came from.

In the morning, the golden sunlight bathed the grove, casting warmth on Big-Headed Son and Small-Headed Dad. The birds in the trees sang joyfully, with one flying down to Big-Headed Son and another to Small-Headed Dad. As they woke up, they stretched, smiled, and basked in the serene atmosphere.

Big-Headed Son exclaimed, "What a comfortable sleep!"

Small-Headed Dad agreed, saying, "Indeed, a

comfortable sleep!"

However, as they turned their attention to the three little trees, they noticed the absence of the three puppies. Concerned, they quickly got up and searched around and up the trees, but the puppies were nowhere to be found.

"They probably went off somewhere to play," reassured Big-Headed Son, though a hint of anxiety lingered in his voice. They shouted together, "Black Doughnut! White Doughnut! Yellow Doughnut!" However, after an extended period of calling, not a single puppy emerged.

Small-Headed Dad scrutinised the ground carefully and suddenly spotted sizable bear paw prints. "Not good, the puppy must have been taken by the big bear!"

Big-Headed Son glanced down and, indeed, exclaimed with a sad face, "Golly, my puppy must have been devoured by the big bear!"

Small-Headed Dad pulled Big-Headed Son to his feet, reassuring, "Don't fret; we'll track the bear's footprints, and perhaps we can still rescue the pups." They sprinted as fast as they could along the bear's trail, calling out loudly, "Black Doughnut! White Doughnut! Yellow Doughnut!" They ran, perspired, stumbled several times, and eventually reached a towering mountain, but the footprints had vanished.

They came to a halt and shouted at the mountain, "Black Doughnut! White Doughnut! Yellow Doughnut!" The mountain echoed, "Black Doughnut! White Doughnut! Yellow Doughnut!" However, the puppy names wouldn't echo back.

Big-Headed Son, tearful, reluctantly followed Small-Headed Dad back.

"Woof woof! Woof woof woof!" Suddenly, the puppies' barking echoed from behind. Big-Headed Son turned around and saw three puppies descending the mountainside. "Look, Daddy! The puppies are back!"

Small-Headed Dad turned sharply to look, confirming the sight: "Indeed! They are the three puppies!"

With great strides, they rushed down the hill to meet the trio. Picking up the puppies, they glanced up and saw the big bear standing halfway up the hill, seemingly bidding farewell to the little ones. The puppies, recognizing the bear, barked at it.

Observing the scene, Small-Headed Dad remarked, "Last night, the big bear must have taken the puppies back to its cave for the night."

Big-Headed Son chimed in, "I believe this mama bear also runs a homestay for little animals. She's so kind!"

Small-Headed Dad interjected, "Wait, are you saying puppies are animals too?"

Big-Headed Son reasoned, "Well, if the puppies weren't animals, the mama bear wouldn't have cared for them." Suddenly, he remembered something and added, "Hey, Small-Headed Dad, how do you plan to compensate Mama Bear for the puppies' lodging?"

Small-Headed Dad scratched his head, pondering the dilemma: "That's a problem; I doubt Mama Bear will ask for money."

As they stood there, the wildflowers on the mountain caught their attention.

Big-Headed Son suggested, "Apron Mum likes flowers, so Mama Bear might too!"

Small-Headed Dad agreed, saying, "Indeed. Let's have the puppies present a bouquet of flowers to Mama Bear."

Quickly, Big-Headed Son and Small-Headed Dad gathered a large handful of wildflowers of various colours, divided them into three bunches, and handed them to the puppies. Pointing to the big bear on the mountainside, they encouraged the three puppies to carry the flowers in their mouths and run towards the mountain as fast as they could ...

Flea Market

In the morning, Big-Headed Son woke up with a hug from his curly-haired bear. As he lay there still half-asleep, Small-Headed Dad held up a whistle and blew it into Big-Headed Son's ear: "Left, right, left …" Following the rhythm, Big-Headed Son climbed out of bed, reaching down to the ground with his hands until Small-Headed Dad stopped the whistle. Opening his eyes with a big yawn, Big-Headed Son said lazily, "Small-Headed Dad, I'm not awake yet!"

Small-Headed Dad shared the exciting news, "I have good news for you; Daddy will take you to the flea market."

Curious, Big-Headed Son asked, "What's a flea market?"

Small-Headed Dad explained, "A flea market is made up of people from the neighbourhood who take things they can't use at home and sell them."

Energised, Big-Headed Son exclaimed, "Really? Are there any toys? If there are Ultraman and Pterodactyls, they must be cheaper than the ones in the toy store."

Small-Headed Dad confirmed, "That's for sure. Hurry up and brush your teeth and wash your face; we'll leave after breakfast."

Big-Headed Son hugged his curly bear and headed to the flea market with Small-Headed Dad. The market, situated on a narrow street, buzzed with people selling a variety of items: old clothes, pots and pans, clocks, vases, shoes, and more. As they moved through the crowd, Big-Headed Son spotted a boy about eight years old selling old picture books and a girl around ten years old selling old rag dolls.

Pausing for a moment, Big-Headed Son tugged on Small-Headed Dad's hand, saying, "There's no Ultraman or Pterodactyls. Let's move on."

However, Small-Headed Dad was soon pulled back by Big-Headed Son, who declared, "Daddy, I don't want the pterodactyls and Ultraman anymore. I want to be like them and sell my old toys too. How fun would that be?"

Encouraging his son's enthusiasm, Small-Headed Dad agreed, "Well, you've only ever bought toys, not sold them.

It's nice to experience it."

Excited, they ran home together to gather Big-Headed Son's old toys for the flea market.

Big-Headed Son gathered all the animal toys from the toy shelf into a sizable bag, and Small-Headed Dad assisted by carrying a stool. Whistling, they made their way back to the flea market together.

Big-Headed Son placed his stool next to the boy's bookstall and arranged the toys on it one by one. Despite adults and children pausing to inspect old picture books or select vintage dolls, nobody showed interest in Big-Headed Son's animal toys. He shifted his stool towards the centre of the street, yet still, no inquiries came. Occasionally, people approached, and just as Big-Headed Son prepared to greet them with a smile, they walked past.

A slight uneasiness crept into Big-Headed Son's heart.

Quietly, Small-Headed Dad remarked, "Seems like no one fancies your toys; maybe it's best to take them back."

"No! I won't take them back!" declared Big-Headed Son.

The girl's rag dolls and the boy's old picture books sold out, leaving them happily counting their earnings before heading home. As darkness enveloped the flea market, everyone packed up, transforming the once-crowded street into a suddenly deserted space.

"Time to go home; no one will be returning to make purchases," suggested Small-Headed Dad.

Big-Headed Son suddenly cried in sorrow, "Why doesn't anyone like my toys?" he sobbed, carefully placing the toys back into the bag one by one.

Early the next morning, Small-Headed Dad once again held a whistle and blew a "left, right, left" to his still-sleepy Big-Headed Son. However, today, Big-Headed Son ignored the whistle and buried his big head under the quilt.

In that moment, a long bamboo pole entered through the door, adorned with a row of animal toys—some old, some new. On closer inspection, these were the original toys of Big-Headed Son, now dressed in tiny clothes, small undershirts, sporting little hats, small boots, and some even with backpacks and belts. The scene became lively and amusing all at once.

Big-Headed Son joyfully climbed out of bed and sat down for breakfast, exclaiming, "Apron Mum, you've dressed up my toys so beautifully!"

Small-Headed Dad chimed in, "Apron Mum stayed up nearly all night trying to craft these little outfits."

Putting down his bread, Big-Headed Son rushed over,

enveloping Apron Mum in a hug, and said, "I love you! Thank you, Apron Mum!"

Big-Headed Son and Small-Headed Dad headed to the flea market together. As they displayed the toys, passersby flocked to them:

"What charming toys!"

"Dressed like little ones!"

...

More and more people gathered around Big-Headed Son at the centre. Happily, he handed over one toy after another, and in no time, all the toys were sold out.

At night, Big-Headed Son gazed at the vacant toy shelf at home and suddenly furrowed his brow.

"Small-Headed Dad, I want to buy back the toys I sold," declared Big-Headed Son as he hurried into his parents' room.

"Why?" inquired Small-Headed Dad.

Tears welled up in Big-Headed Son's eyes as he explained, "Because I miss them very, very, very much right now ..."

Apron Mum approached, gently touched her son's big head, and said, "Now that they've been sold, don't dwell on them anymore."

Big-Headed Son rested his big head against Apron

Mum's arms and pointed to his head, saying, "But ... but I can't control it, ah!" He then burst into a loud cry.

On the third morning, Small-Headed Dad once again held a whistle and blew a "left, right, left" to awaken Big-Headed Son. Big-Headed Son opened his eyes, glanced around, and then cried out again, "I want my curly bear! I want my curly bear!"

Small-Headed Dad took the tearful Big-Headed Son to the toy store. As they approached, they were suddenly taken aback: The window was filled with various animal toys dressed up, the same ones Big-Headed Son had sold yesterday. However, now they appeared even more animated – some on swings, some perched on the crescent moon, and others with their backsides raised high, as if engaged in a playful quarrel.

Big-Headed Son was chuffed to bits, so he dashed straight ahead, and Small-Headed Dad followed closely behind. Just as they stepped into the toy shop, an uncle in a smart black suit emerged from behind the counter. He strolled right up to Big-Headed Son, clutching a photograph: "You're the lad with the big noggin in this picture, aren't you?"

Big-Headed Son glanced at the photo, a snapshot of him peddling toys at a flea market. He grinned and replied, "Uncle, how come I didn't spot you snapping a pic of me?" His smile faded quickly: "But now, I've lost track of where all my animal toys are."

The uncle promptly gestured towards the toys in the store: "Look, they're right here! Only now, they've multiplied." Then, turning to Small-Headed Dad, he remarked, "I really should thank your son; his toys inspired me to dress up my own animal toys in all sorts of fancy outfits, even at night. Business instantly picked up!"

The uncle took Big-Headed Son's hand and said, "To show my gratitude, you can choose any toys you fancy in my toy shop, and I won't charge you a penny."

"Really?" exclaimed Big-Headed Son in surprise.

The uncle nodded in confirmation. Big-Headed Son gleefully selected a blue elephant sporting a denim undershirt, and a little frog with a duffel bag.

Exiting the toy shop with a bulging bag of toys, Big-Headed Son suddenly remembered something and turned back to the uncle who had been so kind: "You must thank my Apron Mum; she's the cleverest mum in the world!"

The uncle responded, "I know, please convey my gratitude to her!"

As they left, the uncle kept his eyes on the father and son.

The Dad Who Can Make Toys

Big-Headed Son eyed a remote control racing car in the toy shop and declared to Small-Headed Dad, "Small-Headed Dad, I want to buy it!"

Small-Headed Dad glanced at the price tag and responded, "It's too pricey!"

Angrily, Big-Headed Son retorted, "If you won't buy me a toy, I don't want you to be my dad!"

"Then who will be your dad?" inquired Small-Headed Dad.

"I'll get the chap who buys me toys to be my dad!"

As they reached the front door of their house, Big-Headed Son abruptly halted and turned towards another dwelling. Small-Headed Dad hurriedly asked, "Where are you going?"

"I'm heading to Big Ears' house. Big Ears' father

always buys lots of toys for him, so I'm going to get him to be my dad too!" replied Big-Headed Son.

With a heavy heart, Small-Headed Dad watched as Big-Headed Son walked away.

Big-Headed Son rang the doorbell at Big Ears' house, and the one who answered happened to be Big Ears' father, a portly man.

"Hello, Uncle, I want you to be my father!" greeted Big-Headed Son.

"Alright, alright, Big Ears currently has no playmate. You come and be my son and be his mate!" beamed Big Fatty.

Big-Headed Son asked, "Will you buy me toys as well?"

Big Fatty pulled him inside, saying, "Certainly, certainly. I'll get you … whatever you want tonight. Quickly tell me!"

Jumping with joy, Big-Headed Son exclaimed, "I want a remote control racing car!"

Big Fatty grabbed his bag and headed towards the door, saying, "Alright, alright, I'll bring it back for you tonight!" Then, he turned to Big Ears and asked, "What do you want?"

After a moment's thought, Big Ears replied, "I already

have a blue remote control race car, so you can get me another one in green!"

Big Fatty then closed the door and left. Big Ears brought out all his top-notch toys for Big-Headed Son to play with, leaving him envious.

"Your dad is so kind!" couldn't help but exclaim Big-Headed Son.

Big Ears nodded, then suddenly shook his head.

In the evening, Big Fatty returned, carrying two large boxes of toys. Upon entering, he exclaimed, "Big Ears! Big-Headed Son! I've bought race cars for you!"

Big-Headed Son and Big Ears were delighted, rushing out to each take a car and play with it. Meanwhile, Big Fatty sat on the side, engrossed in watching TV.

After a while, Big-Headed Son suggested to Big Fatty, "Uncle, why don't you play with us?"

Big Fatty waved dismissively without looking back, saying, "Go play by yourselves in the inner room; I have something to do." He continued watching TV.

Big-Headed Son gazed at Big Fatty for a moment, then turned to Big Ears and said quietly, "If Small-Headed Dad were at home, he would play with me."

Big Ears also whispered, "My dad only buys me toys and never plays with me." Disheartened, they lowered their heads and headed towards the inner room.

At night, Big-Headed Son and Big Ears had to share a small bed.

Standing by the bed, Big-Headed Son looked at the crib, the quilt, the pillow, and suddenly said to Big Ears, "This is not my crib, this is not my quilt, and this is not my pillow." Then he turned his head again and looked around, "This is not my home. I'm going back! I want to go back!" Saying this, he immediately ran out of the hut.

Big Ears chased him with a race car, saying, "This is the race car my father bought for you; don't forget to take it with you."

Big-Headed Son stopped, took the car, but then handed it back, saying, "This is not a toy Small-Headed Dad bought for me; I don't want it." Saying this, he rushed out of the gate.

The light was still on in Big-Headed Son's hut, as if waiting for his return. Big-Headed Son dashed towards the hut.

Huh? The door was open! Big-Headed Son was about to step in but suddenly stood still, quietly peering through the door.

Small-Headed Dad was sweating profusely, with his back to the door, sawing wood. On the table behind him were rows of various wooden carts, brand new and still smelling of wood.

Big-Headed Son was overjoyed and about to rush in when he suddenly stopped, scratched his head, turned around, and spotted a bamboo pole and an iron hook by the door.

Big-Headed Son quietly affixed the hook to the bamboo pole, then raised it to the table, "fishing out" a wooden car.

Small-Headed Dad crafted another one and turned to place it on the table. "Hey, where have all the wooden cars gone?" he inquired, looking around and even checking under the table. Finally, he rushed to the door, peered outside, and exclaimed, "Have all the wooden carts driven away?" Saying this, he walked towards the door.

Big-Headed Son quietly followed Small-Headed Dad and suddenly reached out from behind to tickle him. Small-Headed Dad cried out, "It itches! It itches!" With a quick turn, he scooped up Big-Headed Son, saying, "Big-Headed Son, you're back!"

Big-Headed Son showered Small-Headed Dad with kisses. "Small-Headed Dad, I really miss you."

Small-Headed Dad responded, "Big-Headed Son, I really miss you too!"

"I'm never going to find someone else to be my father again!"

Small-Headed Dad, overjoyed, gave Big-Headed Son a tight kiss. "Really? I'm so happy!"

Big-Headed Son then produced a wooden car from his pocket. "I really like the wooden car you made!"

Upon hearing this, Small-Headed Dad lifted Big-Headed Son into the air. "I did it just for you! I did it just for you!" They headed back inside and continued their activities together.

Small-Headed Dad picked up the last two remaining pieces of wood and asked, "What are these two little pieces of wood for?"

Big-Headed Son took them, examined them, and said, "One for being 'Big-Headed Son' and one for being 'Small-Headed Dad'!"

Small-Headed Dad exclaimed, "Good idea!" He quickly chipped away with his knife, and wood shavings fell from the air like snowflakes, landing on big head and small head.

Big-Headed Son meticulously arranged his fleet of wooden cars in the open space in front of his house. Some cars were adorned with wildflowers, others with branches, and some even carried small stones. Little birds flitted around in the air, seemingly eager to take a ride in the wooden vehicles.

Soon, children with a variety of electric toys started arriving one after another. They were astonished by the wooden cars and couldn't help but stop and inquire, "Big-Headed Son, where did you buy these wooden cars? They look so much fun!"

Big-Headed Son proudly responded, "I didn't buy them; Small-Headed Dad and I made them together!"

"What? Your dad can make toys for you?"

Big-Headed Son raised his head proudly, asserting, "Absolutely."

"But my dad only buys me toys; he doesn't make them for me."

The children all squatted down in front of the wooden cars, eagerly touching them with their hands.

"Big-Headed Son, let's play with the wooden cars too!"

Big-Headed Son contemplated for a moment and agreed, "Okay."

Thus, everyone abandoned their motorised toys and eagerly picked up one charming wooden car after another, as if engaged in a delightful robbery.

Tiger Bear

Auntie and uncle came to visit and presented Big-Headed Son with a large, furry brown bear. Big-Headed Son joyfully accepted it, saying, "So big, like a Tiger Bear!" And from that day on, "Tiger Bear" became the official name for the substantial brown bear.

On that particular day, Big-Headed Son placed Tiger Bear in his backpack, slinging it over his shoulders, and ventured outside to play. As he strolled, two little birds descended from a tree and landed on the bag. However, upon glimpsing Tiger Bear's head, they promptly flew away with a chirp of fear.

"What cowards!" chuckled Big-Headed Son.

Across the street, a cat reclined on a mailbox, observing Big-Headed Son approaching. Yet, when Big-Headed Son drew near, the cat spotted Tiger Bear peeking out from behind him and, with a terrified meow, scurried up the pipe to the roof.

"What a coward!" laughed Big-Headed Son once again.

Come bedtime, Big-Headed Son arranged Tiger Bear on the sofa, the table, and the carpet, but none of these felt quite right. "The Tiger Bear also needs a home where he can sleep," he thought. Surveying the big blocks in the toy corner, he decided, "Yes, I'll build a home for Tiger Bear!"

The large, colourful blocks were stacked together, forming a beautiful little house in no time. Big-Headed Son gently placed Tiger Bear inside. In the moonlight, Big-Headed Son lay down on his cot, contentedly gazing at the little house, and gradually drifted into a dream—

In his dream, Big-Headed Son carried Tiger Bear on his back, wandering through the woods. To his surprise, he stumbled upon a stone house made of large cobblestones. Approaching quietly, he listened closely, squinting to see, and eventually raised his hand to knock on the door, "duh duh duh duh"!

The door swung open, revealing two towering bears!

Big-Headed Son stood frozen, taking in the sight of a bear wearing a flowered turban on its head and a flowered apron around its body, and another bear donning a cowboy hat and sackcloth overalls. To his surprise, they looked at him with smiles on their faces, appearing not scary at all.

The Mama Bear greeted, "Come in, come in!"

Papa Bear added, "We welcome you as our guest!"

Hesitantly, Big-Headed Son walked in and noticed golden dried corn hanging all over the house. When Mother Bear saw him eyeing the corn, she explained, "This is our bears' favourite food. Storing it this way ensures we won't run out in the winter."

As Mother Bear spoke, she spotted the Tiger Bear on Big-Headed Son's back. She reached out, took it into her arms, and exclaimed, "Ah, my child, you've come back!"

The Tiger Bear joyfully shouted "mum" and wrapped its arms around its mother's neck.

Witnessing this heartwarming reunion, Big-Headed Son sat down on a pile of hay in astonishment, causing the hay to scatter around the house. Mother Bear, Father Bear, and Tiger Bear playfully flailed their arms, engaging in a playful hay fight, laughter filling the air. Unable to resist the joyous scene, Big-Headed Son stood up and joined in, clapping along with them.

Small-Headed Dad and Apron Mum were roused from their sleep by a resounding "splash" sound, followed by the distressed cries of Big-Headed Son. They hurried into the room, only to find the cot empty, with Big-Headed Son on the floor, rolling around.

"You're having a nightmare again!" remarked Small-Headed Dad as he gently settled Big-Headed Son back into bed.

At dawn, Big-Headed Son arose and carried Tiger Bear out of the little house. "Come on, I will take you to Bear Mother and Bear Father!" he exclaimed, heading towards the door.

Small-Headed Dad swiftly put on his shoes. "Big-Headed Son! I'll go with you!"

In the early morning, dewdrops glistened on blades of grass and leaves of trees, while the birds' chirping in the woods resonated clearly.

As they strolled, they came across a small tree that had fallen to the ground. Big-Headed Son pointed to it and said, "Look, someone has harmed the little tree again!" He squatted down, stroking the broken part of the little tree with concern.

"It seems like the woods need watching over," observed Small-Headed Dad.

They continued their journey. Big-Headed Son grew a bit anxious, saying, "Why haven't we reached it yet? That stone house is big, big, and it's in the woods."

"Perhaps Bear Father and Bear Mother in your dream were scared of us and hid the stone house," suggested Small-Headed Dad.

"Maybe that's true," pondered Big-Headed Son for a moment. "They might be afraid of getting caught."

"In that case, we'll go back on our own and leave Tiger Bear here. Bear Father and Bear Mother won't be afraid then, and they can come out to take Tiger Bear home," proposed Small-Headed Dad.

Big-Headed Son nodded in agreement. He leaned Tiger Bear against a large tree and, with Small-Headed Dad, headed back home.

In the evening, as Small-Headed Dad returned from work, Big-Headed Son eagerly greeted him and said, "Small-Headed Dad, would you come with me to the grove again to check if the Mama Bear has brought the Tiger Bear home, please?"

"Okay," Small-Headed Dad agreed, turning to accompany Big-Headed Son back to the woods.

Upon reaching the tree, they discovered that the Tiger Bear was no longer there.

"Wow! The Tiger Bear has truly gone home!" exclaimed Big-Headed Son. However, after a moment of contemplation, he furrowed his brow and added, "But who will sleep with me at night now that the Tiger Bear is gone?"

Suddenly, an old grandpa appeared from the other side of the forest, hands behind his back.

"Old Grandpa, have you seen a big stone house? Bear Father and Bear Mother live in it ..." Big-Headed Son rushed over and inquired.

Old Grandpa smiled and shook his head, "No, no. There is only a small wooden house here."

"Cabin? Where is it?"

Grandpa pointed behind him, revealing a newly built cabin.

"Who are you?" questioned Small-Headed Dad.

"I'm the new guy in charge of watching over the woods," replied Grandpa.

Small-Headed Dad remarked, "That's fantastic! With you in charge, the trees won't be cut down."

Old Grandpa turned to Big-Headed Son and said, "I've never seen a stone house, but I have seen a bear." The old grandfather extended his hands from behind, and in his hands was none other than Tiger Bear. "Is this yours?"

"Yes! Yes, yes! It is my 'Tiger Bear'!" exclaimed Big-Headed Son happily as he took hold of Tiger Bear.

Old Grandpa took Big-Headed Son's hand and led him over to the cabin. "Old Grandpa can build any house. Do you want Old Grandpa to build a stone house for Tiger Bear?"

"Yes!" nodded Big-Headed Son. In just a few

moments, Old Grandpa constructed a stone house for Tiger Bear using big and small stones. The stone house was placed right next to the little wooden house.

Big-Headed Son placed Tiger Bear inside, and the bear's head stuck right out of the little window of the stone house. "Look, it looks like Tiger Bear is watching over the woods too," called out Big-Headed Son.

Old Grandpa and Small-Headed Dad both chuckled. After the laughter subsided, Big-Headed Son scratched his head and said, "Grandpa, let Tiger Bear watch over the woods with you during the daytime. Bad guys who want to destroy the trees will run away in fear when they see Tiger Bear here!"

"That's a good idea," agreed Small-Headed Dad.

"That way, I'll have company too," added Old Grandpa.

Big-Headed Son then lifted Tiger Bear high in the air, jumped up, and declared, "My Tiger Bear is going to stand guard in the woods!"

On a sunny afternoon, many children and adults gathered in the grove for a picnic, a party, and games. They noticed Grandpa's cabin and Tiger Bear's little stone house.

A girl exclaimed, "Look, Grandpa and Tiger Bear

watching the woods together, how delightful!"

A boy chimed in, "Because the woods belong to us and to the animals!"

Big-Headed Son added, "We listen to Old Grandpa, and the animals listen to Tiger Bear. If anyone doesn't take care of the woods, animals or people, they have to be thrown out!"

"Right!" echoed everyone.

Under the warm sunshine, the beautiful woods became even more enchanting, filled with the chirping of birds and the laughter of children.

Share the Joy

On Christmas Eve, the storefront was adorned with an array of Christmas gifts: Christmas cards, Christmas trees, Christmas flowers, and red hats worn by Santa Claus.

"Small-Headed Dad, look at how beautiful these Christmas cards are! I want to buy two of them for you and Apron Mum," exclaimed Big-Headed Son, pulling Small-Headed Dad towards the store door.

Reluctantly, Small-Headed Dad picked up a greeting card to take a closer look. Nearby, a group of middle school students had chosen several sheets and were in the process of making their purchases. Small-Headed Dad craned his small head to see and noticed that they had picked the same pattern as the one he was holding.

Without hesitation, Small-Headed Dad put the

Christmas card back, then guided Big-Headed Son aside. "We won't buy it; let's go back and make them ourselves."

Before Small-Headed Dad could finish his sentence, Big-Headed Son abruptly turned, facing away from his dad, and angrily declared, "Cheapskate! You're a cheapskate! You're a cheapskate!"

"It's not that Daddy is being stingy," explained Small-Headed Dad. "Look, what's the point of everyone buying the same greeting card? Why not make them yourself with the computer? You can draw whatever you want on the Christmas card; you can write whatever blessings you want."

"Really?" Big-Headed Son's frown gradually eased into a smile. He turned around and ran forward energetically. "Small-Headed Dad! Let's go home quickly! Go home and make Christmas cards!"

Small-Headed Dad taught Big-Headed Son how to draw on the computer. With Big-Headed Son at the mouse, a depiction of "Big-Headed Son" and "Small-Headed Dad" gradually appeared on the screen, their heads leaning against each other and their backsides playfully raised.

Observing the screen, Big-Headed Son inquired, "What congratulatory message should I write?"

"Write a sentence that is closest to your heart,"

advised Small-Headed Dad.

Big-Headed Son then patted his chest repeatedly, thinking deeply.

"Ah! I've got it. Just write 'I wish you a good laugh every day,'" he exclaimed.

Small-Headed Dad nodded and proceeded to write the phrase in the greeting card on the screen. The green light on the printer illuminated brightly, and the printer emitted a "squeak squeak" sound. Soon, the image from the screen was printed on the paper and slowly emerged from the printer.

Big-Headed Son watched with excitement, exclaiming, "Really fun! Really fun!" He then folded the two Christmas cards, placed them in an envelope, and slipped them into the mailbox outside the door, saying, "You must not open them until the evening when you get the paper!"

"I promise to do that, please don't worry, Mr. Big-Headed!" Small-Headed Dad assured.

However, Big-Headed Son suddenly turned around the house with his hands behind his back, seemingly lost in thought.

"Big-Headed Son, what are you thinking?" inquired Small-Headed Dad.

"I want to give my New Year wishes to more friends,

but who are they?" pondered Big-Headed Son.

Small-Headed Dad suggested, "Besides mom and dad, think about those who have helped you and those who like you and are also liked by you. Think hard, and you will come up with it!"

Only a moment later, Big-Headed Son exclaimed, "I can think of them! There's Uncle Postman, Candy Dentist, Grandpa Kite, Uncle Potato, Grandpa in the Children's Park ..."

The printer started up again, and the Christmas cards rolled out one by one. Big-Headed Son took the cards and rode his little bike to the mailbox, stuffing all the Christmas cards in. Upon returning, he saw his neighbours—Big Ears, Jing Jing, Small Eyes, Grandpa Zhang, Grandma Fatty, Uncle Big, and many others.

Big-Headed Son's bike slowed down, and he thought, "Yes, they are my favourite people too!" He twisted his head to look at them, a smile on his face. Gradually, the bike picked up speed again, and Big-Headed Son was seen leaping straight to his door.

The printer continued singing and printing out many more Christmas cards.

A few days later, one evening, Small-Headed Dad returned home from work and opened the mailbox. To his surprise, there were several Christmas cards, all addressed with "Big-Headed Son" as the recipient.

Small-Headed Dad called into the house, "Big-Headed Son! Come and see! Grandpa Kite and Uncle Potato, they've sent you Christmas cards!"

"Really? Did they really send them to me?" Big-Headed Son ran out of his hut with joy. "Show me! Show it to me!"

Big-Headed Son took the seven or eight Christmas cards, examined them carefully, and embraced them like precious babies. "I can't believe that I send away a Christmas card, and I get a Christmas card. It means I send away joy and get joy—how wonderful! It makes me so happy!"

Small-Headed Dad, stroking Big-Headed Son's big head, remarked, "Of course, you think of others, and others think of you! This is called caring for each other."

Big-Headed Son arranged the Christmas cards one by one on the door of his hut. As darkness fell, Apron Mum arrived home and, from a distance, saw the mailbox stuffed with white envelopes.

"Why are there so many letters?" Apron Mum, puzzled by the situation, called out to the house, "Big-Headed Son, come and see! Our mailbox is full of letters."

From the house, Big-Headed Son's reply echoed, "Hey! I'm coming!"

This time, Big-Headed Son himself opened the mailbox, exclaiming, "This must be from the neighbours, Apron Mum, read it for me."

Big-Headed Son eagerly handed the Christmas cards one by one to Apron Mum, and she identified them, saying, "This is from Big Ears, this one from Big Uncle, and this is from Grandpa Zhang ..."

Joyfully, Big-Headed Son stuck these Christmas cards on the door, forming a colourful collage.

Early the next morning, Big-Headed Son printed out many more Christmas cards and placed them in a big bag.

Small-Headed Dad, poking his small head out of bed, asked with half-closed eyes, "Big-Headed Son, who are you going to send Christmas cards to?"

After grabbing the bag, Big-Headed Son reached out to pull Small-Headed Dad's exposed feet, urging, "Get up, Small-Headed Dad! Get up! Come with me to deliver Christmas cards to the animals!"

"No, no, no, I have to sleep!" Small-Headed Dad hastily covered his head with the quilt.

Big-Headed Son thought for a moment, chuckled, and playfully made a tickling motion, saying, "Cluck

cluck cluck cluck ...” Soon, Small-Headed Dad, tightly embracing himself, rolled back and forth on the bed, pleading, “Don’t, don’t ...” until there was a thud, and he fell to the ground.

Small-Headed Dad and Big-Headed Son, each carrying a big bag, strolled through the alley.

As they walked, they noticed a large spider weaving a web under the eaves of a house.

“I’m going to send a Christmas card to the spider.”

With that, Small-Headed Dad picked up Big-Headed Son and placed the Christmas card under the eaves.

Continuing their walk, they spotted a group of ants crawling near a gutter.

“I’m going to give the ants a Christmas card.”

Big-Headed Son squatted down and placed the Christmas card next to the ant hole.

Further along, they heard a little bird chirping in its nest.

“You want a Christmas card too!”

Big-Headed Son pulled out several cards and instructed Small-Headed Dad, “Put them all in the birdhouse!”

Curious, Small-Headed Dad asked, “Why do you want to put so many?”

Big-Headed Son pointed to the birds and exclaimed, "The little bird can fly and will give Christmas cards to many people we don't know, and they will be happy to receive them too!"

Small-Headed Dad listened, nodded in agreement, and, like flowers, filled the bird's nest with Christmas cards.

They continued on their way, and as they walked, they came across a garden by the side of the road where the waxberries were in full bloom. "Give the flowers a Christmas card too!" suggested Big-Headed Son, sticking the Christmas card by the fence.

Big-Headed Son noticed another patch of dry grass, so he knelt down, gently touched it with his hand, and whispered, "Little grass, are you cold? Spring is coming soon! Here's a Christmas card from me to you, wishing you a happy new year!" He left a card for the grass as well.

As they continued walking, they encountered a neat row of small trees with trunks wrapped in hay. Big-Headed Son took the remaining Christmas cards and placed them in one of the little trees, saying, "May you grow up quickly into a big tree!"

The two bags full of greeting cards were now deflated like two big scarves on their shoulders. The cards were finally delivered.

They returned home happily.

As they were about to enter through the door, they suddenly heard a "hooting and hollering" sound—a flock of birds flew up from the woods, each carrying a beautiful Christmas card in its beak!

Story of the Glasses

On the wall hung a prominent picture of Big-Headed Son and Small-Headed Dad: Small-Headed Dad wore glasses, while Big-Headed Son did not.

Big-Headed Son gazed at the picture and suddenly inquired, "Small-Headed Dad, why do you wear glasses, and I don't?"

"Because my eyes can't see clearly, but yours can," replied Small-Headed Dad.

"But I wouldn't look like your son if I didn't wear glasses!" protested Big-Headed Son.

"That's not necessarily true," Small-Headed Dad countered.

Excitedly, Big-Headed Son rushed to open a tool drawer, saying, "Small-Headed Dad, will you make me a pair of fake glasses? Just create a spectacle frame with no lenses in the centre."

Small-Headed Dad contemplated for a moment, saying, "Hmm, good idea."

Using a green plastic tube threaded through a thin lead wire, Small-Headed Dad crafted a pair of eyeglass frames and placed them on Big-Headed Son, who leaped with joy, exclaiming, "That's great! That's great!"

Accompanied by Small-Headed Dad, Big-Headed Son ventured outside. They encountered an uncle, who greeted Small-Headed Dad with a smile but shifted to a puzzled expression when he noticed Big-Headed Son.

Pointing at Big-Headed Son, the uncle asked, "Who is this?"

"I'm Big-Headed Son!" declared Big-Headed Son proudly.

The uncle, surprised, grabbed his head and exclaimed, "Big-Headed Son? How come it doesn't look like that anymore!"

"Do I look like it now?" Big-Headed Son hastily removed his eyeglass frames.

The uncle smiled and nodded repeatedly, saying, "Yeah, yeah, yeah, that's the Big-Headed Son I know!"

As Big-Headed Son and Small-Headed Dad strolled along, they encountered an aunt. The aunt cheerfully greeted Small-Headed Dad and inquired, "Where is Big-Headed Son?"

Big-Headed Son quickly took off his eyeglass frames, saying, "I am Big-Headed Son!"

The aunt moved closer, examining the eyeglass frames in Big-Headed Son's hands, and remarked, "Oh, your glasses were hiding your face!"

Angrily, Big-Headed Son muttered to himself as soon as the aunt had departed, "It's strange, I wear glasses like you, but people don't recognise me instead!"

Small-Headed Dad chuckled slightly at his son's frustration.

Later in the evening, while organizing his briefcase, Small-Headed Dad suddenly remembered something. He retrieved a roll of drawings from the drawer and said, "Big-Headed Son, please run and deliver this drawing to Uncle Big Li. I promised him today."

Big-Headed Son took the drawings and affirmed, "I promise to finish the job!" He then ran towards the door.

Arriving at a nearby house with steps, he walked up and rang the doorbell, peering through the cat's eye.

"Who is it, please?" came Uncle Big Li's voice from inside.

"I'm Big-Headed Son!"

"What nonsense!" Uncle Big Li's voice grew slightly irritated. "Do you think I don't know Big-Headed Son?"

Big-Headed Son froze and suddenly remembered the "glasses." Hastily, he removed them and stood facing the cat's eye, saying, "I really am Big-Headed Son ..."

However, in the end, the only response from behind the door was the sound of Uncle Li's footsteps.

Reluctantly, Big-Headed Son had to take the drawing back.

At night, he put on his "glasses" and lay in bed, pondering, "Maybe tomorrow everyone will recognise me."

In the dead of night, Big-Headed Son felt the urge to use the bathroom. In a groggy state, he fumbled around to locate the switch but failed. He then squinted in an attempt to find the light, and with a snap, it illuminated a mirror. Startled, Big-Headed Son saw a stranger wearing glasses in the reflection and screamed in terror, racing back to his room. The commotion woke up Small-Headed Dad and Apron Mum, who rushed out to comfort him.

"Big-Headed Son, wake up! It's Small-Headed Dad!" reassured Small-Headed Dad.

"What did you see? Why are you so scared?" inquired Apron Mum.

"I ... I saw someone I don't know in the toilet," stammered Big-Headed Son.

Small-Headed Dad urgently asked, "What did he look like? Tell Daddy quickly!"

"He ... he was wearing glasses," replied Big-Headed Son.

Apron Mum sighed, saying, "Isn't that you yourself?"

"No wonder you couldn't recognise yourself," remarked Small-Headed Dad. "Now you're scaring yourself!"

Big-Headed Son let out an "ah" and touched his face, realizing the frames of his glasses. In embarrassment, he exclaimed, "I forgot. I forgot."

Exiting the restroom, Big-Headed Son removed the "glasses" and declared, "I'll never wear them again!" before returning to sleep.

The next morning, Big-Headed Son woke up, picked up the "glasses" beside him, and had a sudden idea. Excitedly, he called out, "Small-Headed Dad! Quickly come!"

"What's the matter? Daddy's shaving!" replied Small-Headed Dad.

Big-Headed Son suggested, pointing to the large picture on the wall, "Let's both wear glasses and take another big photo as a souvenir, okay?"

A few days later, the two retrieved the new big photo from the photo studio. In the picture, Small-Headed Dad was wearing glasses, and Big-Headed Son also sported "glasses."

Looking at it, Big-Headed Son happily remarked, "I look like Dad this way."

As soon as he arrived home, Big-Headed Son asked Small-Headed Dad to take down the original big photo on the wall and replace it with the new one.

Shortly after, the doorbell rang, and Big-Headed Son eagerly opened the door, exclaiming, "Ah! Grandma and Grandpa are here!" Everyone greeted them warmly.

Grandma brought a box of big and small toys, while Grandpa carried a bag of colourful food.

"Grandma's good baby, you've grown taller again! Did you miss Grandma?" inquired Grandma.

Big-Headed Son replied, "Yes! I missed Grandma very much!"

Grandma, overjoyed, lifted Big-Headed Son and settled on a single sofa without standing still. When she glanced up and saw the new picture on the wall, she inquired, "Who is that? Why do you hang a stranger's picture in your house? Where's the old one? It has my grandson on it."

"That's your grandson!" said Big-Headed Son, pointing shyly.

Grandma immediately stood up and approached for a closer look. She expressed, "How can my grandson look like this? No, no, no, I don't like it."

Big-Headed Son took one glance at the toys and food piled up on the table, then rushed to embrace Grandma, exclaiming, "You like it! You like it! I'll change it right back, okay?" He turned to Small-Headed Dad and urged, "Hurry up, put the original picture back!"

Small-Headed Dad took down the picture and replaced it with the original one. Grandma looked at it and chuckled, "He's the one who's my grandson! He's the little baby I love!" Granny then stood up and piled everything from the table onto Big-Headed Son.

Walking down the street again, Big-Headed Son and Small-Headed Dad encountered the same uncle. Small-Headed Dad greeted, "Hello, Mr. Chen!"

Big-Headed Son followed suit, saying, "Hello, Uncle Chen!"

The uncle took Big-Headed Son's hand and exclaimed cheerfully, "You are really exactly like your father!"

Big-Headed Son scrutinised Small-Headed Dad's

clothes and then his own, asking, "But we look quite different."

Uncle burst into laughter, clarifying, "I mean your dad treats people warmly, and you're warm!"

Understanding the compliment, Big-Headed Son laughed happily. As Uncle walked away, Big-Headed Son remarked, "Small-Headed Dad, actually, I don't need to learn how to wear glasses from you."

Small-Headed Dad agreed, saying, "Right. What you need to learn is that Daddy loves to open his mind, loves sports, and loves to help people ..."

"And also, loves to be the Small-Headed Dad of Big-Headed Son!"

With that, Big-Headed Son giggled and ran ahead, and Small-Headed Dad, a bit stunned, hurried to catch up. The sun rose, casting its golden light upon the earth and the backs of Big-Headed Son and Small-Headed Dad ...

The Hunter Changes His Profession

In winter, the dense forest turned white with heavy snow.

Big-Headed Son and Small-Headed Dad sat on a speeding train. Along the way, Big-Headed Son asked all sorts of questions, and now he turned to Small-Headed Dad, inquiring, "Uncle He is your old friend, how old? Is it true that you were good friends when you were in kindergarten?"

"That's not true," chuckled Small-Headed Dad. "Papa was in the Navy, and so was Uncle He. That's when we became good friends."

The Great Forest of Jiamusi finally came into view,

and as Big-Headed Son and Small-Headed Dad stepped off the train, each carrying a travel bag, they heard a loud voice calling out, "Hey! My Mr. Navy Lieutenant! You've finally arrived!" Big-Headed Son followed the voice and saw a dark-skinned man with a big nose and a beard shouting at them.

Small-Headed Dad rushed forward and shook his hand, saying, "Hello, my Company Commander He! Hello!"

Big-Headed Son thought to himself as he stood looking at them, "Ha, he must be Dad's old friend Uncle He!"

"Hello Uncle He! I'm Big-Headed Son!" Big-Headed Son thought and ran up to say hello.

Uncle He looked at Big-Headed Son with surprise, "Good boy, what a big head!" With that, he stretched out his big palm and shook Big-Headed Son's hand tightly, treating him like an adult.

Big-Headed Son laughed happily.

Big-Headed Son liked this big-nosed Uncle He!

Uncle He led them deeper into the forest. The forest was blanketed in white snow, and various big and small footprints adorned the path.

"Look, these are hare footprints, those are deer

footprints, that's a squirrel's, and those are hound footprints …" Uncle He explained as they walked.

Big-Headed Son suddenly spotted a large, round footprint and asked, "Is this the old bear's footprint?"

Uncle He looked back and smiled, saying, "These are not the footprints of an old bear but of a bear hunter."

"Bear hunter?" Big-Headed Son didn't understand, "What kind of animal is it?"

Now, Small-Headed Dad and Uncle He chuckled together.

Small-Headed Dad explained, "Silly son, a bear hunter is a human hunter. They wear big boots, so their footprints are big."

They entered a small cabin. Big-Headed Son looked around and saw that the walls of the cabin were adorned with the furs of various animals.

Frowning, Big-Headed Son asked, "Uncle He, are you a hunter too?"

"I am not a hunter, but I enjoy hunting. Let me take you both on a hunting outing this time; it's really intense and exciting," Uncle He replied with a smile.

At night, Big-Headed Son and Small-Headed Dad slept together on a wooden bed.

Big-Headed Son tossed and turned, unable to sleep.

"What's bothering you, Big-Headed Son?"

"I was wondering why Uncle He likes to hunt."

"Because hunting can demonstrate a man's strength, and besides, the meat of the prey can be eaten, and the skin can be made into clothes ..."

Before Small-Headed Dad could finish his answer, Big-Headed Son suddenly said, "I don't like hunters!"

The next morning, Uncle He took a hunting dog and led Small-Headed Dad and Big-Headed Son into the forest for a hunt.

As they walked, the dog suddenly barked and ran towards the front. Uncle He immediately said, "Attention! There's something up ahead!" He hid behind a big tree and instructed Big-Headed Son and Small-Headed Dad to hide as well.

After Big-Headed Son hid, he peeked into his pockets and chuckled softly when he found something there. They bent down and proceeded cautiously.

In the distance, the head of a wild deer appeared in the woods, searching for food in the snow. Uncle He raised his gun, saying, "Look out, the prey will be here soon!"

While Uncle He was aiming, Big-Headed Son, hiding in the back, quietly took out his slingshot from his pocket. Sneaking forward, he lifted the slingshot close to the deer and shot, causing the pellets to hit the deer's feet. Startled, the feral deer looked up, then turned and ran.

Uncle He lowered his half-raised gun and sighed, "What's the matter? It's like someone's giving the feral deer a code word."

Big-Headed Son snickered in triumph. They resumed their search, but there was no more sign of the animal. "Come on, let's go back," Uncle He said as he put away his gun. "Bad luck today, come back tomorrow."

That night, Uncle He brought out many shotguns and showed them to Small-Headed Dad and Big-Headed Son. He displayed a variety of bullets, saying, "These are anesthetic bullets. Look how nicely made they are, just like real candy!"

Big-Headed Son couldn't take his eyes off the box of bullets. In the middle of the night, while Small-Headed Dad snored, Big-Headed Son quietly got up and walked to Uncle He's drawer where he kept the bullets. He opened the drawer, found the box of candy-like bullets by the moonlight, and replaced all the bullets with real candies.

On the third morning, Uncle He opened the drawer and took out the box of bullets, exclaiming, "We're going to succeed today! I'm going to shoot a big bear and show you all!"

They ventured deeper into the forest. As they walked, bear paw prints emerged on the snow.

Uncle He pointed to the ground happily, saying, "Great! We found the footprints as soon as we arrived! That's quite a big bear!"

Following the footprints, they reached a large tree, and around to the back of the tree, there was a big hole.

Big-Headed Son was about to stick his head in to look when Uncle He pulled him back, cautioning, "Be careful! If a bear hides in there, he'll bite your head off!"

Terrified, Small-Headed Dad hurriedly hugged Big-Headed Son from behind.

Suddenly, a bear appeared in the distance. It lumbered through the forest and was chewing something in its mouth as it walked towards the tree hole.

Uncle He quickly raised his gun, aiming at the bear, and then "bang" – the shot went off. However, the "bullet" hit the bear's nose, fell to the ground, and the bear picked it up, putting it into its mouth to eat.

"Huh? What's going on here?" Uncle He froze.

The bear ate the "bullet" and continued on its way.

Uncle He removed the bullet from the gun, examined it, smelled it, and then broke it open to see that it was actually a piece of candy. He was so frustrated that he threw it into his mouth and chewed it while saying, "They must have made a mistake! I had to watch this bear run past me. Ugh!"

Uncle He was so angry that he squatted down and beat his fists straight into his legs. Small-Headed Dad suddenly realised that Big-Headed Son didn't say a word, so he deliberately asked him: "Big-Headed Son, do you know who did this?" Big-Headed Son looked at Small-Headed Dad and suddenly lowered his big head. Uncle He looked at Big-Headed Son angrily: "You ..." Small-Headed Dad also got angry and asked: "Why are you playing pranks?"

"I ... I wanted to do the animals a favour." Said Big-Headed Son softly, "I don't want them to be killed by hunters ..." His eyes became red as he spoke.

Uncle He put down his shotgun and said, "Oh, I see, Big-Headed Son doesn't like it when Uncle He hits animals." Big-Headed Son nodded repeatedly, "Uncle He, change your profession, don't be a hunter anymore!"

Uncle He suddenly looked at Small-Headed Dad and said, "Mr. Lieutenant, I hunt just for the love of it, I really didn't think that I would hurt a child's heart!" Then he turned to Big-Headed Son and stood at attention, saluting like a soldier, "Yes, I will change my profession, and I will definitely stop hunting."

"Uncle He! I love you!" Big-Headed Son was so happy that he jumped on Uncle He.

Ghost in the Attic

In the evening, only Big-Headed Son and Apron Mum were having dinner together.

Big-Headed Son, nibbling on a chicken leg, asked, "Can I sleep on the big bed tonight as Small-Headed Dad is not here?"

Apron Mum replied, "No."

"Why?"

"Because you have your own room and your own crib."

Big-Headed Son grabbed another chicken leg, took a big bite, and thought, I'm going to eat more and grow as tall as Small-Headed Dad so I can sleep in the big bed with Mommy!

Later, Big-Headed Son tucked into his cot. Apron Mum gave him a kiss and said, "Good night!" Then she turned off the lights and left the room.

As Big-Headed Son's eyes slowly closed, there was suddenly a "cackling" sound in the house. Startled, Big-Headed Son opened his eyes again. The "squeaking" sound persisted, prompting Big-Headed Son to hastily bury his head under the quilt.

Despite his attempts to block out the noise, Big-Headed Son could still hear the "cackling" in the dark. He covered his ears with his hands, but it persisted; he even put his head under the pillow, but the sound persisted.

"Mom! Come quickly! There's a ghost screaming in my hut!"

Apron Mum rushed into the room and turned on the light. "You're imagining things again. Where's the ghost?"

Big-Headed Son emerged from under the quilt, visibly sweating. "I'm not imagining things. I heard the ghost's cry—it was 'cackle'!"

"That's just the sound of the wind blowing on the leaves," Mom explained as she pulled back the curtains.

Big-Head Son pressed his ear against the windowpane and listened for a moment: "No, no, no, that's the sound of a ghost screaming!"

Apron Mother shone her flashlight under the bed again: "Look, there's nothing! Sleep well." After that, she turned out the light and left.

However, the "creaking" sound persisted, growing louder and more pronounced. Big-Head Son, overcome with fear, wrapped himself in a blanket, silently descended to the floor, and then stealthily crawled towards the door ...

Entering Apron Mother's bedroom, Big-Head Son startled his mother, who was reading in bed, causing her to jump to her feet.

As soon as Big-Head Son pulled his mom back, he explained, "The ghost is making noise in my house again! Why don't you come with me and listen for it, and crawl in quietly like I did."

So, Apron Mother wrapped herself in a blanket and crawled after Big-Head Son towards his hut.

They cautiously pushed open the door and crawled inside.

"Cluck cluck cluck cluck ..." A genuine eerie noise filled the air, causing Apron Mother to shudder with fear as she looked up towards the source of the sound. "The ghost seems to be hiding in the attic ..."

"What? Ghosts like my attic too?"

"Come out here, come out here, I'm scared to death! You'll sleep in the big bed with Mommy tonight!" Apron

Mother had already turned her head and crawled towards the door.

Finally, Big-Head Son slept peacefully with his mom on the big bed.

While Apron Mother drifted into sleep, Big-Head Son's closed eyes gradually opened: "Ghosts also like my attic, so it must not be a scary ghost. I really want to go and see what it looks like."

But then he thought, "It's pitch black at night, and I can't see anything." Big-Headed Son tossed and turned, and suddenly he remembered something. He gently climbed out of bed, opened a drawer, took out a camera, and hung it around his neck. Then he quietly approached the hut.

Big-Headed Son climbed into the hut, and the "squeaking" sound was indeed coming from the attic above. Summoning his courage, Big-Headed Son held the rope and gently climbed up. He raised the camera, aimed at the attic, and took a bold shot. Quickly, he slid down the rope, even rolled and crawled out the door.

The next morning, Apron Mum woke up and said, "I have to call the police; last night was horrible!"

Big-Headed Son jumped up and held the phone down with both hands as soon as he heard that. "No!

Don't call the police!" Then he held up his camera. "I've photographed the ghost in the attic last night, and it might be a very cute ghost for miles! I'm going to develop it now."

As soon as Big-Headed Son left his camera for developing and went out the door, he met Big Ears, Small Eyes, Black Brother, and the others. "I took a picture of the ghost in the attic!"

"Really? What did the ghost look like? Is it scary?" the little ones asked in surprise.

"It's not scary because it likes my attic too."

The little friends followed behind Big-Headed Son, and as more gathered, he, with arms flung around, walked at the front.

They arrived at the photo studio. Big-Headed Son took down the camera, and before he could say anything, his buddies had already jumped the gun:

"What's being photographed here is a ghost!"

"This ghost lives in the attic of Big-Headed Son's house ..."

"This ghost screams 'cackle'!"

The chap running the photo studio, Uncle, slid his spectacles off his nose as he listened: "Is this for real?" He took the camera with trembling hands but hesitated to return it to Big-Headed Son.

Big-Headed Son chuckled and remarked, "This ghost won't bite, don't fret!" Uncle then took the camera and ambled towards the dark room. Big-Headed Son lingered outside with his mates, chatting:

"Is this ghost sizable?"

"Will it take flight?"

"I wonder what it's up to in the attic right now. Perhaps it's having a nap?"

As the conversation flowed, sudden laughter echoed from the dark room, courtesy of Uncle: "Ha ha ... This is a ghost! This is the ghost, ah! Ha ha..."

The kids couldn't resist crowding into the dark room, only to witness Uncle holding a developed photo featuring various images of a large rat.

Big-Headed Son scratched his noggin and found himself at a loss for words. Only his pals were overheard commenting:

"Your attic is terribly filthy!"

"No wonder the mice fancy your attic!"

"Best get back and tidy it up!"

...

It turns out that the "squeaking" sound is the sound of mice.

Big-Headed Son rushed home and cleaned the attic with Apron Mum.

That night, when Small-Headed Dad came home and entered the door, he shouted, "Big-Headed Son! Small-Headed Dad is back!" But after several shouts, there was no response from Big-Headed Son.

"Where is Big-Headed Son? Is he not at home?" asked Small-Headed Dad.

"You go and look for yourself!" replied Apron Mum mysteriously.

Small-Headed Dad searched through the house, even checking the toilet. Finally, he found Big-Headed Son's room, but it was empty.

"Where on earth has this naughty Big-Headed Son been hiding?" Small-Headed Dad wondered aloud. Suddenly, he heard a "squeaking" sound and thought, "Huh, what is this sound?"

He lifted up the bedsheet to look under the bed, opened the cupboard door to inspect inside, and shook the covers out. Still, he couldn't find anything, and the "squeaking" sound persisted and grew louder.

Finally, Small-Headed Dad lifted his head and looked up into the attic. He smiled, grabbed a big stool and a small stool, folded them one by one, then climbed up to peer into the attic. However, he let out a yell, "Ah!" Small-Headed Dad fell onto Big-Headed Son's cot from the stool. The crib "creaked," the bed frame fell apart, and the mattress, teeter-tottering, didn't seem to rest on anything solid. Small-Headed Dad was still lying flat on top of it!

Big-Headed Son, like a monkey, swung holding the rope to the side of Small-Headed Dad, exclaiming, "Small-Headed Dad! Small-Headed Dad! Don't be afraid! I am a fake ghost!" He tore off the ghost mask with force.

"Oh! You ghost hiding above the attic, how did you come up with this idea to tease your Small-Headed Dad like this?" Small-Headed Dad laughed. Big-Headed Son pulled out a stack of pictures of rats, showing them to Small-Headed Dad while narrating the story. As Small-Headed Dad listened to the laughter, he put a picture of rats in front of Big-Headed Son's forehead.

Captain Daddy

Big-Headed Son and three or four children were sitting by the flowerbed, engaged in a conversation.

Big Ears proudly declared, "I love my dad best; he is the general manager and earns lots of money to buy me toys."

Small Eyes chimed in, "I love my daddy too; he is a painter and can draw lots of nice pictures."

Big-Headed Son enthusiastically jumped onto the flowerbed and declared, "My daddy is Small-Headed Dad, and he plays with me every day, so I like him very, very much too!"

The last child to speak was a tiny, pigtailed girl named Maomao, with flowery rubber bands in her braids. She shared, "I love my daddy very, very much because he doesn't come home very much."

The children reacted with laughter:

"You like a daddy who doesn't come home too?"

"He's a bad daddy; I wouldn't like him!"

...

However, Maomao's mood suddenly changed, and she burst into tears, saying, "My dad is a sea captain, and he is in England now, and I miss him very much."

The children's laughter turned to scorn again:

"You are so embarrassed, why are you crying? Why are you crying?"

"Crying is for cowards!"

Big Ears simply turned away: "We don't play with cowards!"

The children all followed Big Ears, and Big-Headed Son hesitated before reluctantly following suit. Left alone by the flowerbed, Maomao covered her face and cried even harder.

At that moment, Small-Headed Dad approached from a distance. As he walked up to Maomao, he paused and inquired with concern, "Little sister, why the tears? Who's been bothering you?"

Maomao looked up at Small-Headed Dad and replied, "I miss my daddy; he's in England now. But the other kids all laugh at me and won't play with me."

Small-Headed Dad frowned, "No need to cry. Come over to my place and play with Big-Headed Son." With that, he took Maomao's hand, and she followed him.

Meanwhile, Big-Headed Son and the other children were engrossed in a game of hopscotch along the path. Spotting Small-Headed Dad approaching with Maomao, Big-Headed Son dashed over, leapt onto him, and gave him a tight hug. Maomao watched enviously, tears welling up once again.

Just then, Big Ears strolled over and pointed at Maomao, teasing, "Coward, are you going to cry again?" He made a face at Maomao.

Small-Headed Dad gently set down Big-Headed Son, picked up Maomao, and addressed everyone, "I believe Maomao is the bravest among you!"

The three children exchanged defiant glances and "hmphed" together. Small-Headed Dad continued, "Because Maomao is cared for only by her mommy, not by her daddy, while you all have both mommy and daddy looking after you."

The children exchanged glances and then collectively turned their attention to Maomao.

Putting Maomao down, Small-Headed Dad continued, "Maomao's daddy is a seafaring captain. He uses large ships to bring all sorts of things from abroad, and then he transports goods from China to foreign countries."

"Does that mean the American Transformers I bought from the toy store were shipped by Maomao's dad in a big ship?" inquired Big Ears, scratching his ears.

"Indeed, that's correct," replied Small-Headed Dad.

Small Eyes followed and asked, "Did the chocolates my mum bought for me also get shipped by Maomao's dad on a big ship?" Daddy Small-Headed Dad nodded his head repeatedly.

Big-Headed Son seemed to remember something and exclaimed, "I know! The 'Adidas' sportswear advertised on TV, tennis rackets, footballs, and so on, must also have been shipped by Maomao's dad on a big ship!"

"So yeah, Maomao is not only the bravest but also the most honourable because she has a really amazing dad!" When Daddy Small-Headed Dad finished, he led the way by clapping at Maomao, and the children followed, their perspectives changing.

That night, Big-Headed Son lay in bed tossing and turning and could not sleep. Early the next morning, he went first to Small Eyes and then together to Big Ears.

"Have you come to play with me?" asked Big Ears as he opened the door.

"No, we have come to see you about something very important," they spoke to Big Ear, one in the left ear, the other in the right ear. Big Ear listened and said, "But I don't want to lend my dad to Maomao."

Small Eyes added, "I don't want to either."

"If you don't want to ..." Big-Headed Son paused, "then I don't want to either."

They stood in the doorway in silence. At that moment, people were coming and going past them, adults and children, men and women. They looked at the pedestrians, and their eyes suddenly all fixed on the men carrying briefcases.

Big-Headed Son called out, "Ah, I have an idea! Let's help Maomao find another daddy!"

Big Ears and Small Eyes squealed with delight, "What a good idea! That's a good idea!"

They jogged together to the side of the path, looking nervous and anxious as they waited. Just then, a plump uncle with glasses approached. "Uncle, would you fancy being a daddy to a little girl?"

Uncle Fatty paused, his glasses sliding up his nose. "Please, say that again."

The Big-Headed Son interjected, "There's a brave little girl whose father is a sea captain and is away most days. She misses her daddy terribly, and we're trying to help by finding her another daddy."

Uncle Fatty adjusted his glasses and responded, "Oh, but I have a daughter of my own. If I become someone else's father, then my daughter won't have a dad." With that, the portly uncle left.

Next, a slim uncle in a hat strolled by. "Uncle, would you like to be a daddy to a little girl, please?"

The uncle stopped, chuckled, and after laughing, he removed his hat, tossing it in the air. "Haha! What a joke! I'm not married yet, how can I be a father?" He caught the hat, placed it back on his head, pretended to be a clown, and departed.

Just then, Maomao arrived, carrying a small bamboo basket filled with several paper boats. "What are you doing here?"

"We're here to find you a daddy."

Maomao was surprised. "Find me a daddy? I already have my own daddy!"

Big Ears explained, "But your daddy isn't home most of the time. What would you do if you miss him?"

Maomao lifted the bamboo basket and remarked, "I fold little paper boats when I miss my dad! Mum said that when I fold a basket full of paper boats, Dad will come back." Maomao finished, smiling and gazing at the paper boats in the basket.

"So ... don't you fancy having another dad?" inquired Big-Headed Son.

Maomao shook her head vigorously, "No, no. I just want my own dad. I'll wait for him to come back!" With that, she folded another paper boat and walked ahead.

The three children stared blankly at Maomao's retreating figure.

Suddenly, Big-Headed Son rushed up, "Maomao! Can I help you make a paper boat together? That way, your dad will come back very, very soon!"

"We'll help you fold it together too!" chimed in Big Ears and Small Eyes.

The four children sat under the tree and folded paper boats, and soon the basket couldn't contain them all. Big-Headed Son suggested, "Let's hang the paper boats on the tree so that Maomao's father can see them from far away." In no time, the big tree was adorned with paper boats, resembling a blossoming magnolia tree from a distance.

The four children happily circled the big tree, and Maomao exclaimed as she circled, "Look! Daddy's big boat is back! Daddy's big boat is back!"

At that moment, a genuine seafaring captain in

a white uniform approached. The captain called out to Maomao before even reaching her, "Maomao! My Maomao!" He shouted and half-crouched down, arms outstretched.

Maomao froze, then suddenly looked at the person calling her name and darted over to him, "Daddy! Daddy!"

Maomao jumped into her dad's arms and hugged him tightly.

Days in the Countryside

In autumn, Small-Headed Dad brought Big-Headed Son to play at his uncle's countryside residence. The uncle's family had a pair of twins, approximately the same age as Big-Headed Son. One was a boy named Yuanyuan, and the other was a girl named Fangfang. Together with their father, Yuanyuan and Fangfang eagerly awaited by the riverside.

"Big-Headed Son! Big-Headed Son!" Yuanyuan and Fangfang spotted Big-Headed Son walking along the river.

Big-Headed Son called out in return, "Yuanyuan! Fangfang!"

A small wooden boat was already waiting on the river. "Let's take the boat! Let's go for a boat ride!" Big-Headed Son rushed to the side of the boat, but when he looked at the wooden planks forming a bridge between the boat and the shore, he suddenly hesitated.

"Look, it's not scary at all!" Yuanyuan confidently stepped onto the wooden board.

Fangfang quickly followed, teasing, "You're a city coward!"

"Who says I'm a coward? Hmph!" Enraged, Big-Headed Son jumped onto the board, causing the boat to tilt, and the board to sway. "Ah!" Big-Headed Son screamed as he fell into the river.

Holding onto the plank, Big-Headed Son floated towards the centre of the river. Small-Headed Dad was about to jump in but was stopped by Yuanyuan and Fangfang's father. "Don't worry, the river is shallow; you don't need to go."

Before their father could finish, Yuanyuan and Fangfang jumped into the river with a thud. They swiftly swam to Big-Headed Son, and the three children clung to the wooden board together. Eventually, the boat also approached. Small-Headed Dad shouted, "Come up! Come on up!"

Surprisingly, Big-Headed Son replied, "No! The water is fun!"

Looking down into the river, Small-Headed Dad saw transparent water with large and small pebbles, small fish, and water plants. Some areas were calm and serene, while others were lively and active.

Uncle swiftly finished his dinner, rose, and declared, "I won't be sleeping at home tonight. One of the lambs is unwell, and I must keep an eye on it."

Upon hearing this, Yuanyuan dropped her bowl of rice and exclaimed, "I'm going to guard the lamb too!"

"I'll go as well!" added Fang.

Big-Headed Son hurriedly approached Uncle and suggested, "Uncle, lambs fancy children. Let all of us go!"

Uncle responded, "Let's do this. The lamb will be in your three hands tonight. I happen to be having a chat with my brother too; we haven't seen each other for a long time."

The three children were overjoyed, jumping up and down and nearly overturning the table.

In the darkness of the sheep pen, Yuanyuan lit a kerosene lamp, and the sheep bleated. Fangfang cradled the sick lamb, saying, "Look at how pitiful it is! It's still shivering."

Big-Headed Son quickly extended his hand and said, "Let me hold it!"

He hugged the lamb, pressed his face against it, and spoke softly, "Little sheep, don't be afraid. You'll soon be fine. Let me tell you a story, okay? When I was sick at home, my Apron Mum told me a story, and listening to it made me feel better!"

"Really? Then tell it to the little sheep quickly!" Yuan and Fang exclaimed together.

Yuanyuan and Fangfang found a space, spread thick hay, and the three children lay down together, encircling the sick sheep. Under the light of the kerosene lamp, Big-Headed Son began to tell a story to the lamb.

As the story unfolded, the lamp went out, and the three children and the sick sheep drifted off to sleep.

The sun emerged, and its golden rays pierced through the openings in the sheep pen, casting a warm glow on the children and the ailing sheep. The unwell animal opened its eyes and stirred. It stretched its neck comfortably before emitting two "bleats" towards the three children who remained in deep slumber. Unfortunately, none of the three stirred; they were still sound asleep!

The uncle arrived, pushing open the sheepfold door and entering. The sick sheep approached him with a bleat. "Oh! Are you truly feeling better?" exclaimed the uncle, lifting the lamb in astonishment. He then turned to observe the three children, saying, "They must have kept you company all night. Look how peacefully they're sleeping now!"

Silently, the uncle carried the sick sheep out of the pen.

Big-Headed Son woke up, stretched, and suddenly recalled something. He twisted his head to look around and exclaimed, "Huh, where's the little sheep?" He hurriedly got to his feet, calling out, "Lamb! Little lamb!" Scanning the sheep pen, he found it empty. He urgently shook Yuanyuan and Fangfang, saying, "Yuanyuan! Fangfang! It's no good, the lamb is gone!"

However, Yuanyuan and Fangfang merely rolled over, burying themselves under the hay, continuing to sleep soundly.

Big-Headed Son grew anxious. "Where is the little lamb?"

Suddenly, his expression tightened. "Perhaps the little sheep wandered off to the river. That's too dangerous!" Big-Headed Son rushed out of the sheep pen and headed straight for the river.

Small-Headed Dad rose and, not finding Big-Headed Son, rushed into the sheep pen. There, he spotted two heads sticking out from under the hay arch.

"Big-Headed Son! Where are you sleeping?" Small-Headed Dad reached out his hands and began searching through the hay.

Yuanyuan and Fangfang woke up, "Huh? Why is Big-Headed Son gone?"

Small-Headed Dad grew anxious and dove under the hay, throwing it behind him as if swimming, "Big-Headed Son! Big-Headed Son!"

Meanwhile, Big-Headed Son couldn't find the lamb at the riverside. Anxiously, he jumped into a small wooden boat alone, rocking and shouting, "Lamb! Little Lamb! Where are you?"

Big-Headed Son scratched and yelled, tears streaming down his face, "Little Sheep! If you fall into the water, grab onto the plank!"

At the same time, Small-Headed Dad, Uncle, Yuanyuan, and Fangfang rushed to the riverside, where Fangfang was holding the little sheep.

"Oh my, how dare Big-Headed Son go on the boat alone?" exclaimed Small-Headed Dad's father in surprise, seeing Big-Headed Son rowing the boat solo.

Uncle chuckled, "Big-Headed Son is quite the quick worker!"

Yuanyuan and Fangfang shouted towards the river, "Big-Headed Son! Come back quickly!"

Big-Headed Son cried in response, "No! I'm going to

find the lamb!"

Small-Headed Dad held up the lamb and chased after the boat, shouting, "Look, the lamb is here! It's not lost!"

Big-Headed Son spotted the lamb, instantly breaking into a smile. He turned the boat around and rowed vigorously towards the shore ...

Big-Headed Son and Small-Headed Dad were heading

home, carrying their luggage.

As they prepared to leave, Big-Headed Son fetched a beautiful sheet of stickers and began affixing them to the cow's horn, the sheep's horn, the pig's tail, and the chicken's body. He repeated, "Bye! Bye!" while attaching the stickers.

Big-Headed Son saved the last two sheets for Yuanyuan and Fangfang's foreheads. "Bye bye, Yuanyuan and Fangfang!"

The boatman rowed the boat to the opposite shore.

Big-Headed Son waved farewell to the children on the shore, as well as to the lamb. "Goodbye!"

Numerous little hands waved from the shore, and the bleats of the little sheep echoed over the water.

Red Chinese New Year

As the Spring Festival approached, families busied themselves buying food, clothes, and firecrackers. Some withdrew money from the bank, standing at their doors to count it joyfully, exclaiming, "After saving money for a year, I can finally use it for the Spring Festival!"

In the midst of the festive preparations, a police officer with a microphone, not far from the bank, announced loudly, "It's almost the Spring Festival! Please be vigilant against thieves!"

Big-Headed Son and Small-Headed Dad walked by, carrying the red paper they intended to use for cutting window decorations. Big-Headed Son glanced at the police officer and asked, "Small-Headed Dad, does the police officer take a break during Chinese New Year?"

"Probably not, because the police want to ensure that

we all have a peaceful Spring Festival!"

"It would be nice if thieves took a break during the Spring Festival so that the police officer could take a break too!"

"What did you say? Let the thieves take a break?" Small-Headed Dad chuckled.

"Yes," said Big-Headed Son seriously, "if the thieves stayed home and didn't come out to steal, then the police wouldn't have to come out to catch them!"

Small-Headed Dad nodded thoughtfully. "That makes sense."

"We're going to cut lots of window decorations and distribute them to everyone, including Uncle Policeman!" declared Big-Headed Son.

"Exactly, whether there are thieves or not, we should still have a happy Spring Festival," agreed Small-Headed Dad.

As they continued their walk, they encountered the police officer who was loudly delivering his message with a microphone. Big-Headed Son suddenly stopped and said to Small-Headed Dad, "Daddy Small-Headed Dad, I have a great idea to let Uncle Policeman rest at home during the Chinese New Year."

"What's your brilliant idea?" Small-Headed Dad

leaned in eagerly.

Big-Headed Son then whispered into the ears of Small-Headed Dad. Small-Headed Dad listened, nodding repeatedly. He hurriedly ran to the police uncle and whispered into his ears. The police uncle listened, smiled, nodded his head, and went to inform the other police uncles.

Big-Headed Son and Small-Headed Dad cut window papers at home. However, instead of creating auspicious designs in compliance with tradition, the 'window papers' they crafted took on the forms of monsters and devils. Together, they distributed these creations to every house and helped everyone paste them on the window glass.

Big-Headed Son said, "If we put these window clings on the windows, the thieves won't dare to come here at night."

Small-Headed Dad added, "Without thieves, our police uncle can enjoy a peaceful Spring Festival at home."

The residents agreed, saying, "This is a really good idea!"

A bit farther from the residential area, there was a dilapidated house where two thieves, one fat and one thin, were hiding, enjoying wine and nibbling on chicken legs.

The fat man exclaimed, "It's a perfect opportunity

tonight."

The thin man inquired, "Why?"

The fat man squinted at him, saying, "Idiot! Tonight is New Year's Eve, and children receive New Year's money from adults after paying them a visit."

The thin man nodded vigorously, "Right, right, right! The children sleep deeply at night, and we'll be able to steal a lot of money!"

The fat man laughed heartily, "The gift money is stashed under the pillow at night, just like when we were kids."

As the echoes of firecrackers subsided, the slender thief stealthily emerged from the dilapidated house, making his way to the residential area. Hiding behind a tree, he cautiously scanned the surroundings, ensuring no one was in sight. With a triumphant chuckle, he declared, "Haha, the Spring Festival – even the police are on vacation! Now I can boldly go and steal the New Year's money!" With a confident flick of his heel, he strutted out from behind the tree, stopping only when he reached the front of a house.

Upon looking up, he encountered a terrifying spectacle on the windowpane – monstrous faces with glaring eyes. Startled, he promptly turned on his heels and dashed towards another house. However, at the second house, he was met with another set of devilish faces on the glass. Panic-stricken, his legs trembled uncontrollably, and he struggled to maintain his composure. "How ... how did window decorations turn into frightening ghost faces ..."

Backtracking repeatedly, he couldn't withstand the fear and collapsed to the ground with a resounding "flop." Rolling and crawling, he scurried back to the broken house.

Fatty, visibly displeased, scolded him, "Useless! You're even frightened by window decorations!"

The slender man, still trembling, stammered, "It's genuinely terrifying! It's like they're about to strip your skin and devour you!"

Undeterred, the portly man donned a hood and headed towards the door, declaring, "Just you wait, watch me!"

Fatty approached the door of Big-Headed Son's house stealthily, glancing around briefly. He then skillfully pried the door open with a large pincer and slipped inside. Upon entering, he immediately sought out Big-Headed Son's dwelling and pushed the door open, stepping inside.

The fat man abruptly paused when he noticed half of Big-Headed Son's head peeking out from under the quilt. Upon closer inspection, he sensed something amiss, muttering, "Such a big head, he must be an adult! Adults don't have New Year's money." The fat man retreated and returned to the room of Small-Headed Dad and the aproned mother.

The entire head of Apron Mum was concealed under the quilt, and Small-Headed Dad's father only had half of his small head visible. The fat man chuckled, "That's right!" Then, his gaze fixed on the pillow, he softly uttered, "Gift money, gift money ..." As he reached beneath the pillow, the fat man's smile vanished, replaced by anger. "What's going on here? Where did this child hide the money?"

Small-Headed Dad rolled over, revealing his entire head, his mouth still chattering in his sleep, "Call the cops. Call the cops ..." The fat man was startled. He turned around and hurriedly fled. Realizing that no one was pursuing him, he paused, musing, "Really strange! How is he an adult?" He patted his head, reflecting on Small-Headed Dad's sleep talk, "Call the cops," and suddenly smacked himself vigorously in the face. "You've become an idiot too; he was talking in his sleep!"

The fat man removed his headgear, straightened his clothes, and returned to the front of the house, lamenting,

"I can't believe I can't steal tonight!"

As he approached the house, he suddenly encountered the horrifying "window papers" in the light. Startled, he retreated and realised that many window decorations now bore terrifying faces with dreadful eyes, all seemingly staring at him. The fat man clutched his head, turned on his heels, and sprinted away.

"I'm scared out of my wits! I'm scared out of my wits! How did those window papers transform into such horrendous ghostly faces!" The fat man collapsed into the broken house.

The slender man remarked, "I remember when we were kids, we had beautiful window papers!"

Fatty replied, "I learned how to cut them from my grandmother."

The slender man said, "Really? Teach me quickly!"

So they worked together to cut the window paper, creating intricate and beautiful designs.

The slender man arranged the window decorations one by one and wondered aloud, "Why do the residents put up such horrifying window papers for the Spring Festival?"

Fatty pondered for a moment, "Probably because of us."

Perplexed, the slender man asked, "Us?"

Fatty slumped to the ground, "You're such an idiot. Didn't we get scared away by those window papers?"

The slender man reflected for a moment, "Right, right, right, it's all our fault, causing everyone to put up such terrifying window displays for Chinese New Year." Then he suggested, "Hey, let's go and change those scary window decorations, okay?"

The fat man looked at him, still not comprehending.

The slender man continued, "We can't let the children nowadays miss out on the window papers that we enjoyed as kids!"

The fat man turned around, fell to the ground, and began to cry, saying, "Now that you mention it, I suddenly miss my late grandmother. I remember when I was a child, she gave me New Year's money and made me a suit of new red clothes ..." The slender man also started to cry.

After shedding their tears, they grabbed the decorative window papers and stepped outside, making their way to each of the houses. There, in front of the windows, they carefully removed the monster faces and replaced them with more auspicious designs. They continued pasting until the stars had retired, the moon had bid farewell, and the sky revealed its pale face.

In the morning, the children emerged from their homes adorned in new clothes. A chorus of claps and cheers erupted as everyone beheld the beautiful window papers: "The window decorations have become so lovely!"

Big-Headed Son and Small-Headed Dad rushed outside to take a look and were thoroughly surprised, "Who did this?"

Examining the altered window papers, Big-Headed Son remarked, "So the thief dares to come and steal again!"

At that moment, a fat man and a thin man approached them, pushing a cart filled with beautiful window papers. The fat man halted and declared, "There will be no more thieves here, I promise!"

The slim man added, "And thieves can change their ways and stop being thieves!"

After expressing their commitment, they pushed the cart forward and continued on their way, chanting, "Window papers for sale! Get your window papers here!" Many residents gathered around to make purchases.

Emergency Rescue

On that day, Small-Headed Dad returned home, bringing with him a little red four-legged stool. Apron Mum took a look and remarked, "What a beautifully crafted little stool, and it seems so sturdy."

"I knew you would like it, so I brought it home," said Small-Headed Dad with delight.

Big-Headed Son rushed out, grabbed the little stool, and held it against his chest, pretending it was a steering wheel. "Tee-hee! Here comes the dump truck!"

Small-Headed Dad was even more pleased. "Looks like you like it too!"

Big-Headed Son chuckled and drove the "car" to his room.

Small-Headed Dad took off his coat and sat down. Apron Mum brought a cup of tea to Small-Headed Dad when suddenly, loud cries echoed from inside the house.

Startled, Small-Headed Dad and Apron Mum jumped up, rushing to the room. Before they could enter, they heard Big-Headed Son crying from inside, his large head stuck in the small stool. "My big head can't come out! My big head can't come out!"

"Take it easy," Small-Headed Dad reassured as he attempted to pull the stool upward with his hands, but it wouldn't budge.

"What can we do? What can we do? We'd better go to the hospital and ask the doctor for help!" Apron Mum exclaimed anxiously.

With Big-Headed Son still attached to the stool, crying all the way, they hurriedly ran to the hospital. Passersby looked on strangely as they passed by.

Upon seeing the peculiar patient, the doctor was bewildered. "What's going on here?"

"Oh, doctor, it's like this," Apron Mum explained hastily. "My child accidentally stuck his head inside the stool and can't get it out. Please help us find a solution!"

The doctor looked towards Big-Headed Son under the stool and said, "I'm not a magician; I can't make the head smaller and the stool bigger ..."

Small-Headed Dad's eyes lit up, and he wiped the

sweat from his forehead, saying, "Yes, yes, yes, we should go ask the magician ..." He pulled up his Big-Headed Son and hurried outside, with Apron Mum closely following.

They rushed into the circus and found the magician. Small-Headed Dad spoke urgently, "Mr. Magician, please help me get my son's head out of the stool! Please!"

The magician rubbed his white-gloved hands together, lowered his head, and glanced both left and right toward Big-Headed Son under the stool. Then he said to Small-Headed Dad, "I'm sorry, I don't dare to perform this magic trick! What if I accidentally lose your son's head?" Small-Headed Dad and Apron Mum, frightened by his words, pulled up Big-Headed Son and hastily retreated.

They ran and ran until they encountered two muscular men. Small-Headed Dad slowed down and quietly said to Apron Mum, "Let's ask them to help us; maybe it will work."

"That's the only way."

The two men were equally tall, fat, and formidable. Small-Headed Dad approached them, bowing his head as if begging, "Sir, please do me a favour and pull this boy's big head out from under the stool for me ..."

The two tough fellows stopped without uttering a word, exchanged glances, and then one picked up the legs of Big-Headed Son while the other grabbed the stool, pulling hard in opposite directions.

"Ouch! My neck is going to break!"

Big-Headed Son let out a yell, startling Small-Headed Dad and Apron Mum. They rushed up in panic, attempting to grab their son, but he exclaimed, "Don't ... don't pull it ..."

The two sturdy men, still silent, exchanged glances before walking away.

Apron Mum bent down to carefully inspect the neck of her distressed Big-Headed Son. "I'm scared to death! If they break your neck, you'll die."

Small-Headed Dad said anxiously, "But now ... what should we do? Big-Headed Son can't carry this stool for the rest of his life!"

Big-Headed Son, in a worried tone, added, "No, no, no! How can I sleep at night? How can I wear a hat in winter? How can I get a haircut when my hair is long? How can I play with children ..."

Small-Headed Dad and Apron Mum were anxious, feeling lost and bewildered. Suddenly, the distant sound of fire engines could be heard – "Wuli Wuli ..." The fire department was on the way. Small-Headed Dad tapped his small head and exclaimed, "Yes, let the firefighters help figure out a solution!"

"The firefighters? Aren't they for putting out fires? Can they really help us?" Apron Mum expressed a hint of disbelief.

"Whatever! Let's give it a try!" Small-Headed Dad pulled Big-Headed Son up and hurried towards the approaching fire engine.

The firetruck came to a stop, and the firefighters were engaged in a practice session. Small-Headed Dad ran up, pointing to the red stool on Big-Headed Son's head, and urgently said, "Quick! Quickly! Please save my son!"

A team member wearing fire glasses mistook the red stool for fire and, thinking quickly, raised a water gun, shooting at Big-Headed Son. However, the water column landed on the stool, drenching Big-Headed Son like a drowned chicken, while the red stool remained unaffected. Panicking, the team member set down the water gun and grabbed a fire-fighting foam, spraying it onto the stool. A mass of foam piled up above the red stool, slowly spreading down and enveloping it. Suddenly, Big-Headed Son sneezed loudly, "ah-choo," and the foam sprayed into the faces of Small-Headed Dad and Apron Mum, revealing the face of the big-headed boy. Apron Mum understood immediately, "They've been practicing for a long time, and they think everything red is fire. We'd better ask others for help!"

They pulled Big-Headed Son up once more, resembling the act of raising a little snowman, and continued running. This time, as they ran, they came across the factory that produced the small stools. Small-Headed Dad had an idea, stopped, and pointed at the factory, saying, "Oh, we should have come here a long time ago. There must be someone here who can help us!"

They rushed towards the inside of the factory. The doorman wanted to call out to stop them but saw Big-Headed Son stuck in the stool, covered in foam, and both Big-Headed Son and Small-Headed Dad's heads and faces were also covered. Nervously, they picked up the phone to call the security guards.

Big-Headed Son rinsed off the foam with water at the door and entered a random workshop, where he found stacks of identical stools.

"Are you ... advertising for us?" an overseer welcomed him, looking at Big-Headed Son with a perplexed expression.

"Not at all," Apron Mum clarified. "My son was stuck in this stool almost all day. Please, you must think of a way to help him get it off."

The supervisor looked down at Big-Headed Son and asked, "What, can't you take it down?"

Big-Headed Son nodded, tears welling up again.

The supervisor expressed regret, saying, "I really didn't think that the little stools we produce could be such a danger to children. I'm so sorry!" He then took out a small saw, aimed it at one of the stool legs, and carefully cut it. In a moment, the stool broke, and Big-Headed Son stretched his head forward, finally freeing himself. "Thank you, Uncle!"

"You're welcome. It's my turn to apologise to you," the older man said. He picked up a new stool, quickly added two horizontal strips of wood between the four legs, and then handed it to Big-Headed Son, saying, "This way, it won't trap your big head!"

A few days later, as Small-Headed Dad and Big-Headed Son passed by the stool store, they noticed that all the stools had been fitted with horizontal wooden bars. Big-Headed Son touched his head and remarked, "Now, my big head and other children's big heads won't get stuck inside the stools!"

As they were discussing this, they heard a "woof woof" from behind. Turning around, they burst into laughter. A large spotted dog had wedged itself into one of the stools and couldn't get out. It was running around, the stool resembling a saddle, with two birds perched on it, competing for a worm they were eating mouth to mouth.

Joint Battle

Early in the morning, Big-Headed Son and Small-Headed Dad each rode a bicycle to the field for a fitness trip, surrounded by mountains, trees, and rivers. They cycled towards the mountain peak road, growing tired and sweaty. When Big-Headed Son couldn't ride any longer, he got off and leaned against a large rock, saying, "Small-Headed Dad, I'm exhausted. Let's rest here for a while."

"Okay." Small-Headed Dad dismounted as well, leaning their bikes against a big tree behind him.

With the sun high in the sky, sunlight filtered through the leaves overhead. They sat, closed their eyes, nibbled on dogwood, and then covered their sunglasses with the brims of their sun hats, appearing as if they were dozing off.

Suddenly, two large monkeys crept out from a gap

in the mountains and leaped into a tree to observe them. The tree rustled slightly, but the two humans remained oblivious.

Two monkeys descended from the tree next to the bikes, turned the wheels and pedals, and then quietly hopped on, each riding crookedly towards the front.

A noise echoed through the mountains, catching Small-Headed Dad's attention. He looked up and was astonished to see monkeys filling the mountains and trees, rushing behind them, screaming, clapping, and several monkeys even attempting to jump straight at them. Small-Headed Dad removed his sunglasses, looked back, and exclaimed in surprise, "Big-Headed Son, this is not good! The monkeys have stolen the bicycles!" He shouted as he scrambled up, "Give it back! Give my bike back to me!" Big-Headed Son quickly followed suit.

The monkeys on the mountain tree saw someone chasing, and they screamed with even more joy. Small-Headed Dad and Big-Headed Son were anxious and started chasing. Two monkeys on bikes lost their way, so they let go of their bikes and jumped up into a tree. Big-Headed Son and Small-Headed Dad then retrieved their bicycles but were already tired and breathless.

They pedaled along, and suddenly, Big-Headed Son

said, "Small-Headed Dad, I want to leave one of our bicycles for the monkey to ride, okay?"

Small-Headed Dad, baffled, responded, "The bike was almost stolen by the monkey, and you're not angry. Now, you even want to leave a bike for the monkey. You ..."

"We like to ride bicycles, and the monkeys like it too!" Big-Headed Son thought for a moment, squatted down, and didn't move. "I can't ride anyway!"

Small-Headed Dad hastily stopped the bike, walked back to Big-Headed Son, and also squatted down, saying, "You must ride this bike back. As for the monkey's bike ... we'll discuss it when we get back."

Big-Headed Son immediately stood up, extending his little thumb, "Come on, you promise!"

After a brief hesitation, Small-Headed Dad reluctantly lifted his hand and linked his pinky finger, making a promise.

A week later, Big-Headed Son and Small-Headed Dad rode their bikes again, embarking on a fitness trip into the wilderness. However, this time, behind their bikes were two slightly smaller bikes, bright and shiny—one red and one green.

Small-Headed Dad turned his head around and said, "Look, it's quite nice. It would have cost a lot more to buy two new ones."

Big-Headed Son also looked back, saying, "Well, the monkeys are going to enjoy them very much!"

They reached the spot where they had rested before, parked the two little bicycles next to the big tree, and then placed their own two bicycles in front of them. Leaning against a large rock, they waited. However, after waiting for half a day, not a single monkey appeared. Small-Headed Dad stood up and suggested, "Let's go around and come back later."

They rode their bikes around the mountain.

As soon as Big-Headed Son and Small-Headed Dad left, several little monkeys emerged from the cracks in the rocks. They jumped and swung in front of the two little bicycles, screaming and snatching them. A fierce scuffle broke out among them. Just as the little monkeys were fighting intensely, the monkey king arrived with a grand swagger. The little monkeys suddenly fell silent, spreading out to make way for the Monkey King, who joyfully rode on one of the bicycles and departed. The little monkeys gathered around the remaining one, only for it to be seized by a larger monkey.

When Big-Headed Son and Small-Headed Dad returned, the monkeys and the bicycles were gone.

They pushed the cart deeper into the mountains. As they walked, in the distance, they heard the sound of monkeys again. Big-Headed Son pointed and exclaimed, "They're up ahead!"

They hastily got on their bicycles and struggled forward.

Finally, they spotted the group of monkeys on the mountain and in the trees. The two bicycles were being ridden by the monkeys. They stopped, watched, and imitated the monkeys by barking, "Oo-ga, oo-ga!" The monkeys paused, glanced at them for a moment, and then resumed their calls.

Big-Headed Son and Small-Headed Dad called out, "Woo-ga, woo-ga!" as they got closer to the monkeys. Surprisingly, the monkeys no longer seemed afraid and didn't run away. Instead, they gathered around.

Suddenly, a small monkey jumped onto Big-Headed Son's big head. At first, Big-Headed Son was scared to move, but then he clapped his hands and shouted, "oo-ga, oo-ga." More monkeys joined them, some jumping on the back seat, stem of the bike, and pedal board. The mountain echoed with a chorus of "wu-ga, wu-ga" noises.

As the sun was setting, Big-Headed Son and Small-Headed Dad descended the mountain, packing the two smaller bikes as they did when they went up.

Big-Headed Son exclaimed happily, "The monkeys have recognised us!"

Small-Headed Dad added, "They also recognise the two bikes we brought them!"

As their bikes sped down the hill, nearing the foot of the hill, they encountered two men, one tall and one short. The tall one asked Small-Headed Dad, "Hey, are there any monkeys on this mountain?"

Small-Headed Dad replied, "Yes!"

The tall man waved his hand to the short one, saying, "Come on, let's go catch some!"

Big-Headed Son, anxious, interjected, "You can't catch monkeys!"

The tall man fiercely retorted to Big-Headed Son, "Mind your own business!" They then ran up the hill. Big-Headed Son wanted to rush up to stop them but was pulled back by Small-Headed Dad.

Small-Headed Dad said softly to Big-Headed Son, "We can't stop them. Quickly, let's sound the alarm for the monkeys!"

"Well! You're signaling the monkeys!" the two villains heard this, rushed down, and covered the mouths of Big-Headed Son and Small-Headed Dad with a cloth. "I'll see how you'll scream!" Then they seized the monkey's bicycle from the back seat, rode on it forcefully, and instructed Small-Headed Dad and Big-Headed Son, "Go, show us the way!"

Small-Headed Dad and Big-Headed Son exchanged glances and rode to lead the way. However, they purposely chose a challenging route, making the two villains exhausted. Gasping for breath, the villains threatened, "Why aren't we there yet? If you dare to play tricks on us, you will be in trouble!"

As they were approaching Monkey Mountain, a loud and prolonged cry echoed through the air.

The taller villain stopped to look up, exclaiming, "Is that a tiger's roar? It's terrifying!"

The shorter one, filled with fear, added, "Well ... it sounds like lions, wolves, tigers, and leopards are all coming ..."

Suddenly, the sounds surrounded them from all directions, and countless monkeys descended on the two villains, grabbing their bicycles. The villains fell to the ground, rolling and crawling towards the mountains to escape. The monkeys in the trees quickly picked a variety of hard wild fruits and threw them directly at the villains' heads and bodies. The two villains, unable to cover both their heads and buttocks simultaneously, were left with swelling on both ends.

Unexpectedly, something hit Big-Headed Son's large head, and upon inspection, it turned out to be a peach!

Big-Headed Son and Small-Headed Dad picked it up and ate it, quenching their thirst.

Now, peaches fell like rain on their heads, almost burying Small-Headed Dad and Big-Headed Son. They sat down and enjoyed the feast.

Small-Headed Dad remarked, "The monkeys are thanking us."

Big-Headed Son added, "The monkeys are hoping that we stay on the mountain and become monkeys too."

Big-Headed Son and Small-Headed Dad ate while hearing the familiar sound of "oooh-gah, oooh-gah" again!

Home on the Map

One afternoon, Small-Headed Dad sat in front of the computer typing. Suddenly, he remembered something, so he stood up and walked to the door, shouting, "Big-Headed Son! Big-Headed Son!"

Big-Headed Son didn't show up, but his remote control car did.

Small-Headed Dad froze for a moment, then snickered. He quietly squatted down and reached out to press the switch on the car, and the remote control car immediately stopped.

"Huh? Why is it not moving?" Big-Headed Son ran out, coming closer to continuously press the remote control in his hand, but the remote control car remained motionless. "It's really strange!"

Worried, Big-Headed Son heard very light laughter

from Small-Headed Dad behind him. He turned his head and said, "Hmph, so it was you who did the mischief!" Understanding the situation, he reached out to turn on the switch and was promptly picked up by Small-Headed Dad.

"Put me down! I want to play with the remote control car!" Big-Headed Son screamed in the air.

"You have to help me go to Uncle Zhang's house to get a file first, and then you can play with it when you come back."

"No, no, do your own things by yourself, that's what you always say." Big-Headed Son twisted his body straight up.

"Then I also said we should help each other! Daddy is just too busy. Don't you want to help me?"

Big-Headed Son finally fell from the air to the ground. "No, just no!"

Small-Headed Dad's eyes twinkled, and he suddenly had an idea: "Hey, I'll draw you a map. You follow the map to find Uncle Zhang's house and see if you can find it."

Big-Headed Son had already turned on the remote control car, and when he heard what Small-Headed Dad said, he rushed to turn it off again. "Okay! OK! You quickly draw one for me, I'll go right away!"

Small-Headed Dad then created a map on the computer. The map included curved roads, flower beds, rows of trees, a few houses, and, most importantly, Uncle Zhang's house.

Once the map was ready, Small-Headed Dad handed it to Big-Headed Son. "Don't go outside the map!"

"I won't!" said Big-Headed Son proudly as he took the map.

Big-Headed Son set off with the remote control car, following the map drawn by his dad. As he walked, he looked at the map and muttered, "Through the path, through the trees ..." He walked and occasionally stopped to look in all directions. "Huh, why aren't there any flower beds?" He looked down at the map, then at the road under his feet, and suddenly understood. He adjusted the direction of the remote control car and said to it, "You took a wrong turn; it should be to the left, not to the right." This time, as he walked, he found the flower bed. "Full speed ahead!" Big-Headed Son shouted, and the remote control car zoomed forward until it was blocked by a house. Big-Headed Son looked up, and it was Uncle Zhang's house as marked on the map. "Ah, I really found it!" He was so happy and he rang the doorbell.

Before Big-Headed Son entered the house with the

information, he shouted, "Small-Headed Dad! I've found Uncle Zhang's house!"

On that day, Big-Headed Son was playing with a hula hoop outside when an aunt arrived from afar, looking around as if she couldn't locate the house, displaying an anxious expression. Spotting Big-Headed Son, she approached and inquired, "Little friend, may I ask where number 34 is?"

Big-Headed Son paused his hula hooping and pointed with his finger, providing detailed directions, "Oh, 34 is just ahead. You need to walk through a meadow, pass three houses, turn left, and then turn right ..." The aunt listened, furrowing her brow.

Observing her confusion, Big-Headed Son's eyes lit up, "Auntie, don't worry, I'll draw you a map. Follow the map, and I'm sure you'll find it." Saying this, Big-Headed Son took out paper and a pen from his pocket, lying on the ground to sketch a map.

Once the map was drawn, he handed it to the aunt, who took a look and remarked, "This drawing is really clear. I can definitely find it. Thank you!" She took the map and walked away.

Big-Headed Son resumed playing with the hula hoop, but soon the aunt returned, saying, "Kid, I've found it!

You drew a great map!"

Big-Headed Son looked at the departing aunt with a grin and smile.

Suddenly, he put away his hula hoop and rushed to a major intersection with a stack of paper and pens. Stretching his neck, he looked into the distance.

Big Ears was coming! Big-Headed Son quickly lowered his head and started drawing on the paper. As Big Ears approached and the map was finished, Big-Headed Son handed it to him, saying, "Big Ears, just follow the map I drew, and you will surely be able to walk to your home too."

"Really? You didn't lie to me?" Big Ears took the map and examined it.

"May lightning strike me down if I lie."

Big Ears then took the map and walked away happily.

Grandma Zhang arrived! Big-Headed Son quickly drew the map again and handed it to Grandma Zhang. "Grandma Zhang, you walk home according to the map I drew!"

Grandma Zhang took the map, looked at it for a moment, and then gave it back to Big-Headed Son. "I don't need it; I know the way home."

"No, if you don't walk home following the map I

drew, I won't listen to you anymore!"

Grandma Zhang quickly took back her outstretched hand. "Okay, okay, I'll walk home according to your map. You won't be angry now, will you?" Big-Headed Son laughed.

In the distance, two more uncles arrived, and this time Big-Headed Son looked at them skeptically. "Where do these two uncles live? How come I don't recognise them?"

The two uncles approached Big-Headed Son and stopped to ask, "Little friend, we want to find a well-known bridge engineer ..."

The other uncle took over and said, "His name is ... Oh, I'll just say that you must know his nickname too. His name is Small-Headed Dad."

Big-Headed Son heard, laughed, and bent over. The two uncles joined in the laughter, and after chuckling, they asked, "Little friend, do you think this nickname is very funny? Please tell us quickly in which building he lives; we have something urgent to find him."

Big-Headed Son, after finishing his laughter, said, "I know!" Then he drew the map again. The two uncles watched Big-Headed Son draw and wondered in their hearts, exchanging glances.

Once the map was finished, Big-Headed Son handed it to them, saying, "If you follow my map, you will surely find it."

The men took the map, examined it, and said, "It's very clear, thank you!" before rushing off.

After drawing a few more maps for other adults and children, Big-Headed Son spotted Small-Headed Dad and those two uncles outside.

"Small-Headed Dad!" Big-Headed Son shouted and ran over to them, "I've drawn maps for people who live here and people who don't live here, and they can find them with the maps I've drawn!"

Small-Headed Dad picked up Big-Headed Son, saying, "Really? My Big-Headed Son has become a map fanatic."

"What? This is your son?" the uncle on the side finally interjected, then turned back to Big-Headed Son and said, "This is your father?" Big-Headed Son and Small-Headed Dad nodded in agreement.

"That's so funny, no wonder you're called Small-Headed Dad, no wonder you're called Big-Headed Son!" the two uncles said in succession.

The uncles walked away. Big-Headed Son followed Small-Headed Dad home, just in time to see a lost cat come purring along.

"Small-Headed Dad, we can draw a map of where people live, but can we draw a map of where animals live?"

"Of course, you can. Daddy will take you to the zoo right now to see a map of the animals."

They walked into the zoo and were welcomed by a large map with various animals drawn on it. Big-Headed Son ran up, pointed, and exclaimed, "Oh, I know, the panda lives here, the zebra lives here, the elephant lives there ..."

Invitation from a Small City

There is a small city with one hundred citizens. Since these citizens know each other, the mayor of the small city is elected by the citizens themselves, once a year, based on who they like and find interesting.

Recently, the citizens of this small city heard many stories about Big-Headed Son and Small-Headed Dad from another city. When the election day approached, someone proposed inviting Big-Headed Son and Small-Headed Dad to become the mayor for one year. This suggestion was warmly welcomed by the people of the city. Some citizens were so delighted that they threw their hats into the air on the spot, while others immediately joined hands and danced a folk dance. The city square that day was filled with songs and laughter.

The next morning, the outgoing mayor wrote an

invitation letter to Big-Headed Son and Small-Headed Dad, explaining the situation and asking if they would like to come and be the mayor.

"Of course, we would love to!" Big-Headed Son and Small-Headed Dad replied promptly to the invitation letter as if the mayor had sent it with a piece of candy.

However, only one person can be the mayor, so who will be the vice-mayor?

"You can be the deputy mayor!" Big-Headed Son pointed at Small-Headed Dad.

"No, you be the deputy mayor!" Small-Headed Dad pointed at Big-Headed Son.

In the end, they had to write a letter to the original mayor. The original mayor decided to let the hundred citizens vote. The final result gave the mayor a big headache: Fifty citizens voted for Big-Headed Son as the mayor and Small-Headed Dad as the deputy mayor, while the other fifty citizens voted for Small-Headed Dad as the mayor and Big-Headed Son as the deputy mayor.

When Big-Headed Son and Small-Headed Dad received the letter, they had to leave promptly. It was approaching New Year's Day, indicating that the new mayor would soon take office.

On that day, in the square of the small city, they came

up with an amusing idea for their mayoral campaign: a "head-to-head" competition, and whoever lost would become the deputy mayor. One hundred citizens learned about this unique campaign method, and ninety-eight arrived early to watch (one citizen was a telephone switchboard operator and couldn't leave, and one small child was getting chickenpox and couldn't go out). They already liked the idea of having either Big-Headed Son or Small-Headed Dad as their new mayor because, truthfully, they were both such entertaining individuals.

The competition began, and forty-nine citizens cheered for Big-Headed Son: "Go Big-Headed Son! Go Big-Headed Son!" Another forty-nine citizens cheered for Small-Headed Dad: "Go, Small-Headed Dad! Go, Small-Headed Dad!" Big-Headed Son and Small-Headed Dad knelt on the ground, head-to-head, from sunrise to sunset. Their heads became concave – Big-Headed Son resembled a big bowl, while Small-Headed Dad looked like a small bowl. The ground became damp with sweat, but there was still no clear winner.

It was the old mayor who finally intervened: "Both of you become deputy mayors! I'll continue being the mayor."

"No!" Unexpectedly, ninety-eight citizens shouted in unison, "Let Big-Headed Son and Small-Headed Dad both be mayors! They are just too funny! They make us so happy!"

And so it was decided: Big-Headed Son and Small-Headed Dad would both serve as mayors. This unprecedented event marked a unique chapter in the hundreds of years of election history in this small town.

Remote Control Toilet

Big-Headed Son and Small-Headed Dad, both now mayors, embarked on a tour of their little city to acquaint themselves with the streets, stores, and houses.

"Small-Headed Dad! I need a wee!" exclaimed Big-Headed Son, abruptly halting.

Small-Headed Dad, hands behind his back, carried on walking. "You're the mayor now; sort out your own bladder issues."

"Small-Headed Dad! I'm desperate!" Big-Headed Son's voice was strained.

With little choice, Small-Headed Dad turned back. If the Big-Headed Son Mayor ended up wetting himself, it wouldn't bode well for his mayoral dignity. "But I don't know where the loos are in this city. We'll have to ask someone or find them before continuing our visit."

Big-Headed Son nodded vigorously. They approached a passerby and inquired about the whereabouts of the restrooms. The citizen enthusiastically guided them, "Keep going, pass seven street lamps, then past five lilac trees and three ginkgo trees. Turn left, pass a pointed hut and a domed hut, and you'll be there."

The two mayors hurriedly counted past seven street lamps and the lilac trees, but Big-Headed Son couldn't hold it any longer. "One, two, three ... Small-Headed Dad, I can't, I can't hold it!" he stopped again.

Small-Headed Dad urged, "You must hold it! Mayors don't pee their pants! If you really can't wait, you'll have to do it next year when you're not the mayor." He pointed a stern finger at Big-Headed Son.

Surprisingly effective, Big-Headed Son suddenly felt less desperate. He quickly followed Small-Headed Dad, continuing under the ginkgo tree.

Finally passing a domed hut, Big-Headed Son rushed into the nearby toilet, successfully preserving the mayor's dignity.

When Big-Headed Son emerged from the loo, ready to resume exploring the city with Small-Headed Dad, he was already pondering ways to revamp the city.

"Small-Headed Dad, we ought to transform the loo

into a remote-controlled contraption," Big-Headed Son declared with gravity, "because the urgency of needing a wee tends to escalate."

Small-Headed Dad quizzically responded, "What? You want the loo to come to you?"

"Yeah," Big-Headed Son nodded, "It'd be brilliant to have a remote control in hand, give it a push, and watch the loo roll over. Just imagine, a toilet on wheels heading my way with a grin." Big-Headed Son's eyes gleamed as if he could already visualise a mobile toilet approaching.

Upon sharing this idea with the public, it was swiftly embraced, particularly by the children who enthusiastically exclaimed, "Great idea! This way, we'll never be caught short during a run again!"

The wheeled toilet was promptly constructed. The two mayors hosted a grand ceremony in the city square, complete with gongs, drums, firecrackers, and they distributed remote controls for the toilet to every child, adorned with a red ribbon. The children clutched these remotes as joyfully as if they were holding a large piece of chocolate.

Henceforth, on the small-town sidewalk, amidst the bustling pedestrians, a wheeled toilet joined the crowd. It maneuvred forward, backward, or stood quietly, resembling an obedient soldier.

During the tenure of Big-Headed Son and Small-Headed Dad as mayors, there were no instances of children wetting themselves in the streets throughout the entire small town.

Scooter City

Today, there was a traffic mishap: a little dog got hit by a car while crossing the street. Big-Headed Son and Small-Headed Dad were deeply saddened, especially Big-Headed Son. He purchased a large bone toy that the puppy liked and visited the pet hospital to check on the little dog. Upon returning, he made an announcement to all the citizens: "No vehicles are allowed during the daytime."

"But what if we need to go up to the theatre for a play?"

"And what about trips to the zoo?"

The citizens deliberated, considering both places were on the outskirts of the city. After a moment of thought, Big-Headed Son suggested, "Ride a scooter! From now on, all scooters can cruise down the streets and cross them!"

"Great!" the children cheered with delight, as previously, they were confined to playing with scooters in the safety of the alley. With eager excitement, they dispersed from the crowd, and soon enough, the streets were filled with children on scooters.

Just as Big-Headed Son was about to join in the fun, the adults and elderly folks who remained in the square called out, "What about us? We don't know how to ride a scooter!"

Small-Headed Dad quickly pulled Big-Headed Son aside and whispered, "The mayor can't leave now." Then he addressed the group, saying, "So be it, all citizens will have a three-day break starting today to learn how to ride scooters!"

"Great!" the adults and the elderly finally found joy, rushing to the scooter store like they were about to stage a heist, squeezing the owner outside the shop in their eagerness.

After three days, all the citizens had mastered the art of riding a scooter. Even the elderly grandparents, initially struggling with arthritis and leg pain, found the learning process challenging but ultimately beneficial. Once they got the hang of it, their joints no longer ached, and they moved as nimbly as children.

One day, a tour bus arrived from another city. As it reached the small city's border, it abruptly stopped. The driver had spotted a large sign proclaiming, "All vehicles prohibited during the day." This posed a dilemma, as the bus was filled with elderly residents from a nursing home. Allowing them to disembark and walk seemed like a recipe for exhaustion and potential harm. The matron of the sanitarium had no choice but to summon the two mayors to find a solution.

"That's too simple; let them ride scooters!" suggested the two mayors.

"Are you joking? They're all sick old folks!" retorted the matron, her hefty face sagging.

Small-Headed Dad reassured her, "Don't worry." He then blew three whistles, and suddenly, dozens of children on scooters emerged from all directions. They surrounded the tour bus. The elderly passengers, unfamiliar with scooters, descended from the bus, curious and encircling the scooters.

"Grandpa, I'll teach you!"

"Granny, don't be afraid; you'll get the hang of it in a minute!"

Some children eagerly ushered the elderly adults to stand behind them, and then they glided away on their skates. Other kids were bouncing around, patiently teaching the elderly how to skate. The seniors expressed their joy, saying, "We usually travel by car, but your city lets us ride these contraptions, and it's so much fun!" They happily followed the children. The tourist bus, now only occupied by the dozing driver and the irate matron, had departed.

To the matron's increasing astonishment and frustration, when it was time to return, only one old man showed up on time. He announced, "The lads wanted me to let you know that they're extending their stay in this scooter-filled city for three more days. When it's time to go back, we'll each have a scooter to scoot our way home!"

The lone old man, brimming with energy, rode the scooter solo. After completing the ride, he turned around and skated away once again.

Eating Apple Penalty

Early in the morning, a group of citizens seized a pointy-headed man and marched to the mayor's office to report, "He pinched a comic book from a neighbour in the dead of night yesterday!"

Small-Headed Dad inquired, "What was the original penalty for stealing?"

"A visit to the orchard to plant ten apple trees!" replied a big-nosed uncle.

"What?" exclaimed Big-Headed Son, "Plant ten apple trees? That sounds like fun! No wonder he's tempted to steal."

"What's enjoyable about planting trees? Then what do you suggest the punishment should be?" asked Uncle Big Nose, engaging in some nose-picking.

"It's more like penalizing him for devouring a

hundred apples in a row."

As soon as Big-Headed Son finished speaking, several small children cheered, "Right! Punish him for eating apples! The more, the better! Let's go plant an apple tree!"

The man who pilfered the comic covered his mouth upon hearing this and thought to himself, "This Big-Headed mayor is really something."

The citizens apprehended the thief and, led by Big-Headed Son, headed to the orchard. Big-Headed Son and the children climbed the apple tree to pick apples first.

"Back home, my mum only gives me apples; she never lets me pick them," remarked Big-Headed Son as he plucked the fruit.

"My mum makes me eat three big apples every day, but I don't know how apples grow," said a little chubby boy whose face resembled a big apple.

A hundred apples were swiftly gathered and divided among three large baskets.

"Bring the thief here to be punished for eating!" commanded Big-Headed Son, and the citizens led the thief in that direction. The thief couldn't contain his happiness, emitting "giggle giggle" sounds all the way.

Big Nose uncle grunted and whispered, "What kind of punishment is this? It's making the thief smile with delight!"

An uncle with meaty bumps on his ears whispered in agreement, "Will this make the thief mend his ways?"

The thief settled beside the basket, gleefully indulging in the apples. Initially, he picked and devoured the larger ones with gusto, causing an onlooker to gulp with anger. The big-nosed uncle's nostrils nearly emitted smoke in frustration.

On the other side, Big-Headed Son and a group of children were busy planting apple trees. Led by a fruit farmer, they diligently dug holes, placed young trees, covered them with soil, and then watered the newly planted saplings. Each child, red-faced and joyful, either dug pits or buried trees, engrossed in their work.

Meanwhile, the thief on the other side continued his apple feast. After devouring the first twenty big apples rapidly and delectably, his pace slowed. He transitioned to picking and consuming the smaller ones, his expression no longer as joyous. By the thirtieth apple, the thief began to cry softly, lamenting, "I really can't eat anymore!"

"No, you must finish it; it's Mayor Big-Headed Son's order!" Uncle Big Nose declared, now in a better mood.

"Oooh ... I shouldn't have stolen someone else's comic book ... I'll be sure to correct myself in the future ..." The thief's cries grew louder, and he sneezed so forcefully that a large spray of apple crumbs shot out of his mouth, nose, and ears. Surprised by the thief's words, Uncle Big Nose and Uncle Meat Pimple exchanged glances. "I didn't realise that eating apples works better than growing them! Mayor Big-Headed Son is marvelous!"

With Big-Headed Son's approval, the thief was excused from finishing a hundred big apples. Despite his resolution to stop stealing, the thief developed a peculiar ailment. He began to cry and scream in fear at the mere sight of an apple.

Haha Laughing Children's Hospital

Big-Headed Son caught a cold today, and Small-Headed Dad accompanied him to the Children's Hospital to see a doctor. As they approached the hospital, they could hear the cries of children and the comforting voices of adults from inside.

"Mayor Big-Headed Son, you need a shot," the doctor said after examining him. Big-Headed Son, usually afraid of shots, forced a smile and declared, "I'm very brave; I don't cry when I get a shot!"

As Small-Headed Dad led Big-Headed Son towards the injection area, they observed many children crying or fleeing as if they had seen a ghost upon encountering the white-clad doctor.

After returning from the hospital, Big-Headed Son suggested to his dad, "Let's build a Haha Laughing Children's Hospital!"

Small-Headed Dad expressed skepticism, stating, "That's impossible; hospitals are places for injections and medicines. Can they be happy?"

"Yes, they can!" Big-Headed Son whispered into Small-Headed Dad's ear.

To surprise the citizens, the two mayors decided to construct the Haha Laughing Children's Hospital in secret. A month later, the mayor's office was flooded with calls:

"Hello, is this the mayor's office? We can't find the children's hospital!"

"Hello, Mayor Big-Headed Son, where has the children's hospital in our city moved to?"

Responding to the inquiries, Big-Headed Son and Small-Headed Dad assured, "It's right where it used to be!"

Confused citizens mentioned that they couldn't see the hospital at its original location; instead, there was an animation city.

"That's not Animation City; that's the newly opened Haha Laughing Children's Hospital ..."

Curious citizens flocked to the hospital and discovered an environment where white was nowhere to be seen. The walls were painted in various hues of pink and adorned with images of animals and flowers.

In the Haha Laughing Children's Hospital, doctors and nurses in white were nowhere to be seen. Instead, doctors wore costumes of animated characters like Donald Duck, Mickey Mouse, Peanut Dog, Robot Cat, Monkey King, and Nezha. The nurses wore fairy-like long dresses and princess-like lace hats, creating a joyful and whimsical atmosphere.

The ailing children initially cried incessantly, but the arrival of the doctors put an end to their tears. Some even burst into laughter, thanks to Dr. Monkey King's entertaining facial expressions.

The sick children eagerly opened their mouths wide, inviting Dr. Donald Duck to inspect their throats or lifting their clothes for the amusing robot cat doctor adorned with an owl stethoscope to listen to their hearts.

Those in need of medicine were particularly cheerful because the medications resembled delightful candies and tasted even better—sweet, sour, and infused with various fruit flavours.

Surprisingly, no child dreaded receiving a shot. The area where shots were administered played the best cartoons, captivating the children to such an extent that they hardly noticed when the shots were administered.

The mayor's office phone rang once more:

"Haha Laughing Children's Hospital is fantastic!"

"Our kids genuinely smile when they visit."

After handling these public calls, Big-Headed Son would proudly turn to Small-Headed Dad and ask, "How about that? Is it working or not?"

Statue of the Mayor in the Square

The year flew by, and today marked the end of Big-Headed Son and Small-Headed Dad's term as mayors.

In the morning, citizens gathered in the square, adorned their scooters with flowers of various colours, creating an atmosphere reminiscent of a celebratory event. Soon, Big-Headed Son and Small-Headed Dad emerged, riding scooters as they had to rush to another city to catch a plane. The citizens crowded around, placing flowers on their scooters.

"Let's go!" Big-Headed Son called out, and together with Small-Headed Dad, they glided towards the airfield on their scooters. The sound of scooters trailing behind them echoed like a collective participation in a sports event.

The whole town resonated with the rhythmic "Wow

– wow – wow" as citizens sang for the departing mayors. The scooter procession traversed seventeen streets and thirty-five trees, reaching another city, then continued over seven more streets and five more trees towards the airport.

Observing the approaching spectacle, the airport security guards suspected something significant was about to happen. Hastily, they closed the airport gates and summoned ten additional tall, stout policemen.

"What do these people want?"

"Are they here to hijack a plane?" wondered the security guards, preparing for an unexpected turn of events.

As they observed with wide eyes and engaged in conversation, a long line of scooters, led by Big-Headed Son and Small-Headed Dad, arrived outside the airport's gate.

"You guys go back, or we won't get on the plane!" Small-Headed Dad cheerfully warned the gathering.

"We'll come back to see you guys later!" Big-Headed Son waved his hand, and the citizens reluctantly turned around and left. Only then did the police open the gates, allowing Big-Headed Son and Small-Headed Dad inside. The police, caught in the oddity of the situation, stared at them so strangely that they forgot to check their plane tickets.

Meanwhile, the citizens who turned away didn't head home; instead, they strolled through the streets of the small town, eager to revisit the unique structures left by the two beloved mayors.

There were the remote-controlled toilets, the animal apartments, and the Haha Laughing Children's Hospital. Along the road, a set of binoculars and microscopes were placed, allowing children to observe the activities of the mother bird in the tree and the type of grain being transported by the little ants to their nests.

"I like the glass house best!" a child pointed out. A transparent, all-glass house stood by the roadside, designed for children to sleep in at night and gaze at the stars.

"My favourite is the story house!" another child exclaimed. Around the corner, there was an old-fashioned steeple house with a chimney on the roof and a fireplace inside. Every night, a kerosene lamp would illuminate the house, and a grandmother would share stories from times long, long ago.

The more the citizens observed, the more they longed for their Big-Headed mayor and their Small-Headed mayor. Some were so moved that they couldn't hold back tears. In response, someone proposed, "Let's erect statues in the square for Mayor Big-Headed Son and Mayor Small-Headed Dad. It'll feel like they're still with us." The suggestion received immediate approval.

Before long, the statues were standing tall. Can you guess their pose? In truth, Big-Headed Son and Small-Headed Dad weren't depicted standing or sitting. Instead, they were lying on their backs, with the big head against the small head.

From that day forward, as people passed by the statues, they couldn't resist touching the big head and the small head, which inevitably led to grins and laughter.

Path at Night

In the evening, Small-Headed Dad was bringing Big-Headed Son back from the countryside when, unexpectedly, the bike tire broke halfway. Given the late hour, finding a car repair store was out of the question, so they had to push the bike towards home.

"Do we have to walk a long, long way?" Big-Headed Son worried about the distance.

"It's not far; we'll take a shortcut through the path. It only takes ten minutes!"

"A path? Is that the path in the woods? Could there be ghosts there?" Big-Headed Son expressed concern, as the ghosts Auntie talked about were usually associated with the woods.

"Ha, it's good to have ghosts. Ghosts sleep during the day and come out at night; maybe their repair store is still open. Then we can ask the ghosts to fix our bikes for us!" Small-Headed Dad said with ease.

As they entered the path in the woods, there were no streetlights. Initially, they could see the road by the moonlight filtering down between the leaves. However, as they progressed, the leaves overhead became denser, blocking the moonlight. Big-Headed Son felt as if he was walking at night with sunglasses on.

"Dad, I can't see anything!" Big-Headed Son admitted feeling a bit scared.

"Now we are in a hurry, not at a toy fair; we don't need to see anything." Small-Headed Dad appeared braver than his son.

Suddenly, Small-Headed Dad stood still for a moment and slowly raised his head to look up a tree.

"What's the matter, Small-Headed Dad?" Big-Headed Son leaned in close to his dad, his voice already shaking.

"You, you listen to ...," Unexpectedly, Small-Headed Dad's voice also started shaking, and Big-Headed Son heard the sound of "dudududu—" coming from the tree.

"Are you also afraid?" Big-Headed Son asked worriedly.

"I am not afraid! But we'd better be polite and not frighten the ghost," said Small-Headed Dad. After saying this, he crouched down and walked on gently and softly. However, the "tuk-tuks" in the trees seemed to be watching them, following wherever they went.

"Thump!" Small-Headed Dad suddenly tumbled and collapsed on the ground along with his bicycle. Big-Headed Son was on the verge of crying out but was hushed by Small-Headed Dad: "Don't make a sound; there are many ghosts, and we are few." Only then did Big-Headed Son refrain from crying out.

"Big-Headed Son, did Auntie teach you how to catch ghosts?"

"Yes, she told me not to be afraid of ghosts, just stand still and spit in all directions, and the ghosts will run away."

"Oops, why didn't you say so earlier?" Small-Headed Dad hastily stood still, turned his body, and spun four times. The "Duk Duk Duk Duk Duk" sound ceased entirely.

"Hey, that's a pretty good trick. Let's use it to catch ghosts!"

Small-Headed Dad dropped his bike, took a few steps forward, spun around, and spat four times; then took a few more steps, spun around, and spat four times again. Big-Headed Son followed suit. Fear no longer gripped them, and they even shouted into the dark trees at the top of their voices: "Ghost! We're not afraid of you! If you have courage, come out!" Not content with shouting, they kicked the trees with their feet, producing a "tom-tom" sound as if they were trying to kick the ghost out of the tree.

"Pfft ..." Suddenly, something flew out of the tree.

"Small-Headed Dad, look, the ghost has escaped!"

"It turned out to be a flying woodpecker ghost!" Small-Headed Dad and Big-Headed Son laughed heartily together.

Super Sleepy King

On Sundays, Small-Headed Dad enjoyed sleeping in, resisting all of Big-Headed Son's attempts to rouse him. Whether it was using a toothbrush on the soles of his feet, threading hair into his nostrils, or playfully riding on him with two hands to scratch an itch, Small-Headed Dad would remain undisturbed. The final resort for Big-Headed Son was to shoot him in the face with a water gun, prompting Small-Headed Dad to jump up, yelling, "You stinking Big-Headed Son, couldn't you see I was lying here on my bed?"

Big-Headed Son, ducking away, would reply, "No! You were having a lie-in on your bed."

An angered Small-Headed Dad wiped off the water droplets with the quilt and resumed his sleep, but not this week's Sunday. When Small-Headed Dad woke up around eleven o'clock, the surroundings were still quiet. He couldn't find Big-Headed Son or hear his usual antics. Had Big-Headed Son suddenly become a good boy, showing sympathy for his hard-working father? Puzzled, Small-Headed Dad climbed up and entered Big-Headed Son's cabin, only to find him sleeping soundly on the cot.

"Hmph, so you can sleep in late too? Today, I'll give you a taste of being caught while sleeping!"

Small-Headed Dad used various antics, from brushing the soles of his feet to pawing an itch, but Big-Headed Son remained motionless, deeply immersed in slumber.

"Huh? Does this stinky Big-Headed Son sleep more soundly than I do?"

Unconvinced, Small-Headed Dad grabbed a water pistol, aimed it at Big-Headed Son's head, and sprayed water. The head, pillow, and bedsheet got wet, yet Big-Headed Son continued to sleep.

"Hmph, can't I wake up this stinky Big-Headed Son?"

Determined, Small-Headed Dad grabbed the sheet, lifted it, and dragged Big-Headed Son from the shed to the big house, and even into the living room. Despite the dragging, Big-Headed Son remained in a deep slumber.

Enraged, Small-Headed Dad let out the three puppies from their cage, and shoved Big-Headed Son into the dog's tiny enclosure. The puppies growled outside the cage, anxious about losing their nest, but Big-Headed Son just laughed in his sleep, possibly dreaming about some amusing encounter with the three puppies.

"Hmph, I don't believe I can't wake you up, you stinky Big-Headed Son!"

Small-Headed Dad found a large hemp rope, tied one end to the four corners of the bedsheet, threw the other end over the door, and pulled it down hard. Big-Headed Son was left hanging in the air. However, not only did Big-Headed Son fail to wake up, but he also slept even more soundly!

Small-Headed Dad's frustration grew, and he gritted his teeth and stamped his feet in anger. Eventually, he left Big-Headed Son hanging on the door, ignoring him completely.

At 3 o'clock in the afternoon, Big-Headed Son finally woke up after a good stretch and yawn.

"Small-Headed Dad! I had a dream that I was sleeping in a hammock, and it was very, very cozy! I'm going to have that dream again tomorrow!"

Small-Headed Dad entered the room and remarked, "Starting today, I'm naming you the super sleepy king of our house!"

"And what's the prize?"

"What do you want?"

"A hammock!"

First Day of Kindergarten

Big-Headed Son is heading to kindergarten, and Small-Headed Dad's dad holds his hand as if sending him to another city. Small-Headed Dad is particularly uneasy and keeps reminding him along the way, "If you miss your dad, just call, and he'll come right away to pick you up!"

Big-Headed Son promises and inquires, "Why haven't we arrived at the kindergarten yet?" "Coming soon," replies Small-Headed Dad, adding hastily, "Your cell phone is in the inside shirt pouch pocket, so be careful the teacher doesn't find it!"

Big-Headed Son promises again and asks once more, "Why haven't we arrived at the kindergarten yet?"

"Look, the iron gate is right in front," points Small-Headed Dad.

"Why is there an iron gate here too?" Big-Headed Son

recalls the big iron gate of the zoo.

"Because ... because it doesn't let the kids escape!" Small-Headed Dad responds.

Big-Headed Son doesn't ask further; he suddenly stands outside the big iron gate of the kindergarten, seemingly reluctant to go in.

Small-Headed Dad is secretly pleased, saying, "If you don't want to go, we can go back now!"

After a moment's thought, Big-Headed Son decides, "I'll go in and have a look!"

The kindergarten's grassy area is vast, resembling a park with numerous fun attractions. There's a rotating slide, a small basketball hoop, various big and small fitness balls, and all sorts of cars to sit in and drive. Suddenly, Big-Headed Son starts running, making a beeline for a large blue crane truck to sit in.

Later, Small-Headed Dad dropped Big-Headed Son off at the classroom and left. However, he lingered outside the big iron gate for a long time, seemingly waiting for Big-Headed Son to come out. But Big-Headed Son didn't come out; he was already enjoying kindergarten!

Big-Headed Son had a delightful time in kindergarten, relishing his lunch and eagerly anticipating naptime.

However, on this particular day, when he returned

home, Small-Headed Dad seemed unusually unhappy. Despite Apron Mum calling him to lunch, he didn't eat. When she suggested he rest for a while, he refused. Small-Headed Dad's father anxiously hovered by the telephone, but after a considerable time, the phone remained silent.

"Is the telephone broken?" pondered Small-Headed Dad's father. He repeated this seven times, yet every time he picked up the phone, he only heard the dial tone. The phone was in working order.

"Why hasn't Big-Headed Son called back?" Small-Headed Dad wondered. "Could it be that the teacher took away his cell phone? Oops! That's possible. Let me try calling him."

Unable to wait any longer, Small-Headed Dad decided to call Big-Headed Son himself.

In the quiet kindergarten bedroom, suddenly, the sound of music filled the air. Teacher Bei, overseeing the kindergarten, followed the unusual music and discovered it emanating from Big-Headed Son's cot. Teacher Bei carefully retrieved the cell phone from Big-Headed Son's shirt pocket and answered it, saying cordially, "Hello!"

When Small-Headed Dad's father heard the voice on the phone, realizing it was indeed the teacher, he became so scared that he hastily hung up.

Later that day, when Big-Headed Son returned from kindergarten, he handed the cell phone back to Small-Headed Dad and declared, "I don't want to bring my cell phone!"

Concerned, Small-Headed Dad asked, "Did you get scolded by the teacher?"

Big-Headed Son explained, "There are lots of fun things to do in kindergarten. I don't want to play with my cell phone!" It seems like Big-Headed Son found plenty of enjoyment in the activities at kindergarten and preferred them over the electronic device.

Strange Gardener

On this day, after the morning exercises in the playground, Big-Headed Son and the other children stayed behind for some free time.

Big-Headed Son chose a toy green jeep to drive around the big playground, racing along the circle of concrete road.

As Big-Headed Son started his second lap, he noticed a gardener in the distance next to a holly tree. The gardener, wearing a straw hat, raised his hand in a straight gesture. Perplexed, Big-Headed Son stopped the jeep and looked at him. Bi Xiaohu, driving a toy sedan nearby, was informed by Big-Headed Son, but he just glanced and remarked, "He is beckoning me. I'm not going," before driving away.

A while later, when Big-Headed Son was enjoying the

slide, he saw the gardener again, this time raising both hands and waving. Excited, Big-Headed Son informed Fan Dawei, who also looked but dismissed it, saying, "He is waving at both of us; let's ignore him," and then proceeded to slide down.

After sliding down, Big-Headed Son swung on one of the swings and then climbed the climbing frame. When he reached the top, about to descend, he remembered the gardener again. Looking over, he saw the gardener anxiously stretching his arms, as if wishing he had a long rope to pull Big-Headed Son over. Feeling a bit scared, Big-Headed Son ran to inform Ms. Bei, pointing in the gardener's direction. However, Teacher Bei looked and said, "That gardener is cutting the holly tree with his head down; he didn't wave at you!" It turns out that Big-Headed Son had misunderstood the gardener's actions.

Big-Headed Son glanced, and indeed, the gardener had stopped waving. A little later, the teacher rang a small bell, signaling the children to head into the classroom. As Big-Headed Son ran past, he caught sight of the gardener taking off his straw hat, revealing his face.

"Ah! It's Small-Headed Dad!" exclaimed Big-Headed Son in surprise. He then informed the children running past him, "Look! That's my dad!" Several children ran after Big-Headed Son, finding it quite novel that the kindergarten gardener was the father of one of the children.

Small-Headed Dad dropped his straw hat, picked up Big-Headed Son in his arms, and said, "Daddy was so worried that he wanted to come and see you!" Feeling embarrassed in front of the children, Big-Headed Son insisted on coming down. As he did, the excited children surrounded him, chanting, "Big-Headed Son! Small-Headed Dad! Big-Headed Son! Small-Headed Dad!"

Their loud voices reached Ms. Bei, who came over and asked, "What are you all doing here? You're interfering with Uncle Gardener's work!"

"He's Big-Headed Son's father!" the children eagerly informed Ms. Bei.

"I, I happen to be the gardener here ..." Small-Headed Dad hastily replied, putting his straw hat back on.

"Huh? Aren't you the engineer who built the bridge?" wondered Big-Headed Son.

Small-Headed Dad quickly answered, "Today, today daddy is the engineer who builds gardens ..." However, the next day, the engineer who built the garden resumed his role as the engineer who built the bridge.

The Boat on the Floor

When Ms. Bei entered the bedroom, she discovered that none of the children had gone to bed for their nap. Instead, they were all wearing socks and joyfully sliding around on the floor as if it were an ice rink, bumping into each other. Some were still learning and kept falling, while others skated back and forth confidently. Among them, Big-Headed Son showcased exceptional skill, weaving through the crowd, bending over, going around, never falling.

Rather than getting upset, Ms. Bei applauded, signaling for everyone to stop. She asked, "Who invented this game?"

"It's Big-Headed Son! It's Big-Headed Son!" the children shouted.

But Big-Headed Son insisted even louder, "I didn't invent it! My father did! He can even make a boat on the floor." At this point, Big-Headed Son wished that Small-Headed Dad could demonstrate his skills to the children and Ms. Bei, anticipating their praise: "Small-Headed Dad is great! Small-Headed Dad is great!"

However, Small-Headed Dad was still at work and wouldn't be able to pick up Big-Headed Son until the afternoon.

Ms. Bei continued, "Our children love the games invented by Big-Headed Son and Small-Headed Dad. It's nap time now, so let's play it when we wake up, okay?"

"Okay!" the children answered in unison, then quickly went to bed.

Upon waking up, Ms. Bei allowed the children to wear socks and skate on the floor for a while. Even she joined in, taking off her shoes and skating with the children. However, Ms. Bei accidentally fell, prompting many children to rush to her aid. Despite this, Ms. Bei found the situation amusing, sitting on the ground and laughing heartily.

After the children had a snack and a drink of water, they played in the classroom while awaiting their parents to pick them up. Big-Headed Son, however, didn't join the games; instead, he stood at the window, eagerly awaiting his father's arrival.

One by one, the children were picked up by their parents, but Big-Headed Son's dad had not arrived yet. Big-Headed Son grew anxious and stood up on a stool, finally spotting Small-Headed Dad running in from outside.

"What took you so long, Small-Headed Dad?" Big-Headed Son said, pulling him over to Ms. Bei. "Ms. Bei, my dad can make a little boat on the floor!"

Teacher Bei responded, "Good, let your dad show us one!"

However, Small-Headed Dad seemed reluctant, stating, "No, no way."

"I won't go back with you if you don't perform, humph!" Big-Headed Son, displeased, threatened his father.

Small-Headed Dad thought about it and had to comply. He took off his shoes, sat on the floor, raised his legs in front, placed his hands on the floor, and pushed backward. His buttocks slid forward, and he skated swiftly, even faster than the children wearing socks on the floor.

The children cheered, "Small-Headed Dad is really great! Small-Headed Dad is great!" Big-Headed Son, listening and watching, couldn't have been happier.

Ouyang Dad

Small-Headed Dad had been particularly unhappy lately because Big-Headed Son consistently chanted "Ouyang Dad": "Our father Ouyang is very powerful, he can perform acrobatics, martial arts, and ..." Almost every day, Big-Headed Son would come home from kindergarten talking about the new male teacher, imitating Ouyang dad even in his mannerisms. What infuriated Small-Headed Dad even more was that Big-Headed Son had discarded the way Dad taught him to take off his sweater and instead adopted Ouyang Dad's method of first withdrawing his head and then removing the sleeves.

"Teacher is a teacher; why do you have to call him Daddy Ouyang?" Small-Headed Dad disliked it when Big-Headed Son referred to someone else as Daddy.

"Ouyang Dad didn't ask the kids to call him Ouyang

Dad; we did it ourselves. Ouyang Dad said that we can call him whatever we want, as long as we like it," explained Big-Headed Son. He then took out a paper airplane from his pocket and added, "This is a reward from Daddy Ouyang for my good somersault today!" He launched the plane into the distance.

"What's the point of having a lousy airplane like that? I'll make you an even better one." Small-Headed Dad's father fetched a piece of snow-white printer paper, which he was reluctant to use, and swiftly folded a rocket airplane with a pointed head and upward-pointing wings. "Look at this!" he exclaimed. Small-Headed Dad threw the plane into the distance, but unexpectedly, perhaps due to the heavy head, the plane quickly plummeted.

"Dad, you can't do this!" Big-Headed Son didn't even bother looking and continued playing with Ouyang Dad's airplane.

Having fallen asleep at night, Big-Headed Son suddenly climbed up and rummaged through the closet.

"What are you looking for?" Apron Mum asked.

"Looking for my red hat." Big-Headed Son's voice came from inside the closet.

"I thought you didn't like hats?" Apron Mum was a little surprised.

"I love wearing hats now, very much!"

Small-Headed Dad heard it and came over, saying, "It's probably because that Ouyang dad of yours wears hats, so you like wearing hats too!"

Big-Headed Son hurriedly withdrew from the closet, saying, "Right, right, right. How did you know, Dad? Our father Ouyang wears a red hat every day, so he's very smart, just like a football star!"

The hat was finally found, and Big-Headed Son finally lay down.

At night, Small-Headed Dad couldn't sleep, he decided to go the next day to meet the "Ouyang dad".

That afternoon, when Small-Headed Dad's father went to pick up Big-Headed Son, he saw Ouyang Dad lifting his sleeves up high and showing his triceps to the children. The children were all stretching their necks and their eyes were wide open as if they were watching Superman.

Small-Headed Dad thought to himself: What kind of skill is this?

Unexpectedly, Ouyang Dad saw Small-Headed Dad coming over and suddenly said to him, "You are the father of the little child, aren't you? Please cooperate; I would like to show the children the sport of arm wrestling."

Small-Headed Dad nodded in a panic.

The result turned out to be that Small-Headed Dad won, and Ouyang Dad lost.

"Not counting! It doesn't count!" Unexpectedly, the children yelled out; they all didn't like the result.

What further fuelled Small-Headed Dad's anger was when Big-Headed Son said on the way home: "Our Ouyang Dad must lose to you on purpose because you are the father of one of the kids and also a guest ..."

You Adults Are Weird

Small-Headed Dad came back early at noon today because later on he had to go to a parent visitation day in the kindergarten: "Small-Headed Dad, you mustn't be late!" Big-Headed Son had repeatedly reminded him when he left in the morning.

"Why don't you go yet!" Apron Mum urged several times, but Small-Headed Dad was still turning around in front of the mirror, changing into a black suit one moment, and a white suit the next.

"Just go, right away!" Small-Headed Dad finally decided to wear a white suit, and then took a camera and hung it around his neck, and hurried towards the kindergarten.

Wow, the parents were already there. Small-Headed Dad found Big-Headed Son in the classroom and winked at him to show that he had arrived, and Big-Headed Son squeezed his nose at Small-Headed Dad to show that he was happy.

The open class began. The children sat in the front, and the parents sat in the back. Small-Headed Dad was sitting in the last row, his white suit was very conspicuous, and the black camera on his chest was even more conspicuous.

Ms. Bei faced the children and took out a wrench, asking, "Do you know what this is?"

A few children answered: "It's something to open bottle caps!"

A few children answered: "It's a wrench!"

Big-Headed Son did not answer anything; his eyes stared straight at the wrench in Ms. Bei's hand, wanting to take it into his own hands to take a closer look at whether it was fun or not.

Ms. Bei continued: "Yes, this is a wrench, it is used to open the cap of a bottle. If we take a bottle of water with us on a trip and forget the wrench, we can't open the bottle and drink it ..."

"We can!" Big-Headed Son suddenly put his hand up in the air, "My dad can open the bottle cap with his teeth!"

Ms. Bei laughed, and the parents joined in, but the

children remained silent, all turning their heads to catch a glimpse of what kind of dad Big-Headed Son's dad was.

After the laughter, Ms. Bei continued, "Of course, if we happen to be out and forget to bring a wrench, and we're thirsty, then we have to think of other ways to open the bottle cap. But children are still young, and they're not allowed to bite the bottle cap with their teeth ..."

Once the open class concluded, Big-Headed Son happily accompanied Small-Headed Dad home.

"Small-Headed Dad, I really wished Ms. Bei would give me the bottle, and then I would pass it to you, and you could bite it for everyone to see. Everyone would be amazed!" Big-Headed Son exclaimed.

However, Small-Headed Dad wasn't pleased to hear that and retorted, "I'll never attend your parent visitation day again, anyway!"

"Why?" Big-Headed Son didn't understand.

"Because you embarrassed me! Look at the teachers and parents laughing at me, and the children staring at me as if I had a mouthful of wolf's teeth ..." Small-Headed Dad's expression hardened.

"But you were biting bottle caps on the train!" Big-Headed Son protested.

"I did it because you were dying of thirst!" Small-

Headed Dad quickened his pace.

Big-Headed Son was left frozen but had to follow and walk again. In frustration, he added, "You adults are weird!"

Very Stupid Idea

Big-Headed Son thought that everything was good in the kindergarten, except that he didn't want to take a nap when he had to.

"Small-Headed Dad, go and talk to Teacher Bei about not letting me take a nap every day." Big-Headed Son saw Liu Lili's father discussing with Teacher Bei about not letting Liu Lili do gymnastics every day, and Teacher Bei agreed because Liu Lili has a heart condition.

Small-Headed Dad said: "It won't work. Liu Lili has a reason."

"I also have a reason! Because I don't want to sleep!" shouted Big-Headed Son.

Later, Small-Headed Dad came up with an idea for Big-Headed Son, and Big-Headed Son smiled and nodded his head straight when he heard it. Then he followed his father to kindergarten.

Just after lunch in the kindergarten, Big-Headed Son yawned desperately: "I really want to take a nap!"

Ms. Bei looked at him and asked: "You didn't sleep last night?"

Big-Headed Son said with his eyes half closed: "I kept dreaming about playing with the scooter when I went to bed last night, which is the same as not sleeping! Ah-" He let out another big yawn.

Ms. Bei said: "Since you're so sleepy, go ahead and take a nap in the bedroom!"

"Huh?!" Teacher Bei's words seemed to bring Big-Headed Son into the spirit, and the boy happily stood up and went straight to the bedroom.

Instead of sleeping on the bed, Big-Headed Son slept under the bed. He pulled the sheets and quilt down from both sides to cover them, and it was dark under the bed, as if it were a basement.

Big-Headed Son in the basement imagined that he was in a bunker. When the cavalry came in on his left, Big-Headed Son stretched out his left arm as a machine gun and fired: "BURST BURST BURST ..." When a tank came on the right, Big-Headed Son stretched out his right arm as a bazooka to bombard it: "Bang ..." Ha-ha! The tank rolled over! The troopers turned around and ran away! Big-Headed Son was playing so much that he didn't even know when he fell asleep. He still didn't know!

That was, after the children woke up from their afternoon nap, they gathered on the playground after eating snacks. After a while, ten firefighters uncles lined up neatly and came to the children to perform climbing rope ladder, jumping fire, fast clothing, and other skills. The children enjoyed it so much that they shouted and kicked their legs so much that they wanted to fly into the air and have a better look...

But there's no Big-Headed Son among all these happy kids. Big-Headed Son was still in the bedroom, still sleeping in his imaginary bunker under the bed. In fact, when the teacher found him, she wanted to wake him up, but he slept so well that she really thought he didn't sleep well last night, and thought that he would make up a good sleep!

"It's all your fault! It's your stupid idea! You told me to sleep under the bed, so I didn't see the fireman's uncle's performance!" When Small-Headed Dad came to pick up Big-Headed Son, Big-Headed Son was just putting on his shoes, while all the other children were already in the classroom talking about the performance they had just seen while waiting for their parents to come and pick them up.

"It was you who said you couldn't sleep, so I taught you to hide under the bed and play, but you obviously could sleep, can you blame me?" Small-Headed Dad wasn't buying it.

But when he took a nap, Big-Headed Son never slept under the bed again because he didn't want to miss something that he would regret for days!

Let's All Escape Inside

It was summer vacation, and Big-Head Son felt incredibly bored staying home every day.

"Dad, why don't you show me the kindergarten!" Small-Head Father finally got up.

Small-Head Father, walking towards the toilet, remarked, "What are you doing in the kindergarten with the door closed?"

"Go check it out! Anyway, the big metal door is covered with cut-outs, and you can see the big slide and the climbing frames on the playground from outside. Maybe we can even see the little zebra in our classroom window!"

Small-Head Father emerged from the restroom, saying, "Okay, go take a look if you say so, and when you're done, you can go play in your house, okay?"

Big-Head Son looked at Small-Head Father and nodded his big head.

The big iron gate of the kindergarten was closed, the playground was very quiet, and all the sports equipment had been repainted, looking beautiful and fun. Big-Head Son suddenly felt his hands itch, his feet itch, and he couldn't help but grab the iron gate, causing it to shake with a "clunk clunk clunk" sound.

Observing Big-Head Son, Small-Head Father asked in a hushed voice, "Do you want to go in and play?"

Big-Head Son's eyes lit up at once: "Yes, I want to, too much! What good idea does Small-Head Father have?"

Without saying a word, Small-Head Father looked around and then lifted Big-Head Son up, sending him towards the top of the iron gate: "Climb up, Daddy will hold your buttocks." Big-Head Son made a great effort and managed to ascend.

However, he found himself stuck sitting on top of the iron gate and couldn't get down: "Daddy! Dad!" Big-Head Son wasn't scared, but he was in a hurry.

"Hold still!" Small-Head Father looked around again, then threw up his hands, jumped upwards, and hoisted himself up to the iron door. He turned around and jumped inside, holding Big-Head Son down: "What's the use? You want to play, but you can't climb!"

Big-Head Son didn't care about Small-Head Father's comments; he ran anxiously inside. First, he climbed up backward under the big spiral slide, then came down holding the slide pole, went on the swing and seesaw.

"Small-Headed Dad! Fancy a go on the teeter-totter with me!" Big-Headed Son couldn't play alone.

Just as Big-Headed Son and Small-Headed Dad merrily seesawed, letting each other energetically "spring butt," they suddenly heard a whistle. They halted and traced the sound: What? Outside the hefty iron gate stood a burly policeman, who blew his whistle and waved his truncheon at the duo.

"Oops, the police are coming to nab us," exclaimed Big-Headed Son, quite frightened.

But Small-Headed Dad remained unfazed, dismounting the seesaw and strolling towards the iron gate.

From a distance, Big-Headed Son observed Small-Headed Dad saying something to the policeman through the iron gate. Then he saw the policeman climbing in as well, smiling and approaching Big-Headed Son. Oh my goodness! The policeman hopped on the seesaw and teeter-tottered with Big-Headed Son, thoroughly enjoying themselves!

Subsequently, the policeman dismounted from the seesaw and said to Big-Headed Son's Dad: "You've got a point, keeping the only child at home after the summer vacation can be really lonely. The kindergarten should open the hefty iron gate ..."

Then the policeman descended from the seesaw and remarked to Big-Headed Son's Dad: "You're onto something. After the summer break, the solitary child at home can get quite lonely. The kindergarten should open the hefty iron gate ..."

"Exactly!" Big-Headed Son was so delighted to hear this that he leaped up from the seesaw and nearly toppled over. "Open the big iron gate of the kindergarten and let all of us escape in!"

Uncle Policeman and Small-Headed Dad chuckled happily.

Indeed, the next day, the substantial iron doors of the kindergarten swung open, and many children, who had felt lonely during the summer vacation, joyfully played together once again!

Two Ears on a Big Bed

"Little Biscuit" ain't a biscuit, she's a two-year-old little sister. Little Biscuit's mum and dad are heading abroad, so they've stashed her in Big-Headed Son's place for a bit.

"I'm gonna be a brother! I'm gonna be a brother!" Big-Headed Son chirped happily to the teddy bear a few times, then dashed to the balcony to share the news with the birds flitting about. He eagerly anticipated every day, leaving heaps of grub for Little Biscuit.

On that noon, Little Biscuit indeed arrived, but Big-Headed Son was nowhere in sight!

"How peculiar!" Small-Headed Dad scanned all around, but Big-Headed Son was elusive.

Apron Mum remarked, "He's probably in the loo!" She hurried to check, and sure enough, Big-Headed Son was in there.

"Out, out! It's the gents' now!" Big-Headed Son was occupied in the toilet with his bare bottom.

"What on earth are you up to?" Apron Mum rapped loudly on the already locked door. "Do you resemble a brother?"

A short while later, Big-Headed Son emerged – whoa! He'd undergone a complete transformation. The sky-blue fleece jacket was swapped for a dark blue suit that trailed on the floor; the blue and white plaid trousers were exchanged for black and grey striped ones that covered his feet.

"You ..." Apron Mum was too astonished to speak.

"Do I look like a big brother now?" Big-Headed Son asked proudly. Suddenly, "flop", he stepped on his own trouser legs and stumbled. On the brink of tears, he held back, for Big-Headed Son is now a big brother, and big brothers don't cry when they tumble.

Little Biscuit stared blankly at her oddly dressed brother. Suddenly, she sniffled and exclaimed, "Wah-wah!" She then repeated, "I'm scared! I'm scared!"

Throughout the afternoon, Big-Headed Son continued to sport the Small-Headed Dad's suit. He didn't play with toys, skipped napping, and refrained from using spoons to eat. He brushed his own teeth, washed his own face, and changed his own pyjamas.

Wait a minute! Where does Little Biscuit sleep at night? Big-Headed Son suddenly pondered this question. He rushed out of his room, checked the living room—no Little Biscuit. Kitchen—no Little Biscuit. Study—no Little Biscuit. Could it be that Little Biscuit is snoozing in the closet? Big-Headed Son swung open the closet door, but it was pitch-dark, and he couldn't see a thing inside.

Next, he dashed to Mom and Dad's spacious bedroom to inquire. However, as soon as he walked in, he froze, and then his mouth curled up. "No ..." he cried out, and Big-Headed Son finally returned to being Big-Headed Son. Turns out, he spotted a small bed on one side of Mom and Dad's massive bed, resembling an awkward ear, which made the big-headed son feel genuinely uneasy.

"You lot fancy Little Biscuit and not me, ooh, ooh ..." he cried sadly, pushing Little Biscuit held by his dad away. "Get out! Out! They're not your mum and dad!"

Eventually, Small-Headed Dad had to relocate Big-Headed Son's crib to the small room and place it right next to the big bed. Big-Headed Son then exclaimed happily, "Look, the big bed grew two ears!"

The "Big Bear" on the Quilt

A week later, Small-Headed Dad moved both cribs into Big-Headed Son's little room. After dinner, it was finally bedtime. As soon as Apron Mum closed the door and left, Big-Headed Son rolled over, quickly got up from his own cot, grabbed the rail of Little Biscuit's bed, stepped in at once, and slept next to Little Biscuit.

"What are you doing, brother?" asked Little Biscuit, curiously and happily.

"Can I tell you a story?"

So, Big-Headed Son recounted the tale of the Big Bad Wolf, a story Small-Headed Dad had told him before. However, as he narrated, Big-Headed Son felt it was dull because Little Biscuit didn't laugh or express fear. Big-Headed Son rolled over again and climbed out of Little Biscuit's crib: "I will play hide and seek with you!"

This game brought joy to Little Biscuit, who turned around inside the bed to find her brother. When she found him, she laughed. Meanwhile, Big-Headed Son sought out hiding spots—sometimes under the bed, sometimes at the head of the bed, sometimes at the foot of the bed. They played energetically.

Huh? Little Biscuit's laughter gradually faded and eventually ceased! Big-Headed Son peered into the small bed carefully; Little Biscuits lay there and had fallen asleep.

Big-Headed Son had to return to his own bed to sleep. He was likely tired from playing and soon drifted off.

However, in the middle of the night, Big-Headed Son suddenly woke up, sensing something was amiss, but he couldn't pinpoint it. Oh, it seemed to be his buttocks. He reached out and touched it, finding the quilt was wet. However, the bed was dry last night. It was probably too hot, and his butt was sweating. Big-Headed Son turned around, attempting to go back to sleep, but the damp quilt was too uncomfortable. Hey, Big-Headed Son recalled that he had received a shot in his buttocks yesterday afternoon; perhaps the medicine liquid leaked out again ...

But the medicine liquid was only a small amount; how could it wet such a large area?

Big-Headed Son suddenly sat up, as he recalled a dreadful incident. He turned his nose to a damp spot and sniffed – ouch, it was stinky; it was that dreadful thing – Big-Headed Son had wet the bed!

Quickly, he threw the quilt over the soaked mattress, fearing the embarrassment if Little Biscuit were to see it! Fortunately, Little Biscuit remained asleep. But how to handle the wet blanket? When Apron Mum walked in the next morning and caught sight of it, she'd surely exclaim, "Oops! Big-Headed Son, why are you wetting the bed?" Little Biscuit would hear that for sure.

Big-Headed Son sat on the bed pondering, contemplating, until he finally came up with a cunning plan.

In the morning, as Apron Mum entered the small room, she noticed a mat under the bed where Little Biscuit lay, featuring a large spread of bear-like wet prints in the middle. Big-Headed Son didn't wait for Apron Mum to inquire; he promptly pointed at the Little Biscuit beneath the quilt and declared, "It's the urine that leaked from Little Biscuit's bed! It wasn't me who peed! It's definitely not my pee!"

Seeing No Animals at the Zoo

After lunch, Small-Headed Dad and Apron Mum took Big-Headed Son and Little Biscuit to the zoo to check out the animals. Apron Mum brought a stroller for Little Biscuit, which intrigued Big-Headed Son so much that he gripped the handlebars and pushed it as fast as he could. This constant motion had Little Biscuit in stitches, while Apron Mum and Small-Headed Dad were in a constant state of exclamation: "Watch out!" "Slow down!" "Don't hit anyone." Every time mom and dad shouted, Big-Headed Son eased up a bit, but as soon as Little Biscuit's laughter subsided, he resumed pushing the stroller at top speed.

Approaching an uphill section, Big-Headed Son exerted more effort, and the stroller couldn't ascend quickly, slowing down considerably. However, going downhill was a different story. Even if Big-Headed Son stood still, the stroller would glide forward. Witnessing this spectacle, the throngs of tourists dispersed to make way, and the stroller, with Big-Headed Son in tow, raced to the bottom of the slope far from where Small-Headed Dad and Apron Mum were in the vast crowd.

As they descended, Big-Headed Son got separated from his parents. This situation left him anxious, forcing him to push the stroller more slowly while scanning the surroundings for his mum and dad. Little Biscuit, possibly feeling bored, began to cry to be taken out of the stroller. Big-Headed Son had no choice but to carefully lift her off the stroller.

An uncle noticed this and asked Big-Headed Son if he had lost his parents. Big-Headed Son thought to himself that he couldn't disclose the truth; if the uncle knew, he might cause trouble. So, he hurriedly shook his head and said, "No, not lost. My mum went to buy milk for my sister, and my dad went to buy orange juice for me!"

Uncle listened, smiled, and then walked away. Little Biscuit, full of joy, came to the grass, sometimes squatting down to pull grass, sometimes standing up to chase butterflies, and occasionally falling forward with a "flop." This kept Big-Headed Son busy as he had to take care of the cart and Little Biscuit running all over the place. Suddenly, his cart disappeared, which was odd because he had been pushing it all along. Big-Headed Son wanted to stop and look back, but he couldn't; Little Biscuit had already stumbled and run ahead again. Big-Headed Son had to follow her in a hurry. If he didn't find his mom and dad soon, he would surely be scolded!

At that moment, the radio in the zoo unexpectedly broadcasted an announcement. Big-Headed Son didn't pay attention to it, but an aunt approached him and said, "Listen, little brother, are you the two children being searched for on this radio?"

Upon hearing this, Big-Headed Son realized that indeed, they were the ones being sought. Since the radio was already on, it didn't matter if he confirmed it, so he nodded at the aunt. The kind aunt then escorted them to the radio room, where Apron Mum's anxious face turned red, and Small-Headed Dad was visibly scared.

"You ..." When they saw Big-Headed Son and Little Biscuit unharmed, with no missing arms or legs, there was nothing more to say. They gathered them into their arms with relief.

"But, but I lost the stroller!" Big-Headed Son exclaimed, emerging from the Small-Headed Dad's embrace with fear.

"It's okay, you can look for it at the lost and found; it should be there," said Small-Headed Dad reassuringly. They did indeed find the stroller at the lost and found.

However, the unfortunate incident meant they didn't get to see any animals that afternoon. As darkness had already set in, they decided to head home.

It Was So Much Fun to Paint!

Small-Headed Dad purchased a small box of coloured pencils for Big-Headed Son and Little Biscuit. Big-Headed Son stretched out on the white paper, teaching Little Biscuit how to draw the sun, the moon, clouds, and more. Initially, she happily followed the little brother, but soon boredom set in, and she started looking around and putting the coloured pencils in her mouth.

Small-Headed Dad then shifted the long couch in the living room, revealing the white wall behind it. "Big-Headed Son, take your sister to the wall to draw!"

Little Biscuit regained interest and joined her brother in drawing big houses, cars, and people on the white wall. However, as she drew, her enthusiasm waned, and she resorted to putting the coloured pencils in her mouth to bite.

Big-Headed Son looked around and couldn't spot Small-Headed Dad anymore but noticed Little Biscuit's white dress, white sweatshirt, and white socks sitting on the couch.

"Let's draw on the clothes, okay? This dress has no colour on it, it doesn't look good!" Big-Headed Son suggested. He started by painting colourful dots on the white sweatshirt, and Little Biscuit found it easy and followed suit.

"Look, how pretty it is now! It looks like colourful rain." Big-Headed Son placed the coloured dots on Little Biscuit's head as well.

"Now let's paint the skirt." Big-Headed Son smoothed out the folds of the skirt and drew colourful circles on it. "This is a colourful snowflake!" he declared, placing the painted skirt on Little Biscuit too.

Finally, he turned his attention to the socks. After a brief moment of thought, he drew a strip of colour on the white socks. "This is coloured wind; you'll fly when you wear these socks."

Once Little Biscuit had happily put on the socks as well, Big-Headed Son took her to the big mirror in the bedroom. "Look, how pretty you are!"

But Little Biscuit pointed to her face and exposed arms, saying, "This is not pretty!"

"That's alright, sister. Brother will draw on you, and you'll look pretty in no time," said Big-Headed Son, grabbing the coloured pencils and proceeding to draw on Little Biscuit's face, arms, and legs. Once he finished, he took her into the kitchen to show Apron Mum. Mother was so surprised that she opened her mouth wide, unable to close it for a long time. She then dragged them both into the study.

"Look at your son, drawing Little Biscuits like ghosts!" Apron Mum scolded Small-Headed Dad angrily.

Small-Headed Dad turned around, laughing, and rushed to grab his digital camera, snapping dozens of pictures of Little Biscuit.

A month later, the cover of the Photography Magazine featured the photo of Little Biscuit, and they sent Small-Headed Dad three hundred yuan. This made Small-Headed Dad very happy, and he used the money to buy Big-Headed Son and Little Biscuit each a big box of coloured pencils.

Apron Mum saw it and said, "Hmph, wait until you regret it!"

Sure enough, one day, Small-Headed Dad woke up

from his nap and looked in the mirror. He found that a green sock had been painted on his left cheek, and a black cell phone had been painted on his right cheek.

A Total of 25 Big Bags

Today is the busiest and happiest day for Big-Headed Son and Small-Headed Dad because they had to organize a lot of things for their trip to the big beach!

"Organize your own things!" Small-Headed Dad reminded Big-Headed Son multiple times. Consequently, they ended up sorting a total of 12 large bags – 5 for Small-Headed Dad and 7 for Big-Headed Son.

"Goodness! Where did you two get all that stuff!" cried Apron Mum, holding her chin as if it were about to fall off.

"What's the fuss? We've got everything we need, so you can be empty-handed when you come tomorrow." said Small-Headed Dad, loading the twelve large bags into the cab.

Big-Headed Son enthusiastically hugged one of his Winnie the Pooh travel bags and said, "Apron Mum, you just need to bring your own makeup when you come tomorrow!"

The cab, loaded with 12 big bags, a big-headed child, and a small-headed adult, drove off towards the ocean.

However, from nine o'clock onwards that night, the telephone at Apron Mum's bedside rang incessantly: "Hello, honey, I forgot my pyjamas; remember to bring them to me tomorrow!"

Apron Mum, her face adorned with fresh cucumber slices, had to carefully raise her head to fetch Small-Headed Dad's pyjamas. When she returned, the phone rang again: "Apron Mum! I forgot to bring replacement socks! Please bring them to me tomorrow! Bring a couple of extra pairs!"

-Ding- "Honey! I forgot to wear my watch ..."

-Ding- "Apron Mum! I forgot my swim trunks ..."

And so the phone continued ringing until Apron Mum fell asleep on the couch in the middle of the night, too tired to hear it anymore! Cucumber slices were no longer on the sleeping Apron Mum's face; they had all fallen on the floor and carpet as she moved back and forth, getting things.

The next day, when Apron Mum headed to the beach, she carried 13 big bags, one more than what the father and son had brought. Of the 13 bags, 2 were for makeup, 3 for spare dresses, and 3 for shoes to match the dresses (all belonging to Apron Mum). The other 5 were for items that Big-Headed Son and Small-Headed Dad had forgotten to take.

When the cab arrived at the beach with 13 big bags and an Apron Mum, Big-Headed Son and Small-Headed Dad eagerly pounced on the bags containing their belongings.

"Oops! This is not good!" Apron Mum suddenly yelled, "It's all your fault! I was told to bring this and that, and I forgot my own bottle of super sunscreen! It's your fault!"

"Hurry up and call home!" Big-Headed Son and Small-Headed Dad said simultaneously.

"Like there are still ghosts in the house!" Apron Mum, infuriated, turned and ran toward the hotel, shielding her head from the sun's rays with her hands as if they were a giant thunderstorm. "I'm just going to have to stay in the hotel and make it through this vacation!"

Before Apron Mum could reach the hotel, Big-Headed Son and Small-Headed Dad had already changed into swimming trunks provided by Apron Mum and enthusiastically jumped into the cold sea with a "flop! flop!"

Pants Kite

During the summer, the beach attracted many swimmers and kite enthusiasts. Big-Headed Son, inspired by the activities around him, wanted to swim and fly kites. However, after searching through 25 bags, he couldn't find a kite. Remembering it was behind the big wooden box in the closet at home, he suggested calling home and asking the ghost to deliver it.

"Don't worry, let me make one for you!" reassured Small-Headed Dad.

They crafted a small kite from old newspapers found in the hotel. But, there was no string. Big-Headed Son rummaged through the bags again, finding nothing. Small-Headed Dad then pointed to an open red bag.

"What's that?" he asked.

"That's full of Apron Mum's stuff!" thought Big-

Headed Son, finding Small-Headed Dad's question strange.

"You silly Big-Headed Son! " Small-Headed Dad playfully tapped his nose with his index finger and took a big bag out of the red bag.

"That's all. Apron Mum's stockings!" Daddy said, grinning.

He poured out all of Apron Mum's stockings, about thirty pairs, and then tied them together one by one. Big-Headed Son quickly understood. "Small-Headed Dad is so smart!" he exclaimed, as delighted as if he were about to eat a stocking.

"Keep it quiet! Don't let Apron Mum hear!" Small-Headed Dad reminded Big-Headed Son hastily. If Apron Mum discovered they were using her stockings as kite strings, she might get angry and scold them, perhaps even demanding that they wash their own socks and underwear every day, make their own beds, and neatly fold their quilts every morning as punishment.

Sixty stockings strung together. It's really long, wrapping it around the TV remote control makes it as big as a ball. Big-Headed Son no longer needs to worry about it being too short and not being able to fly the kite to the sky.

On the way out the door, Apron Mum pointed to the newspaper kite and said, "If there were no sun, I would really like to go with you to see how high this kite can fly!"

Luckily, the sun was high and bright, like a red light at an intersection, and it "blocked" Apron Mum's feet. Big-Headed Son and Small-Headed Dad ran to the beach as if they were running away.

Oops! The kite wouldn't fly at all because the string made of stockings was too heavy, and the kite made of newspaper was too light. Big-Headed Son was so disappointed that he was about to cry. Small-Headed Dad suddenly smiled and said, "I have a solution, it's up to you if you want it."

"Yes!" As long as the kite is allowed to fly into the sky, there is nothing that Big-Headed Son is not willing to do.

"You can use your pants instead of a kite." Small-Headed Dad stared at Big-Headed Son's beach shorts with a squinty eye.

Big-Headed Son looked down at his cool shorts, "Okay! I'll wrap my butt in a towel!" He agreed readily and then quickly took off his pants, letting Small-Headed Dad transform them into a pants kite.

It was great! The pants kite flew really high! The gusts of wind on the beach blew many kites up and down in the air, but only the pants kite held steady, because pants are heavier than paper, and the stocking holding it was thicker than the string.

The pants kite soared higher and higher, as if it wanted to fly to the sea to show off. Big-Headed Son held it and ran over and over, as if he wanted to fly up to the sky with the pants kite!

Cold, Cold Night

Big-Headed Son and Small-Headed Dad were both keen on spending the night at the beach.

"Anyway, we have a tent!" asserted Small-Headed Dad.

"Anyway, we've brought our tents!" echoed Big-Headed Son.

"Anyway, I've already told you that you're going to catch a cold sleeping on the beach at night!" warned Apron Mum before heading into the bathroom for a shower. Upon her return, she found that Big-Headed Son, Small-Headed Dad, the blue and white tent, and the bread, milk, and ham sausage from the refrigerator had all disappeared.

It wasn't completely dark yet, and the big red sun seemed like it was preparing to take a bath in the sea, gradually descending.

"Small-Headed Dad, awesome! We're awesome!" exclaimed Big-Headed Son, brimming with excitement. He laid out all the food, placing it on the napkin Small-Headed Dad had prepared, and initiated a delightful picnic.

The aroma of grilled sausages attracted numerous seagulls. Tossing pieces of bread into the air, the seagulls formed a chaotic flock, screeching and snatching. Big-Headed Son revelled in the joy of the moment.

As darkness set in, they retreated to their tent to sleep.

"Small-Headed Dad, I'm not afraid. What about you?" inquired Big-Headed Son, listening to the soothing sound of the waves.

"I'm a bit scared; it sounds like a wolf's howl," admitted Small-Headed Dad, squeezing Big-Headed Son's side. In response, Big-Headed Son reached out and patted him.

Attempting to drift off to sleep, Big-Headed Son found it challenging as the night grew colder and colder.

"Apron Mum was right, it is cold at night at the beach!" Small-Headed Dad wrapped his arms around Big-Headed Son, but Big-Headed Son still complained, "I'm freezing."

"Apron Mum is so comfortable now; she is in an air-conditioned room with a quilt!" Big-Headed Son said enviously.

"Yes, we won't be so cold if Apron Mum cooks a pot of steaming chicken soup and brings it to us for drinking," Small-Headed Dad suggested, licking his lips.

"I don't want Apron Mum to bring us chicken soup; I want Apron Mum to bring us duck down quilts and woolen blankets. That will keep us warm!"

As they talked and imagined these comforting things, they slowly fell asleep. In their dreams, they felt warmer and warmer until they were awakened in the early morning by the fishermen's song.

"Huh? It's not even dawn yet; why is someone singing already?" Small-Headed Dad opened his eyes and looked around, finding it pitch black.

Big-Headed Son suggested, "Let's open the window and see." He sat up, pulled open the curtains on the tent, and exclaimed, "Huh? What's this?" There seemed to be a thick layer of something blocking the outside of the tent.

Small-Headed Dad quickly reached out and touched it. It was hairy and rough. Curiously, he drilled out of the tent, pushing through the hairy and rough material until he finally got outside and saw the glowing white sky. "Big-

Headed Son, quickly come out to see! Our tent is covered with a 'quilt,' so we are so warm! That's why we're so warm!"

Big-Headed Son dug out to take a look and indeed found a very, very large fishing net folded several layers over the tent. "Uncle Fisherman must have covered it for us!" Big-Headed Son turned around and pointed at the fishermen casting nets on the beach.

The fishermen's song drifted over again, like a warm wind blowing!

Catch a Big Fish

During dinner at the hotel in the evening, Apron Mum inquired, "Are there any fish in this sea?"

"Of course there are," replied Small-Headed Dad. "Where else would the fish in the hotel come from?"

"So why don't you guys catch a big fish? How great it would be if we went down to the beach and grilled it after the sun went down!" expressed Apron Mum, pausing with her chopsticks.

"No problem," assured Small-Headed Dad. "Come to the beach tomorrow evening, and we'll catch a fish that's sure to be bigger and bigger than your leather shoes. You can just come and grill it then!"

Early the next morning, Small-Headed Dad and Big-Headed Son took their rented fishing rods and went to the seashore to fish.

However, they spent the entire morning until noon without catching a single fish.

"The fish have probably all gone traveling!" Big-Headed Son exclaimed, keeping his eyes fixed on the sea. He then desperately sprinkled breadcrumbs into the sea again, but the softened breadcrumbs remained untouched by any fish.

"Let's change to another spot!" suggested Small-Headed Dad, folding his fishing rod and moving further out.

Fortunately, this time they caught a small fish, not too big – perhaps as long as Small-Headed Dad's thumb.

"It's not a big fish, hey! What should we do?" Big-Headed Son expressed happiness and concern.

"Never mind, let's quickly feed it some food. It might grow a lot bigger by the end of the day," said Small-Headed Dad. Big-Headed Son threw the entire croissant into the fish bucket upon hearing this.

"It won't eat at all. It probably wants a big crab," Big-Headed Son speculated to Small-Headed Dad. Small-Headed Dad went crab hunting and caught a crab significantly smaller than the fish. However, the fish showed no interest in the crab; it swam around as if afraid.

"No, no, no, the fish will be even smaller if it swims

like this," Small-Headed Dad hurriedly caught and released the crab. By the afternoon, the fish in the bucket was still tiny, and by the time the sun went down, it hadn't grown a bit.

"Oops! Apron Mum is coming!" Big-Headed Son called out, spotting Apron Mum wearing a navy-blue dress, happily strolling to the beach to enjoy grilled fish. Small-Headed Dad quickly bent down and whispered into Big-Headed Son's ear. Together, they carried the bucket of fish and approached Apron Mum.

"What? Is this the...big fish you caught?" Apron Mum's surprised expression resembled seeing them catch a whale.

"We did catch a big fish," Small-Headed Dad hastily explained, "but then we let it go."

"Because, because we thought that such a big fish must have lots of babies ..." added Big-Headed Son, continuing the story, "and I would be very sad if Apron Mum was caught and eaten by a fish!"

"That makes sense," Apron Mum thought for a while and then said, "If Big-Headed Son was caught and eaten by the fish, I would go crazy. Why don't we just let the little fish go too!"

"Yay!" shouted Big-Headed Son and Small-Headed

Dad happily, tossing the little fish back into the sea. Later, they cut the bread into various shapes resembling big and small fish, sat on the beach, and baked the bread fish to eat. Apron Mum also enjoyed the treat with delight. Small-Headed Dad couldn't resist feeling pleased, so he sneakily pinched Big-Headed Son's buttocks. Big-Headed Son let out an "ouch" scream, making Apron Mum even more joyful!